A
TRIO
OF
TROUBLE

Books by Michael Jenet

FICTION
(THE DI SCOTTE MYSTERIES)
Trouble Comes In Threes
A Trio of Trouble

SELF IMPROVEMENT
MOTIVESTIONS - The Missing Key to Living Your Best Life
(Originally published as: *ASK: The Questions to Empower Your Life*)

A Better Life

CONTRIBUTING AUTHOR
Imagine: 29 Days To A Better You

Peanut's Legacy

A TRIO OF TROUBLE

MICHAEL JENET

Wordbinders Publishing
Journey Institute Press
Colorado, U.S.A.

Wordbinders Publishing
An imprint of Journey Institute Press,
a division of 50 in 52 Journey, Inc.
www.journeyinstitutepress.org

Library of Congress Control Number: 2024950421
Names: Jenet, Michael
Title: A Trio Of Trouble
Description: Colorado: Wordbinders Publishing, 2024

Identifiers: ISBN 978-1-964754-14-7 (hardcover)
978-1-964754-23-9 (paperback)
978-1-964754-24-6 (ebook/kindle)

Subjects: BISAC: FICTION / Mystery & Detective / Women Sleuths |
FICTION / Thrillers / Crime |
FICTION / Crime

First Edition

Printed in the United States of America

1 2 11 37 41 54 69 73 80 99

This book is typeset in Garamond / Minerva

Cover Design by WiggleB Studios
Editing by: Jessica Medberry - InkWhale Editorial LLC

This is a work of fiction. Names, characters, places, and incidents er are the product of the author's imagination. Any resemblance to actual persons, living or dead, businesses, companies, events, or locales is entirely coincidental.

CONTENTS

To Dafna, my reason and my love, always.

BOOK 1

THE DOMINION MURDERS

CHAPTER 1

It was an innocent comment. "Hello honey," a voice said, interrupting Amelia Hamza's thoughts. Honey. The nectar of bees, a term of endearment used between people who are close. Something sweet. Little did she know, but this innocent term would be the last thing she would hear before the horror she would face later that day.

Before this interruption, Amelia Hamza, journalist for the digital newspaper Daily Coast, had been sitting alone at a table by the window. Pouring a small amount of the golden nectar into her tea, she stared out at the people darting in and out of the rain.

She turned to see who had spoken. A young man—at least younger than her—was standing with a cup in his hand and smiling down at her.

She considered him for a moment, holding the plastic tube of honey in her hand, then said, "Sorry, you'll have to try harder than that, mate." She glared at him before looking back down at her open laptop.

The young man, unperturbed, shrugged and walked off.

Amelia knew that most men, and a more than a few women, considered her good-looking. She was used to being approached, propositioned, and flirted with. That didn't mean she enjoyed it. In fact, it was all a bit tiring.

It didn't help that her luck with men had been less than stellar of late.

If she was honest with herself, the gray skies and flooding streets she saw out the window matched her mood. She was tired of it all. The slog, the long hours of work, the loneliness.

Not that she minded her job; she enjoyed it most days. Lately, however, things had been more of a grind than the exhilarating journalistic reporting that she yearned for. She knew much of that had to do with her current nonexistent personal life.

She sighed heavily and looked at her watch. Time to get moving. She had somewhere to be.

***

In the New Forest, several miles from the café where Amelia Hamza was packing up, a lone bicyclist was braving the weather and dangerously speeding along the narrow pathways.

Jillian Scotte didn't mind the rain. In many ways, she preferred riding in the rain. There were fewer people, and she was going to work up a sweat anyway, so getting soaked didn't really bother her.

She knew her bike and her limits, and unless she hit a stray wet leaf or some such thing, there was little chance she would get hurt. It was part of the allure, pushing herself and her bike to the point of danger without encountering it.

She craved the rush, the surge of adrenaline, as much as she craved the exercise. Jillian had never been much of the gym membership kind of woman. She wanted solitude, time to think, as much as she wanted the health benefits. Running was too slow; she needed something with speed. Cycling was the perfect fit.

Her job as head of the Violent Crime Unit for the South of England was stressful at the best of times. Her first few cases had been nothing but one harrowing investigation after another.

She had a great team, though they remained one down, with Detective Sergeant Listun still on limited duty. He was finishing his physiotherapy after having had much of his shoulder blown into fragments several months ago.

Jillian rounded a corner and got up out of the saddle to speed up as she entered a long straightaway amid an almost tunnel-like section of the bike path. The narrow path, covered by overhanging trees, was not soaked, and her tires gripped the drier pavement, giving her a much-needed burst of speed.

Her breathing was coming in a steady rhythm now and her lungs were pumping full of oxygen as her legs pedaled faster and faster, shooting her like a rocket down the straightaway.

***

Amelia struggled to see through the windshield. The weather called for rain all day.

Having few friends was nothing new for her. Her parents had left their home in Pakistan soon after Amelia was born, so although she grew up in England, she could never shake her birthplace.

In school, she had been teased mercilessly by girls who were jealous of her looks and by boys who were too immature to know how to talk to her. At the first sign of interest from one of the cliques, what few friends she had tried to make always seemed to desert her, fearing ridicule for being friends with "that Paki girl."

University had been little better, and while she had made a few friends, they had all scattered across the globe, and she only saw them on social media.

Jinani had been one of the few friends she'd been able to make since moving south. Jinani had recently arrived from Pakistan when they had met at a local restaurant run by two expat brothers. The food was authentic and the clientele mostly immigrant.

She and Jinani had jelled almost immediately, and they quickly became friends. Life and work, for both, kept them busy—Amelia with her journalism, Jinani with her job at a large import–export firm where she was the assistant to the CEO. Still, they got together whenever they could.

Jinani had met Jonathan about a year ago and was smitten immediately. Amelia had met them both for dinner after almost three months of hearing how great he was.

He wasn't Amelia's type, but Jinani loved him, and he seemed to reciprocate, though he was a little too possessive for Amelia's taste.

About a month ago, something happened that had Amelia concerned for her friend. Jinani had changed. The spark was gone from her eyes; her joie de vivre was no longer in her voice when they talked on the phone. No amount of coaxing could get her to divulge what happened, but Amelia knew something was wrong.

Pulling up in front of Jinani's flat, she parked in a spot for visitors and prepared to make the dash through the rain from the car to covered safety. One way or another, she was going to find out what was wrong with her friend.

As she approached the door, she found it wasn't completely closed. It looked like it had just been pulled to, but not actually latched. She knocked on the door, which just caused it to open further.

"Hello," she called out. "Jin? It's Amelia."

No response. Stepping inside, she closed the door behind her.

"Hello," she said again, louder this time, but the house was quiet. It had that feel about it, like when you walk into a place and know by the quiet that no one's home, but that wasn't right—she'd gotten a text from Jinani this morning saying she was looking forward to seeing Amelia at nine.

It was 8:59 a.m.

Amelia cautiously walked through the entryway door into the sitting room that doubled as the dining room in the small flat.

Everything was as she remembered it, if messier than the way Jinani normally kept her home. The mantle above the electric fire had a photo of her and Jonathan, smiling at what looked like someone's garden party. She looked happy. He had his arm around her, pulling her close as he, too, smiled at the camera.

Amelia called out again, but her words seemed to seep into the empty walls of the small flat.

She could see the open door to the bedroom across the room. Beyond that lay the toilet. Sighing loudly in the small space, she walked across and opened the door to the kitchen, just to be thorough.

She immediately wished she hadn't.

Blood was everywhere.

There was her friend, and equally covered in blood was Jonathan.

Amelia was not new to death and blood, not with her job. This was different. This was her friend. She could feel the bile coming up and ran to the toilet.

***

Jillian was facing the brunt of the rain. Having just crested a small incline, she was now gliding down the other side, careful not to go too fast, but enjoying the brief respite from the climb.

Her earbuds were playing some Bach when suddenly the robotic tone of her phone changed to an incoming call.

Not just any incoming call. It was detective constable Kara Devanor's ringtone.

CHAPTER 2

The kitchen always seems to be where people gather. The smell of the cooking, the nibbles before the meal. Everyone always ends up in the kitchen.

It was an odd thought, Jillian Scotte mused as she stepped into the brightly lit room where the crime had taken place.

It seemed longer than an hour since her phone had buzzed during her early-morning ride. It felt like an eternity since she'd heard the robotic voice in her ear coming from her phone—*incoming call from kara day van oar*, which was how her phone pronounced Detective Constable Devanor's last name.

Jillian had taken the call. Her DC would not be calling this early on a Sunday without good reason. Breathing hard from the climb on her bike, she asked, "Kara, what's up?"

"Sorry to bother you, guv, there's been a double murder."

This was nothing out of the ordinary. Even a violent crime on her day off happened more often than not. There were people on shift to handle it—which made Jillian slow down and bring her bike to a halt.

"Kara. You're not on this weekend, and why are you calling me?"

"I got a call from the desk sergeant, mum," her DC responded. "The call was phoned in by the person who found the body."

Jillian waited, knowing she would not like where this was headed.

"It was Amelia Hamza, mum."

"Shit." The reply came out of Jillian's mouth before she could stop it.

She had hurried back to her car, thrown her bike in, and rushed home to change. She hadn't bothered to shower—she just toweled her hair to give it the semblance of being dry, threw some clothes on, and headed to the scene.

The scene of crime officer, or SOCO, was already there with an entire team wearing disposable blue pull-up suits over their clothes. Kara Devanor approached Jillian as she got out of her car. Her face was grim.

"Morning, guv," she said politely as they made their way under the police tape, the duty constable noting their names, as well as those of everyone who went into and out of the flat.

"Rather rough, I'm afraid," Kara said, looking at her notes. "The flat is owned by a Jinani Rasool, one of the victims. Ms. Hamza was supposed to come over for a chat this morning. They're friends."

"You said *one* of the victims," Jillian said as they climbed the stairwell of the complex, making their way to the third floor.

"Yes," Kara answered, "the other victim is Jonathan Blakesly, boyfriend."

"Do we know anything about the time of death?" Jillian asked as they approached the front door of the flat.

"Prelim from the doctor, sometime late last night."

"Where's Amelia?" Jillian asked.

"On her way to the Tof, mum," Kara answered, wondering if they should have kept her here.

Her boss looked briefly at her and then nodded.

"Okay. Let me have a look. Get back there and wait till I arrive before interviewing her."

"Yes mum."

DI Jillian Scotte put on a blue coverall and stepped into the flat. When she entered the kitchen, the scene was like something from a movie. Blood was everywhere, but it wasn't the sight of the blood that unnerved her.

Both bodies were tied to chairs. Hands zip-tied behind them. Ankles also zip-tied to the legs of the chairs. Bodies stabbed multiple times in the chest.

Jillian took in the scene as the photographer's camera clicked and its powerful flash illuminated the scene in bright bursts like strikes of lightning.

Both bodies were naked. The man had deep cuts above and below his left kneecap.

The woman's breasts had been sliced, with two deep cuts on each side forming an X over each one. It was then Jillian noticed her nipples were gone. They had been cut off.

This was a brutal murder. A deliberate and violent act.

What sent a chill down her spine most of all was that the participants had been made to watch. The chairs were facing each other.

***

Back at the Tof, Kara followed her boss into the interview room. Both women sat down opposite Amelia Hamza, and Kara switched on the digital recorder, announcing everyone present.

"Hello Amelia," Jillian said, setting her cup of tea down as Kara opened her notebook, ready to take notes. "I'm sorry to have kept you waiting, and before we begin, is there anything we can get you?"

Amelia looked back with a mix of shock, exhaustion, and a healthy cautious wariness. She simply shook her head slowly and silently back and forth.

Jillian, showing genuine concern, said, "Okay. Just let us know if you change your mind. We'll keep this as short as possible. Is there anyone we can call to come and get you afterwards?"

Kara knew these were standard questions when interviewing family members, or witnesses, or friends of someone who had been killed. Still, she was curious to see how carefully Jillian would handle the journalist. Given that she had found the bodies, she was still technically a suspect.

Again, Hamza shook her head.

Jillian, who had been leaning forward at the table, now straightened up. "Right. Can you please tell us how you knew Jinani Rasool and Jonathan Blakesly?"

When she spoke, Amelia's voice was low, but she enunciated clearly. "I didn't know Mr. Blakesly very well. I'd only met him once. Jin . . . Jinani kept telling me about her new boyfriend and how great he was, and after the second or third time of asking me over for dinner, I finally accepted."

"And was he?" Jillian asked.

Amelia, who had been staring blankly down at the table, looked up. "What?"

"Was he great?"

Amelia returned Jillian's stare for a moment before answering. "He was . . . I don't know, he seemed all right. Jinani clearly was infatuated with him, and he seemed . . ." She considered for a moment, then said, "Normal. Like a regular bloke."

"Did you have any reservations about him?" Jillian asked.

"No."

Switching tack, Jillian asked, "And how did you come to know Jinani Rasool?"

"We met through an immigrant group I belong to. People from Afghanistan who live in Southern England."

"What's the name of the group?"

"Ex-Pakistani UK. Hardly original, I know," Amelia said, a thin smile crossing her lips. Her green eyes were bloodshot from the tears she had shed.

"How long ago was this?" Jillian asked, keeping her voice neutral.

"A bit more than a year, eighteen months. I don't remember exactly."

"I understand you were scheduled to meet Ms. Rasool this morning?" Jillian asked, and seeing a little stiffening from Amelia, she added, "Meaning you weren't just dropping by unannounced?"

"Yes," Amelia added, though her voice was terser than before.

Jillian paused, sharing a quick glance with Kara before adding, "What was the purpose of your visit?"

"Just a catch up. I hadn't seen Jin in a while."

Changing topics once again, Jillian said, "Can you think of anyone who might wish to harm either of them?"

Amelia, her eyes once again gazing off into the distance, slowly shook her head.

The interview lasted another half hour, after which time Jillian asked Kara to arrange a lift for Amelia back to her flat.

"We'll be in touch as soon as we know more," Jillian said as they walked Amelia to the door. "Try to get some rest, Amelia. You've been through a shock today."

It was unclear if Amelia had heard her or not. Her eyes still seemed to look off in the distance as she slowly nodded.

Kara walked into Jillian's office after she had placed Amelia in a car.

"What do you think?" Jillian asked.

"She's hiding something," Kara responded immediately.

Jillian looked at her young detective. "Yes, I agree. The question is what?"

CHAPTER 3

Rain from the overnight storm still hung in the air and made the streetlights look mottled through her window as Jillian Scotte drove into work before dawn.

Dr. Daniella Morales, Jillian's romantic partner, was working the graveyard shift, and they had been mostly ships in the night for the past fortnight. Jillian hadn't wanted to be home when Daniella arrived. She didn't want to go through the case and admit how much she didn't know, because Daniella would want to help, and right now Jillian needed answers.

She got to the Violent Crimes Unit building, or the Tof as the team called it, before anyone else. Jillian turned on the coffeemaker. Hanging up her wet coat and grabbing a steaming cup of coffee, she sat down at her desk. It wasn't quite six o'clock yet. The sky was just beginning to show signs of light.

She went through her email and answered a few, including two from her boss, Superintendent Maryanne Sanderson, asking for updated overtime reports that Jillian had prepared yesterday after returning from the crime scene but had been too preoccupied to send.

Within a minute, her computer buzzed with an incoming call on the internal Metropolitan Police video conferencing application, METV. Putting down her coffee and running her hand through her messy hair, she clicked the answer button.

Superintendent Maryanne Sanderson looked like she'd just stepped out of a high-priced spa treatment, her hair perfect and her maroon jacket and cream blouse well pressed. No doubt she smelled like lavender, Jillian thought. "Hello boss," she said pleasantly.

"What are you doing in so early?" Sanderson asked, getting straight to business.

"I could ask you the same thing," Jillian shot back. Superintendent Sanderson was a direct, strong woman who didn't suffer fools easily. Jillian would not play the overworked junior to her. She would stand her ground, and Sanderson liked her for it.

True to form, a quick smile crossed Sanderson's lips before she said, "Fair enough. Is everything okay? Things with Daniella all right?" Despite the icy demeanor most of the male officers at the Met accused her of, Superintendent Sanderson was exceptionally perceptive about people's lives and never forgot important dates, significant others, or children's names. It was something Jillian knew she needed to get better at.

"Fine. Dani's fine too, she's just working graves and we need to make some headway in this new case."

"Right. This is the double murder in the kitchen?"

"Yes, mum," Jillian said.

"The reporter was the one who found them?" Sanderson asked, though Jillian knew her boss wasn't as unsure as she sounded about the question. She likely had the preliminary case file pulled up already on her second screen. Unlike Jillian, who spent as little time as possible on her computer, Sanderson practically had a control center setup on her desk, with multiple mounted screens she could move and pivot as she wanted.

"Yes," Jillian replied, "Amelia Hamza, mum."

"And this is the same reporter that you have been cultivating a relationship with since you arrived?"

She never missed a beat, Jillian thought. Although given that the VCU and Jillian's post as its head had been Sanderson's idea, it made sense that she would take a closer interest in everything.

"Yes, mum," Jillian said. "She has been helpful in the past."

"How is she?"

"She was quite shocked. The female vic was a friend, apparently."

"Any chance of involvement?" Sanderson asked.

Jillian waited a breath before answering, "Too soon to tell, mum, but I don't think so."

She could see her superintendent mulling this over. "Mmm, well, don't close doors you haven't looked into yet." She didn't wait for Jillian to respond, adding, "Where do things stand now with the case?"

Jillian filled her in on the preliminary work the team had done the previous day. Financial records were being looked into. Work and friends were being interviewed. It was too early for forensics, and she was hoping the coroner's report would come in sometime today. It was all early days, and yet, Jillian was all too aware that time was not on their side. Statistically, if they were going to find a trail, it would be in the first two days, three on the outside. Today was already day two.

They spoke for another ten minutes, catching up on parts of the job that Jillian hated most, but that had to be done. Budgets, reports, other cases. The drudgery that went with being in charge of an elite unit of coppers assigned to track down violent crime suspects in Southern England.

Two hours later, with the rest of the team knee deep at their desks, Jillian had made headway on her paperwork. Her desk looked like the Tasmanian Devil had been let loose with stacks of paper and had a right good old time with it.

Kara had run the morning meeting. She was the acting DS while Listun was still working from home, though he dialed in and participated remotely. Jillian was trying to get him to cut back, even speaking directly to his wife, who said, "You know what he's like—might as well try telling the tide to stop coming."

So, he dialed in for meetings, sent packets of emails, and did his best to run things through Kara. To her credit, she didn't mind the extra work and was extremely patient and kind with him, though Jillian wasn't sure how productive or efficient the system was. She'd have to have a talk with them about it.

When Jillian was back in her office, Kara knocked and came in, her nose buried in some papers she was reading. "Boss?" she said, finally looking up as Jillian raised an eyebrow in response. "The team's been looking into the male victim Jonathan Blakesly's bank records. There are regular payments for something called Historinaccuracy Research. The payments are weekly and they're not small, going back two years."

Jillian took the pages and scanned the highlighted areas. "Did you look them up?" she asked.

"That's the thing, guv," Kara responded, her arms now folded across her chest. "I can't find them. No website, no mention of them at all on social media. They have a National Insurance number and are in HM Revenue and Customs. Address is in Basingstoke."

Jillian chewed her lip as she scanned the pages.

"Thought I might go have a look," Kara said, hopefully.

Jillian looked up. "I'll go with you," she said, and the two women headed off on the three-quarters-of-an-hour drive up to the address for Historinaccuracy Research.

On the drive up, Kara wondered aloud, "What do you think of the name, Historinaccuracy Research?"

"What do you mean?" Jillian asked, looking over quickly and then back at the road.

"Well," her acting DS said, "is it History in Accuracy or History Inaccuracy or Historin . . . no, that wouldn't be right." Her voice trailed off in thought.

"We'll just have to ask them."

With the night's rain a memory, the gray clouds were cold but dry as they pulled up across the road from the address. Both women got out of the car and looked at the building. It was nondescript and set between two other buildings. What was noticeable was that there were no windows. Where once they might have existed, they had been filled in. The entire facade of the building was painted a muted black. The door, a large wooden affair with black studs and heavy black iron hinges, provided the only color.

There was no knocker or buzzer that they could see, and after trying the handle to determine it was locked, Jillian pounded on the door with her fist.

After twenty seconds, she did it again.

And again.

Finally, they heard a bolt sliding, and the door opened slightly.

A large, imposing man filled the gap. He was bald and wore dark blue jeans with a black T-shirt that was one size too small and looked as though about to burst from his larger-than-average arms and chest. He looked at them with soulless black eyes. He said nothing, just looked back and forth from Jillian to Kara.

Jillian pulled her warrant card and showed it to him. "I'm DI Scotte, this is DC Devanor. Do you work for Historinaccuracy Research?"

The man simply stared back without speaking. Nor did he move or open the door any more than he already had. Finally, he said to Jillian, "No one's here."

Jillian repeated, "But this is Historinaccuracy Research?"

"No one's here." His accent was English, though it sounded more Manchester than Southern England.

Kara said, "Well, you're here."

The man flicked his eyes toward her for a moment. Jillian saw something flicker briefly behind them as he said, "Not talking to you, am I?" and then he returned his intense gaze to Jillian.

Jillian said, "Can we come in?"

The man didn't even blink. "Do you have a warrant?"

Jillian slowly shook her head.

"No," he replied.

"Can I ask your name?"

"No," the man said.

Jillian considered pushing the issue, but she finally reached into her bag and pulled out a business card. Handing it to him, she said, "When someone comes back, your boss perhaps, please have them call me as soon as possible."

The man took the card and retreated, slamming the large wooden door firmly. Bolts could be heard sliding into place.

As they walked back to the car, Jillian turned and looked back at the door. "What'd you make of him?" she asked.

Kara Devanor stopped by her side of the car and looked over the roof at her boss, frowning. "White supremacist," she said plainly.

Jillian cocked her head. "Really? Just like that?"

Kara took a deep breath. "When you grow up in my shoes, you learn to spot them rather quickly."

Ouch, thought Jillian, she'd deserved that. She trusted Kara a great deal, and she should have recognized that being black, and a black woman at that, this was something Kara knew far better than her. Seeing the frown on her detective's face, she said, "Something's troubling you. What is it?"

Kara looked back across the road at the doorway. "I dunno. Something's not quite right about it."

It wasn't until they were halfway back to the Tof when Kara said, "Hmm," almost to herself, but loud enough for Jillian to say, "What?"

"It's nothing," Kara responded, "just realized what was throwing me off."

After she didn't elaborate, Jillian looked across at her briefly again and said, "And?"

Kara turned and looked at her boss. "No tattoos," she said plainly. "Usually, these guys have them up their neck, on their bald heads, down their arms, on their knuckles, everywhere. This guy had none. At least no visible ones."

CHAPTER 4

Yoga did not come easy for Kara Devanor, but she had to find something to do for exercise, and it was something she could do in the privacy of her own home.

She had tried going to the gym, but she was tired of men who thought it was the perfect place to hit on women while throwing their testosterone around like confetti.

She was not a cyclist like her boss. Kara tolerated jogging, but had never been one to get up every morning for a run. Her schedule just wasn't that predictable, and yet she needed something to keep herself fit for her work and her own sanity.

It was a juxtaposition of her life that while she was at ease out in public behind the mask of her warrant card, in her personal life, she was very much an introvert. All the classes and group activities most people joined were perfect for making new friends or, gyms aside, meeting lovers, but Kara hated crowds.

After trying two different yoga classes, she had once again run up against her work schedule. The studios offered classes at all hours, but the thought of having different instructors and participants every time she went made her stomachache. Then she found online courses she could do on her own, in private.

Since she was not particularly limber, it had been difficult at first, but in time she found herself getting quite good at it. She didn't buy into the Eastern philosophy of some courses, so she kept searching until she found a set of online courses that stuck simply to the "work" of yoga, which suited her well. Her primary focus was on building her core strength and stretching. She incorporated some of her own exercises with small weights to build muscle strength.

Having built up a bright sheen of sweat from her early-morning session, she stepped into her shower. Even as the hot water washed away the effect of her workout and steam coated her skin in a warm embrace, Kara shivered.

She hadn't been able to get the man from Historinaccuracy Research out of her mind. His gaze when he'd looked her up and down had felt like ice shooting down her spine. She knew that Jillian, normally attuned to everything around her, hadn't seen what Kara did. It wasn't something you saw or felt unless you'd grown up with the hatred white supremacists had for you just because of the color of your skin.

There was something purely evil in the look, in the subtle shift behind the eyes, in the muscles of the man's neck. The way he had forcefully swallowed when he first saw her as though trying to keep down bile rising in his throat.

It didn't matter that he'd never met her before, knew nothing about her, had no idea what her beliefs were, what she stood for, or what she cared about. None of that mattered. It was simply and solely because of the color of her skin.

Wherever this case would lead, Kara knew it was going to be deeply rooted in something dark, something vile, something evil, and no amount of sweating or hot water was going to make her feel warm until it was over.

***

While Kara was finishing her shower, Detective Inspector Jillian Scotte was sitting down in a café she often frequented when meeting with Amelia Hamza. She set one cup she'd been carrying in front of the journalist.

Amelia looked like she hadn't slept since she'd stumbled into the double homicide murder scene of one of her friends. Her green eyes were bloodshot; her jet-black hair, normally straightened, looked a mess. She thanked Jillian for the coffee and absentmindedly took a sip.

"How are you coping?" Jillian asked warmly.

Amelia looked up, but her eyes weren't really looking at Jillian. There was an emptiness to them, and Jillian knew she was looking into her mind's eye at the carnage she had walked into. Finally, her eyes focused briefly on Jillian. "I'm not," she said, sounding disheartened.

Jillian didn't know Amelia well enough to know what she could do to help her. They weren't friends, not even acquaintances, really, merely peers in the world of police and press. They might work to benefit one another, but she'd never really spent much time with the journalist beyond exchanges of information.

Still, Jillian's heart went out to her. She couldn't imagine walking into that kitchen expecting to talk to a friend and finding them like that. Finally, she said simply, "I'm so very sorry, Amelia," and meant it.

Amelia looked back up from her coffee, and a thin smile briefly crossed her lips. She nodded slightly.

They sat in silence for a while. Amelia, in her grief, and Jillian wondering how best to handle this. She couldn't quite decide if the woman sitting across from her was a suspect, witness, acquaintance of one of the deceased . . . Her mind was stuck not knowing which track was best to go down.

Finally, she decided on none of them. Instead, she reached out and placed her hand on top of Amelia's, causing the journalist to jerk her head up. Jillian felt Amelia's hand begin to pull back, but she pressed her palm gently down, holding it in place.

Looking Amelia in the eye, she said, "Tell me about her. What was she like? What made her laugh?"

For the next fifteen minutes they just talked about Jinani Rasool—single woman, expat from Pakistan, friend. Amelia let her tears fall silently amid small bursts of laughter as she recalled something funny or the time they both stumbled home from one too many drinks at their local pub.

The coffee cups now empty and the stories exhausted, Amelia took a deep breath. "Thank you," she said, her voice ever that of the stern journalist, but with a tinge of appreciation mixed in.

They both gathered their coats and bags and stepped outside into the cool gray morning.

As they turned to each other to say goodbye, Jillian said, "Amelia. When you were in the interview room . . ."

Amelia's eyebrows knitted closer together. Jillian continued, "I just had a feeling . . . it's probably nothing . . . but I felt there was something else you wanted to say."

She'd said it offhandedly, almost as an afterthought. The effect had Amelia thinking; Jillian could see her eyes tighten slightly and look up to her left, a sign she was recalling a memory. Finally, Amelia shook her head gently. "I don't know, it was just . . ."

Jillian stood still, saying nothing. Sometimes it was best to just wait.

Finally, Amelia said, "I met Jonathan about nine months ago. Jin kept going on about how great he was."

She was looking off again, remembering. Jillian pushed slightly. "You didn't think so?"

Refocusing once more, Amelia seemed unsure as she cocked her face slightly to one side. "Not quite. I mean, he's not my type, all business and a little too overbearing, but she seemed happy, so who was I to say?"

Once again, Jillian went quiet, waiting patiently.

As though concluding some internal struggle, Amelia straightened herself up a little. "Something happened about a month ago. Jin changed."

"Changed how?"

Again, Amelia shook her head. "Don't know. She was just different. She wasn't herself. It's why I was going to see her. I wanted to know what happened."

"Do you think it had something to do with Jonathan Blakesly?" Jillian asked.

Amelia shrugged. "I thought so. I mean, what else could it have been? But then, seeing them both . . ." The memory came flooding back, and Jillian could see the pain on Amelia's face.

Jillian reached out and gently grabbed her shoulder. "I'm going to do everything I can to find out who did this. I give you my word."

Amelia looked up, and a softer, more genuine smile fleetingly crossed her face. Then, sensing awkwardness, she said, "I have to go. Thanks for the coffee."

Jillian watched her walk away for a few moments before turning and walking in the opposite direction to her car.

As Jillian walked into her office at the Tof, Kara hung up her desk phone from a conversation. "Mum?" she called out. Jillian turned as she hung up her coat.

"Just got a call from a man called Derek Winston. Says he's the director of Historinaccuracy Research."

Jillian raised her eyebrows. Her DC went on, "Says he'd be happy to talk to us, but he's at home with his family and can't come in at present. We are welcome to come to him." Kara looked up from her notepad, and Jillian knew that she'd just been reading a quote from Mr. Winston.

Taking her coat back down off the rack, Jillian said, "Right. Let's go and have a chat with Mr. Winston then."

CHAPTER 5

Hats. Some days, Jillian Scotte lost count of how many different hats she wore.

Detective Inspector, lover, friend, manager, boss, employee, head of the Violent Crimes Unit, occasional babysitter to grown adults who didn't know how to behave, comforter to the bereaved, negotiator with miscreants and criminals—the list went on and on.

As she and her detective-constable-slash-acting-detective-sergeant headed outside, Jillian figured she needed to add another hat to her growing collection. This one, however, she wasn't even sure what to call.

As Kara pulled the car out of the Tof parking lot into traffic, Jillian asked, "Have you eaten this morning?"

Kara glanced over. "No. Got in a bit early. Not much was open."

"Right. Slight detour then," Jillian said, and began giving Kara directions—left here, right at the roundabout—until they pulled up near a business-laden part of Southampton. Jillian told Kara to park just behind a food truck. "Be right back," she said, hopping out of the car.

She soon returned with two large foil-wrapped items and two cups of coffee. The food turned out to be breakfast burritos from a vendor Jillian had stumbled upon a few months ago and often sidetracked to visit on her way to work. The Tof, having been remodeled from an empty warehouse, had a kitchen, but not a proper canteen like Southampton Central's Constabulary building. So, unless you brought food with you, there was likely nothing to eat. Not even a vending machine, something many of the team had been grumbling about for weeks.

"Let's eat first. Mr. Winston will wait."

Kara didn't need telling twice. Having taken her first smell of the burrito, she seemed to realize she was famished. She took several large bites in succession before pausing long enough to have a drink of coffee.

Jillian spent the quiet time thinking as they ate. When the Black Lives Matter protests had gone global, she'd studied enough and spent enough time in introspection to know that there was a lot she didn't know. She'd read articles, watched some online videos, gone through the Met's mandatory (and useless) new training, all to conclude that as an individual, no matter how much she thought she treated people fairly, she had a lot to learn.

"Kara," she said, getting her junior's attention. "Look, I'm probably going to screw up saying this, so please forgive me."

Kara stopped chewing and looked over at her boss.

Jillian started slowly. "I have a feeling with this case that we're going to get into a world I know little about, but I suspect you have . . ." She paused, trying to choose her words carefully. ". . . I suspect you have been exposed to it far more than I have."

Making sure her DC understood the direction she was going in, she plunged forward. "What I'm trying to say is that it's quite likely that I'm going to miss things that you won't, and while it pains to think that, right now is not the time for me to address it. What I . . . what we need to do is focus on this case."

Again, Jillian paused slightly as Kara nodded gently. "So, if I miss something, I need you to tell me. Don't assume I saw it or heard it or . . . whatever. If I don't bring it up, tell me, even if you think you're sure I must have observed it, okay? Does that make sense?"

Kara nodded solemnly. "Yes mum."

After a few more bites of food, as they were putting their rubbish into a plastic bag, Jillian said, "And Kara . . ."

Starting the car, DC Devanor looked over once more as Jillian continued, "When this is over, I'd like to sit down with you. I'd like to talk with you about what it's like from your perspective." Taking a deep breath, she added, "I may not be able to do anything, or maybe I will. I don't know. But I do know that until I learn more and understand more, I won't ever be able to be a good ally."

Kara was struck speechless at this direct request. She'd never had anyone ask for her perspective before, not from someone white, anyway, and certainly not from a copper, much less a boss. Blinking several times, she merely nodded before concentrating on driving as she pulled into traffic.

They pulled up to the address in a rather new cluster of homes with a half-circular drive in front. Though not quite a mansion and with neighboring homes on either side, the yellow brick home still seemed impressive, with a well-maintained hedge following the drive. The drive continued down one side of the home to a two-car detached garage in the back.

A woman with blond hair down to her shoulders, wearing a blue skirt and white top with a cardigan draped over her shoulders, answered the door with a wide smile.

Jillian and Kara flashed their warrant cards and said they were told Mr. Winston was expecting them.

"Of course." The woman, still smiling, added, "Please, come in," and directed them to a sitting room with furniture that looked like it had never been sat in and carpet that still bore marks of a vacuum. "I'll let Derek know you're here."

If it hadn't been for the conversation earlier in the car and Jillian's private musings, she would have missed it, but when Derek Winston came round the corner a minute later, he smiled broadly at Jillian, but as his gaze swept over Kara, something changed.

It was ever so slight; even his gait almost paused mid-step. He didn't stop or even slow down, but there was a change in his cadence. The smile, still plastered on his face, never left, but something about it shifted. It was his eyes that betrayed him the most. His pupils constricted, and his eyes widened before quickly resuming their previous form.

Jillian said, "I'm DI Scotte. This is DC Devanor. Thank you for making some time for us, Mr. Winston."

"Please," he answered, shaking her hand but not even offering to shake Kara's. "Call me Derek."

Everyone took a seat on the new-looking furniture.

"Now, how can I help you?" he asked, his gaze firmly on Jillian, his smile fully in place, as though painted on.

"As I understand it, you are the director of Historinaccuracy Research?" Jillian asked, her hands resting gently on her lap. She knew without looking that Kara was taking notes.

Winston sat back in his chair a little. "Well, I wouldn't quite put it like that, but yes, I am responsible for running things."

"How *would* you put it?"

Winston paused, clearly giving his answer some thought. "As I say, I am responsible for the organization's day-to-day."

"What is it exactly that Historinaccuracy Research does?"

His smile widened, though until that point Jillian would not have thought it possible. "I should think the name was self-evident, *Detective*." He emphasized the last word as though mocking her title. "We research the accuracy, and often inaccuracy, of history as it pertains to the United Kingdom."

"To what end?" Jillian said, as if asking about the weather.

Winston, his legs crossed, reached down and plucked some invisible piece of something off his gray trousers and flicked his fingers. At that moment, the woman who had opened the door came in bearing a tray with a tea kettle and some biscuits on it. She carefully and gently set it down on the coffee table before them without making a sound.

"Tea?" Winston said. Jillian said no thank you. Neither the woman nor Winston bothered to look at Kara for a response.

The woman left without saying a word. Winston reached over and poured himself a cup, added some milk, and took a biscuit, leaning back in his chair and taking a bite.

Jillian waited without saying a word, letting Derek Winston chew both on his thoughts and his tea biscuit. Finally, he said, "We are a private member's organization, Detective. Our work is for the benefit of our members."

"Was Jonathan Blakesly a member of your club?"

Winston did not like hearing the word "club," which was, of course, why Jillian had used it. His smile faltered a little. Leaning forward, he set his teacup down. "I'm afraid our membership directory is privileged information, Detective Inspector. I cannot divulge membership information without their consent."

"Mr. Winston," Jillian said, purposefully not using his first name, "we are investigating a double murder, with Mr. Blakesly being one of the victims. As I can hardly ask him for his permission, I'm sure you could agree that his membership in your organization will not affect him one way or the other now."

Winston didn't miss a beat. "That's as may be, Detective, but if I were to break our membership rules, it would have an effect on other, and future, members. They might think we would easily give out their own information when any Tom, Dick, or Harry came knocking."

"I can certainly get a warrant to compel you." Jillian let the threat hang in the air.

"To which I would happily comply. Our rules permit us to divulge information when legally bound to do so."

"But not when morally bound?" Jillian taunted.

Winston did not reply, choosing instead to simply look at her and smile.

"Well, thank you for your time," Jillian said, standing up. Kara did the same, closing her notebook and putting it in her handbag.

"I'm sorry I couldn't be more helpful, Inspector," Winston said, clearly not meaning it.

As Jillian and Kara got back in the car, they studied the front windows of the home. They could see Winston standing by the sitting room window, looking at them.

"Get the warrant, Kara," Jillian said, staring back.

"Yes mum."

"We both know it will show Jonathan Blakesly was a member, but let's tick off that box." Then, after a pause, Jillian added, "He didn't even try to hide it, did he?"

Kara paused with the key in the ignition. "We were in his home. His turf. He doesn't have to be civil; he can do as he pleases."

Jillian shook her head in disgust.

"Guv?" Kara said, turning the key to start the car.

Jillian looked over.

"Did you see the children in the other room?"

Jillian tilted her head slightly. "Yes, three of them at the dining table. Looked like they were doing schoolwork or something."

"Yes, but did you notice how they were dressed?"

Jillian frowned, searching her memory. "Not particularly."

"They were dressed like their mother. Very proper. The boy had a shirt and tie under his cardigan. The girls had skirts I'd swear were ironed, just like the mother's."

Jillian contemplated these words, nodding absentmindedly as Kara added, "When have you seen a home that immaculate with three young children of that age? Not a thing out of place. No toys. No noise. The house was as quiet as a church."

Jillian turned and looked back at the window. Winston was no longer there watching them, but a shiver ran down her spine just the same.

CHAPTER 6

Invisible strings. It was the best way Jillian Scotte could describe the feeling as she lay in bed with Daniella early on Monday morning.

Daniella lay sideways and propped up on one elbow, her hand holding up her head. Her long, black hair was tousled from sleep, the sheets barely covering her naked body as her other hand twirled around Jillian's hair. "What do you mean, invisible strings?"

"I can't explain it." Jillian sighed contentedly, turning to look up into Daniella's deep black opal eyes. She couldn't help but smile before adding, "It's just a feeling. We served the warrant, and of course Blakesly was listed as a member, but we already figured that. We've been chasing the money, but everything seems to come to dead ends."

"So why the invisible strings?"

"Because I can't help feeling like every time we look one way, someone is pulling us in that direction on purpose, like a marionette controlled by some unseen, all-seeing manipulator that controls our every move."

Daniella frowned. "That seems unlikely, though, doesn't it?"

"Yeah," Jillian said, sighing heavily again.

"Maybe you should start looking where the puppet master doesn't want you to look," Daniella said, letting her fingers trail down Jillian's stomach.

Jillian gave her the equivalent of the "gee, why didn't I think of that" look but was too distracted by Daniella's fingers to give much more of a response.

Half an hour later, with Daniella's hair even more tousled, Jillian got out of bed and padded to the shower, mumbling something about being late.

"Are you complaining?" Daniella said in a mockingly hurt voice.

Jillian stuck her head back out of the bathroom door. "Only about having to go to work."

Showered, dressed, and filling up a travel mug with coffee to head out the door, Jillian looked at Daniella, who had a rare day off and stood leaning against the counter in a fluffy white robe.

"What?" she asked.

Daniella shook her head. "Nothing, you just looked like you were someplace else. I was wondering what you were thinking."

Giving her a quick kiss, Jillian said, "I was thinking about what you said about where the puppet master doesn't want me to look."

As Jillian opened the door to leave, she caught Daniella raising her eyebrows and looking away pointedly.

"What is that for?"

Daniella turned back, smiling. "Nothing. I know that look on your face." Then she added, "I wouldn't want to be that puppet master, that's all."

***

Detective Constable Kara Devanor walked into her boss's office, having been summoned by a yell through the door. "Yes, mum?" she asked, taking a seat, her notepad out and pen at the ready.

"What do we know about Jinani Rasool?" Jillian asked.

"Nothing more than before, I'm afraid," Kara responded, flipping through her notebook. "I have Stacey doing historical digging, but so far, she seems rather boring."

She was referring to Stacey Alston, one of their administrators, and a wiz at doing background research. If she couldn't find anything unusual, it meant there wasn't anything.

Jillian's cell phone rang. After looking at the caller ID, she glanced at Kara. "I'd better take this."

Kara took her cue to leave, but before turning to go, she said hesitantly, "Mum, DS Listun called to say he was coming back next week."

Picking up her cell with her finger poised to swipe, Jillian said, "Did the doctor say he's ready?"

"Sounds more like he and his missus are ready regardless," Kara answered, and walked out the door.

Jillian half smiled; Detective Sergeant Stephen Listun would drive her bonkers after two days, let alone months. She swiped her phone. "Hello."

"Good morning," said the unmistakable voice of Sebastian Hughes, the well-dressed head of syndicated gambling in Southern England. Intelligent, charming, and simultaneously unnerving all at once.

"Good morning to you, Mr. Hughes," Jillian said. She was never sure how she felt about Sebastian Hughes. He was, after all, a criminal, and yet he had saved her life and always seemed to be more concerned with helping her than harming. Still, she had to remind herself that this was a man who had killed before and was not afraid to do it again. "To what do I owe the pleasure of this call?"

"How is Daniella doing?" Hughes asked, ever the gentleman.

Jillian's mind flashed back to the events of the morning, and her faced flushed. Taking a breath, she said, "She's great." She realized she knew next to nothing about Sebastian's life. She couldn't ask about anyone in particular, so she said, "How are things with you?"

"Very well, thank you," he replied. After a pause, he said, "I wanted to ask you something a bit . . . delicate."

"Go on," Jillian said cautiously.

"It has come to my attention that your colleagues have been looking into the financial affairs of some of my . . . ah . . . more influential clients."

Jillian said nothing, waiting for more.

After another pause, Sebastian said, "I was just wondering if this had anything to do with my business or something I should be concerned about?"

Jillian took a moment to pause before saying, "Can you give me some names?"

She knew he was weighing whether to give her the names, knowing it would confirm that they were connected to his gambling operations in some fashion. Still, he had called her about them, so he knew she was checking on them already.

Hughes was silent for a while. Jillian lifted the phone away from her ear to make sure the call had not dropped. When she heard his voice, she put it back to her ear and wrote down three names. She vaguely recalled seeing them on the membership list, but they meant nothing to her.

"I'm not aware of any connection to you," she said, choosing her words carefully. "Just a coincidence from another line of inquiry."

"Would you have told me if it had been connected to me?"

The question caught her off guard. She thought about it for a moment. "I'm not sure."

She wasn't sure how she knew, but she felt like she could feel him smiling down the phone.

"Sebastian," she said, her voice lowering a bit, "what do you know about something called Historinaccuracy Research?"

"Not much. I know it's some sort of private club for radicals, mostly ex-prison white nationalist gang members, if I recall."

"What about a man called Derek Winston?"

"Hmm." Hughes pondered. "I've heard the name before, but I couldn't say where. It's possible I heard Slater say it or something. Why?"

"Nothing," Jillian said, wondering now if his former boss, Greg Slater, had somehow been connected with Derek Winston. "Just wondering. Listen, I've got to go."

"Of course," Hughes said. "Thanks for taking my call."

"Any time," Jillian replied, meaning it.

"Oh, and Jillian?"

That got her attention. Sebastian rarely called her by her first name. "Yes?"

"Be careful if you go up against the white nationalist people. They don't play about."

Jillian hung up the phone and got that same shiver down her spine that she had felt when leaving Winston's house.

CHAPTER 7

Eyes of gold stared back at her in the mirror. Kara Devanor had always liked her eyes. Sometimes they were more brown than golden brown, but other days, like today, the golden hue shone brighter. She knew most men found her attractive, and she worked hard to stay fit, but she felt her eyes were her most distinguishing feature. Men were always looking her up and down, but it was rare that someone bothered to approach her, which was partially why she was still single.

Well, that, and her job. Most blokes ran as soon as they learned she was a copper. It was funny how women loved a man in uniform and thought being a copper's girlfriend was exciting. Not so with women in the police. Men were frightened of them.

Kara had been in love once, or at least thought she had. Long ago, at university. She had taken her broken heart with her after graduation into the police academy and, with it, a renewed passion for work. That left little room for anyone else. Except for those she worked with. Since her days at the academy, every place she had been, someone had tried hitting on her at work.

That was not going to happen here, Kara thought, having freshly showered after her morning yoga and a quick cup of tea. On her way to work, she shifted her attention from her determination not to date other coppers to the case at hand.

Something just did not add up, and she wanted to talk to Jillian about it.

***

Jillian was just getting to work when she received a message from Superintendent Maryanne Sanderson, her boss, asking for a video call first thing.

Once they were connected, Sanderson asked how things were going. Jillian gave her an update, such as it was. Then Sanderson said, "Okay, Jillian. Look, I've got an MP breathing down my neck that insisted on an update personally. He wanted to come down and talk to you, but I convinced him to do it this way. He'll be joining us in about four minutes. Just tell him what you've told me."

Great, Jillian thought. This was why she would never rise higher than her current position of Detective Inspector. Even the mountain of paperwork that she already loathed at this level was nothing compared to her loathing of politicians. And perhaps even more, the politics of policing at her boss's level.

Presently, Minister of Parliament Rupert Chiswick joined their call. He looked the part of a politician—all smiles, dark hair, brown eyes, and the stereotypical slimy demeanor. He began with the usual congratulations for all her hard work, how much he admired the Met and all that they stood for. Finally, he got around to the point and asked about the case, explaining that the crime had occurred in his district, and he had constituents calling him constantly for updates.

Jillian doubted his phone was ringing off the hook as he claimed, given that hers had not rung once. And she was likely to get more calls about it than a politician who spent as much time in London as he did in his district. Still, she filled him in on their lines of inquiry and their progress, minimal though it was.

He asked one or two more questions, then said, "So, what has this historical group got to do with the case?"

"I'm not quite sure, Mr. Chiswick. It is just one of our lines of inquiry."

"Yes, Inspector," he replied, "I understand that. I certainly don't mean to tell you how to do your job."

Which Jillian took to mean that he was about to.

"But the last thing I need right now is to draw attention to white nationalists or create a race media circus because someone of color was murdered."

"We are being discreet, sir."

At this point Sanderson chimed in, saying that all lines of inquiry needed to be followed, and of course they would do everything in their power to keep the media away from this angle of their investigation.

"Thank you, Superintendent," he said—condescendingly, Jillian thought. "I trust you will keep me apprised of any updates on the investigation?"

"Yes, of course," Sanderson replied—equally condescendingly, Jillian was pleased to hear.

The call ended, and Jillian bent her head back to her second-least-favorite task of paperwork.

Kara knocked on her boss's door.

"Come in," Jillian said, looking up from the piles of folders, reports, and papers on her desk. "What have we got on the double murder"?

Having scanned the overnight emails on the way in, Kara said, "Nothing new. We're still going through financials of both victims and trying to work our way through the labyrinth of the members of Historinaccuracy Research, such as it is." The list they had been given was far from complete, and many of the names and addresses did not even seem to exist. It was a wild goose chase they had to follow, as frustrating as it might be.

Jillian sighed loudly and rubbed the bridge of her nose.

"Boss," Kara said, "something's been bothering me."

Jillian dropped her hand and looked at her DS. "Go on."

"Well," Kara said, "we know that the male vic was a member of Historinaccuracy Research."

Jillian nodded.

"And it would certainly seem, from what little we know, everything points to that club being a haven for people who believe in white supremacy."

Again, her boss nodded.

"So, what was Jonathan Blakesly doing in a relationship with a Pakistani woman? Someone neither white nor English?"

Jillian studied her for a moment. "You're suggesting that the crime may have been racially motivated?"

Kara shrugged. "Dunno. It just doesn't fit, does it?"

"Jonathan Blakesly was white and English, and he was murdered as well," Jillian pointed out.

"I know," Kara said slowly, formulating her thoughts. "At first, that's what kept me going down the usual paths—money, power, sex, et cetera, but . . ."

"But what?" Jillian asked.

Kara seemed nervous, then she finally blurted out, "You asked me to point things out if I saw them."

Jillian now leaned forward, resting her forearms on her desk, her hands clasped as she stared directly at Kara. "Yes, I did."

"The idea that a man who was a member of an organization of white supremacists would have a relationship with a woman of color, an immigrant at that . . ."

"Go on," Jillian prodded.

"Well, I began looking at the crime scene a bit differently. The two victims were made to watch each other's torture, and one of them, the eventual death of the other."

Jillian nodded slowly.

"It's as though it was both a lesson and a message," Kara said.

Jillian sat back in her chair, thoughtful.

Just then, Jillian's cell phone rang. Not recognizing the number, she swiped it and, holding it up, said, "Jillian Scotte."

"Hello, Ms. Scotte," the voice said on the other end. A woman's voice accented but not heavily. "This is Lilian Delacroix. I wondered if you had a moment?"

Jillian raised her eyebrows at Kara and said, "Hello Ms. Delacroix. Yes, of course, how can I help?"

Kara raised eyebrows of her own at the mention of the eccentric madam, whom they had met some months ago on another case.

"Actually, I was calling because I think I might be of some help to you," Delacroix said. Jillian opened her mouth to say something, but the woman continued, "At least, indirectly."

"I'm not sure I understand," Jillian said, shrugging at Kara.

"It has come to my attention that you are interested in an organization known as Historinaccuracy Research?"

"How do you know that?" Jillian said, slowly standing and half turning to look out her office window at the slight drizzle that began to fall.

Ignoring the question, Delacroix continued, "I have, or rather, had, someone in my employ who was, shall we say, tangentially associated with them."

Jillian was pondering what to say next when Delacroix said, "She would be willing to speak to you, off the record."

Jillian turned back to facing Kara and said simply, "She?"

After a few minutes of logistical conversation, Jillian hung up the phone.

"It would seem that Ms. Delacroix has a connection to someone from Historinaccuracy Research who would like to speak with us. Get your coat, we're going to pay the Madame another visit."

CHAPTER 8

Oranges were piled high on a dark brown wooden bowl in the middle of the coffee table. Once again, Detective Inspector Jillian Scotte and Detective Constable Kara Devanor found themselves in the well-appointed library of Lilian Delacroix, the madam they had met when a prostitute had been brutally murdered on a previous case.

The gray stone building looked much the same as before, though two additional large cement plant holders had been added to the front entryway, effectively creating a barrier that only pedestrians could pass through. Jillian silently wondered what had precipitated the added security.

The library, with its roaring fireplace, was a warm welcome on the wet, chilly day.

Lilian Delacroix walked in, tall and slender, with her light brown hair pulled back in a bun. She wore a dark gray suit with a vanilla-colored blouse and matching flat shoes.

She shook hands with Jillian and Kara. "Nice to see you again, Inspector, Detective," she said, addressing them each in turn.

"And you," Jillian said.

Ms. Delacroix sat down on the smaller of the two sofas while Jillian and Kara took the larger one opposite. "Can I offer you some tea? Coffee?"

Both policewomen accepted tea. Delacroix simply nodded to the butler, who bowed his head and retreated from the room, closing the door behind him.

"Lilian, I'm curious how you learned about our interest in Historinaccuracy Research?" Jillian said, immediately getting to the point.

Ms. Delacroix smiled, looking down at the oranges before plucking one from the bowl and beginning to peel it. "I have my sources, Detective," she said simply. Before Jillian could say more, Delacroix added, "Could you please elaborate for me on what your interest in them is?"

"We're investigating a brutal double murder. Their name came up in connection with one of the victims."

"That would be Jonathan Blakesly," Delacroix said matter-of-factly, carefully placing her orange-peel pieces in a small pile on the coffee table. She placed a slice of orange in her mouth, delicately chewing as she looked across the table at the two detectives.

Jillian raised one eyebrow and turned her head slightly, though she kept her eyes on Delacroix with a "how could you know that" expression on her face.

Swallowing her orange, Delacroix said, "The murder was in the papers, online, and on the telly. Of the two victims, only Mr. Blakesly would have been connected with that organization." She placed another slice of orange in her mouth.

Jillian decided to take charge of the conversation. "You mentioned on the phone that you had someone who wished to speak to us."

The door opened at that point, and the butler returned with a tray ladened with tea, cream, sugar, cups, and saucers. Ms. Delacroix poured tea for everyone, then turning to her butler she said, "Can you please fetch my laptop from the office for me?"

Bowing slightly again, the man said, "Certainly, madame," and once again departed.

After adding cream and a bit of sugar to her tea, she took a sip. Satisfied, she placed the cup back on its saucer. "Some time ago, a woman came to me needing protection," she said.

"Protection from whom?" Jillian asked.

Ignoring the question, Delacroix said, "I took her in and gave her shelter. I was in a difficult position, you must understand. Because of the danger she was in, she could not work."

Jillian and Kara stayed quiet. Delacroix continued, "It quickly became clear that she could not stay here. We came to an . . . arrangement . . . in which I would help her find somewhere to live, and she would recompense me over time. Thus, we have stayed in touch."

Taking another sip of her tea, she said, "When the murders happened, she heard about it online."

Kara looked at Jillian, but her boss kept her gaze focused on their host.

"When I heard you were making inquiries around that dreadful organization, I contacted her," Delacroix said, just as the butler returned with her laptop. Placing it on the coffee table in front of her, she opened the cover, pressed a few keys, and smiled briefly.

Looking across the table at the two women, she said, "Her safety is my primary concern."

"Of course," Jillian said.

"You will have to take my word that what she has to say is true," Delacroix said before spinning the laptop around so the screen faced the two detectives.

Jillian and Kara leaned forward. The screen had a video conference engaged. They saw the silhouette of a woman with long hair in front of a brightly lit window. She was sitting on a plain wooden chair. No other furniture or discernible items were in the frame. The window was covered with a plain white curtain that obscured the view outside, though it allowed enough light to create the silhouette.

"Hello," a voice said. It was low, clearly being modified digitally. It almost sounded male, though the detectives knew that this was because of the digital voice-altering process.

Jillian and Kara exchanged glances. "Hello. My name is Detective Inspector Scotte." Then nodding next to her, she added, "This is detective constable Devanor."

"I know who you are," the voice said.

"What can you tell us about Historinaccuracy Research?" Jillian asked.

"Nothing you don't already know," the voice said. Then, "They're not who you're looking for."

Jillian pulled back a little, sitting up straighter, but before she could say anything, the voice went on. "They are just enforcers. The ones responsible for what happened to your victims are with something called Dominion."

Kara, writing in her notebook, exchanged another look with Jillian. This time Kara said, "What do you mean, something called Dominion?"

The woman on the screen took an audible breath. "I was involved with someone a while ago. Occasionally, over dinner, the name would come up. I tried asking about it. At first, I was told it was nothing. The man I was seeing brushed it off. Once I pushed him on it and he became angry, telling me it was none of my business."

The woman paused. Jillian and Kara said nothing, waiting.

"I came to find out Dominion is some sort of group. They believe in something they call the TELL. It stands for True English Living Lineage. They believe English blood has been diluted over the decades through immigration and interracial marriages with those of non-Anglo-Saxon heritage."

Kara's pen stopped in midair. The voice continued, "One night, the man I was seeing told me we were going out for a surprise. I thought he meant dinner. He took me on a long drive. The further we drove, the wearier I became. Finally, he told me we were heading somewhere special, that I was going to have the honor of meeting the head of Dominion."

Again, the voice paused before continuing. "I insisted he stop the car and wanted to know exactly what was going on. That is when he told me the truth about what Dominion was. He said there would be an enormous party and that we had been especially invited."

The pause this time was longer. When the woman continued, her voice had changed. Even though the voice-altering synthesizer still masked it, there was something subtly different. "You must know from Ms. Delacroix that my profession means I am not new to sexual variety."

Jillian nodded, but said nothing.

"He told me we were being specially invited to what sounded like a party whose primary purpose was an orgy. He then said that the reason we were meeting the head of Dominion was because he was looking for potential breeders for the next generation of the true English lineage"—here she waited a beat before adding—"with him as the breeder."

Kara couldn't help herself. "You're joking."

Jillian shot her a quick look to keep quiet. Turning back to the screen, she said, "Did you meet this head of Dominion?"

"No. I got out of the car and ran. He tried to chase me, but I can run quite fast. He eventually gave up and went back to his car. It took half the night for me to find somewhere I could call from and get back to my flat. That's when the threatening phone calls began."

"From the man you were seeing?" Jillian asked.

"At first, yes," she said. "Then I would have someone stop me in the street to tell me I had better keep my mouth shut. They were people I had seen from events at Historinaccuracy Research. That's when I ran and came to Ms. Delacroix."

Kara knew the answer before she asked, but it had to be done. "What was the name of the man you had been seeing?"

"Jonathan Blakesly," the voice said.

CHAPTER 9

Dark clouds blanketed the sky. An ominous warning if ever there was one, Jillian thought as she wrapped her arms around herself, hugging her coat closer to her body as she walked across the street to the café.

Amelia Hamza had asked to meet her, no doubt to ask how the investigation was going.

The past few days had been somewhat of a blur, like the neon lights of the café reflecting on the puddles of water in the street. The visit to Madame Delacroix's home had been filled with more questions than answers.

Jillian and Kara had been taken aback by the revelation about the organization called Dominion.

"It seems the white supremacy of Historinaccuracy Research is more an enforcement arm of this Dominion thing," Jillian had said, thinking out loud.

"Yeah," Kara responded, "that whole breeding the next generation thing is a whole new level."

As they made their way back to the VCU headquarters, Jillian mused, "It's like they took that old tale of droit du seigneur and ran with it."

"The what?" Kara asked.

"It has been called 'first night,' or 'right of the lord.'" Jillian said, looking out the window of the car. "Back in medieval times, noblemen claimed they had the right to spend the first night with newly wedded brides in their fiefdoms." After a pause, she added, "It was a continuation of what has always been. Using positions of power for sexual conquest."

"Whatever it's called, still sounds like rape to me," Kara said, her face grim as she drove.

Jillian looked over at her DC. There was something more to the comment, she was sure, but she decided now was not the time.

Back at their office, Jillian called the team together. "I want everything we can find on a group called Dominion. Also, we need more background on the male victim, Jonathan Blakesly. Check with known associates, work mates, et cetera. I want a thorough analysis of Derek Winston. There is something much bigger here than Historinaccuracy Research, so let's shift our focus."

DS Listun, still relegated to desk duty on doctors' orders, got everyone moving, assigning tasks, and making sure everyone kept to them.

It was nice to see the office humming again, Jillian thought, watching from behind her desk. Although Kara had done a great job in his absence, she had been pulled in too many directions to keep everyone on task, the job of her DS.

Two days later, her two-star detectives came into her office for an update. Kara, as usual, had her notebook at the ready. Listun did not look pleased as he sat down heavily in one of Jillian's guest chairs.

Listun began somberly. "Guv, we haven't been able to find anything of note on Dominion. As it relates to this case," he clarified.

"What? Nothing at all?" Jillian asked, surprised.

"No," Listun said, shaking his head. "The only website with that name is a commercial property agent's, which is a nonstarter. Of course, 'Dominion' was the status of all commonwealth countries prior to 1939, so there's loads of information about that, and of course those blasted election machines from the 2020 elections in the United States, but otherwise, absolutely nothing."

Kara spoke up, consulting her notes. "Likewise, mum, nothing much on Mr. Blakesly. At least nothing we didn't already know. Further inquiries into his finances show nothing new either. A dead end, I'm afraid."

"And what about Winston?" Jillian asked, frustrated.

Listun looked over at Kara, who consulted her notes, flipping pages before speaking. "His primary employment comes as the director of Historinaccuracy Research, for which he receives a larger than usual salary, but otherwise nothing out of the ordinary."

Jillian stared at her two detectives, knowing they wanted her to give them new directions to go in, but she was stumped. She had been sure something would have come up from their searches. To be completely blank was odd at best, and disheartening at worst.

She got up and half turned to stare out her office window, mostly to buy some time while she was thinking. There had to be something they were missing.

"Okay, let's keep expanding our radius. Check Winston's family, look into the female victim again, her peers, work mates, et cetera. We are missing something, and we have to find it."

Having given her team their orders, she grabbed her coat and headed for the café to meet with Amelia.

Jillian stepped through the door and spotted Amelia near the back. Normally, she would have expected to see the journalist's laptop and papers all over the table, but not this time.

Amelia Hamza looked tired. Her shoulders were slumped, and her smile didn't quite reach her deep green eyes as Jillian sat down.

Jillian asked how she was doing, but Amelia's answers were too rehearsed, as though she had been asked the question a thousand times since she discovered the brutal murder of her friend.

"How is the investigation coming?" the journalist asked, getting to the point quickly.

"Amelia," Jillian said hesitantly, "you know I can't discuss an ongoing investigation with a reporter, especially given that . . ."

Amelia stared straight at Jillian; her eyes unblinkingly fierce. "I've been put on leave to let me have time to grieve." As she said the last four words, she made air quotes with her fingers.

Jillian weighed her options, then told her about Blakesly's former girl-friend, or at least the experience.

"How do you know this?" Amelia asked.

"I can't tell you," Jillian said.

"But," Amelia stammered, "that can't be right?"

Jillian just waited.

"It makes no sense," Amelia said. "He couldn't have been a white supremacist."

Jillian said nothing, knowing what was going through the woman's mind. It was the same thing Jillian and Kara had gone over after their video call at Madame Delacroix's.

"Jinani was Paki," Amelia said. "She was brown, he . . . why would . . ." Amelia looked up at Jillian with confusion and anxiety written all over her face.

"We don't know," was all Jillian could say.

"Amelia," she asked gently, "have you ever heard Jinani, or Jonathan, for that matter, ever mention the word Dominion?"

Amelia's brow furrowed. "Dominion? No, why?"

"How about a man called Derek Winston?"

Amelia straightened up in her chair. "No. Who is he? Did he kill Jinani?"

Jillian held her hands up. "Hold on. I didn't say that. He's just part of the inquiry."

Amelia didn't look like she bought it but instead said, "What is Dominion? Is it someone's name?"

Jillian sighed. "I'm afraid I don't know. We don't think it's a name, more the name of something, a group maybe. We can't seem to find out anything."

Jillian stayed for another fifteen minutes, letting Amelia ask all her questions. She felt a little guilty, knowing with the names of Winston and Dominion in her head, the journalist would look into them. It was, perhaps, not the right thing to do, and certainly not the most ethical, but Jillian was running out of time and ideas. She already had another call from Superintendent Sanderson to return, and if she didn't get some answers soon, there would be hell to pay.

***

Back at the Tof, the team were in the incident room. Listun wanted everyone to go over every detail they had been working on. He knew that sometimes sharing information could lead to something, and he was hoping it would now. He was right.

PC Stella Dawson was going over some of the information on the Winston family, but much of it everyone already knew.

"What about the Historinaccuracy Research side of things, any joy there?" Listun asked.

Kara and Stacey Alston, their principal police administrator, had been poring over financial records and digging into some of the hidden companies that seemed to both donate money and receive donations from the research company. It was a daunting task.

"We're still trying to track down some of these shell corporations, sarge," Kara said. "I'm sure some have laundering written all over them, but we're compiling a list of owners and names associated with them. So far, nothing that connects them to Winston or Blakesly or even the girl Rasool. Nothing remotely resembling the name Dominion either."

Listun sighed loudly. Looking up at their board, he searched for some thread to follow. "What about the rest of the Winston family?" he said, looking back at PC Dawson.

Flipping through her notebook, she said, "Nothing much, sarge. Sarah Kolvan, the wife . . ."

"Not Winston?" Listun asked.

"No sir," Dawson said. "On the marriage certificate she kept her maiden name."

Kara was frowning. "What was her name again?"

"Sarah Kolvan," Dawson said.

Kara and Stacey exchanged glances. "We've seen that name before."

CHAPTER 10

When evening's shadows fall, most people look out their windows and feel the yearning to close down their work and go home. Not Detective Constable Kara Devanor, or, for that matter, most of the members of the Violent Crimes Unit.

Kara and the chief VCU administrative assistant, Stacey Alston, had been poring over hundreds of documents and printouts for most of the day. They were looking for a name: Sarah Kolvan.

A name that, so far, had eluded them.

Jillian stopped by the incident room, where they had everything spread out and two computers running, to check in. "How's it going?"

Both women sighed loudly.

"That good, is it?" Jillian said with a weary smile.

"We know we've seen that name, mum," Kara said.

"Sod all if I know where, though," Alston added.

"Let's pack it in for tonight," Jillian said. "It's been a long day and you've been at it nonstop. Try again in the morning with fresh eyes."

Later that night, at their small, but cozy cottage, Jillian and Daniella lounged together on their small sofa. Jillian, at five foot five, was slightly shorter than Daniella. Jillian was sipping on a glass of wine with a throw pillow on her lap, upon which Daniella's head was resting.

"How are you getting along at work?" Jillian asked.

Daniella, having recently joined the coroner's office in Southampton, was working under the chief coroner, Michael Thorsby. It was a change from being by herself and effectively in charge when she was up in Cumbria. Southampton was a much bigger city and saw all manner of bodies go through the morgue on any given day.

"Not too bad," Daniella said, her eyes closed contentedly as Jillian gently stroked her hair. "Dr. Thorsby is really talented; I'm actually learning quite a lot from him."

"He's not intimidated by your stunning good looks, top-of-the-marks intelligence, and hyper-drive ambition?" Jillian said, looking down and smiling.

Daniella opened her eyes with a "you've got to be joking" look on her face. "I think that describes you more than me, love," she said, reaching up and poking her lover in the ribs.

"Mmm," Jillian replied, taking another sip of wine, "I think you under-value your abilities, Dr. Morales. If I were Michael Thorsby, I'd watch my back before I lost my job to the younger lesbian."

Daniella giggled, then adroitly changed the subject. "How is the investigation going?"

"Nowhere," Jillian replied. "We've hit a dead end, really. Something will turn up in time, but it's frustrating not doing anything."

Daniella, always attuned to her partner's mood changes when she was entrenched in a case, began asking questions. Jillian knew she had changed the subject on purpose, as Daniella was never one to enjoy talking about herself, but Jillian also welcomed the chance to talk through the case with her. It always helped settle things in her mind.

"This Winston bloke sounds like quite the patriarchal arsehole," Daniella said.

"You should have seen him in his home. Like he was a king, and his wife, all prim and proper, with the children out of sight and quiet, *as they should be*." Jillian held up air quotes with her free hand to emphasize the last four words.

"You're sure there isn't anything more to this Historinaccuracy Research?" Daniella asked.

Jillian shook her head. "No. Looks like mainly muscle for this group, Dominion. We're trying to find the paper trail. There are hooks into a few dummy corporations with various enterprises, most of which border on just the right side of legal, but so far not much in the way of clues."

"Well," Daniella said, "like you always say, there are only two trails you can follow."

Jillian looked down affectionately.

Daniella looked back up, smiling warmly, and said, "Follow the money or cherchez la femme."

As it turned out, it would be both.

✳✳✳

The next day, the VCU team was hard at work by the time Jillian came in, having languished far too long for her own good before getting out of bed.

She grabbed some coffee and headed over to the incident room, where DS Listun was looking over Kara's shoulder.

"Morning, guv," Listun said as she came in.

"Good morning."

Kara looked up from her computer. "We're putting together a new strategy so we can be more methodical in our search."

Jillian always loved the passion with which Kara threw herself into any task. Still. "Right, well, one more day, but that's it. If you don't find her today, we'll need to focus our efforts elsewhere."

Kara didn't like the deadline, but she understood it. She nodded curtly to her boss as Listun and Scotte left the incident room to talk about the rest of the team's progress.

Kara turned to Stacey Alston. Stacey just nodded once, a determined look on her face. Together, the two got to work.

Jillian spent much of the day returning messages, filling out the never-ending pile of reports, and attending the equally laborious meetings that her job demanded.

It was midafternoon. A brief splash of sunlight poked through between the ever-present storm clouds, casting a swath of light across Jillian's desk when Kara and Stacey walked into her office.

Jillian glanced up, then dropped her pen and straightened herself in her chair. The two women looked like the cat who just swallowed the canary, so big were their smiles. Jillian raised her eyebrows questioningly.

"We went through every transaction, every business associated with Historinaccuracy Research," Kara began. "We looked at those who gave money and those to whom the *research* company gave." Kara used air quotes and a fair amount of sarcasm with the word *research*. "We tried to track down anyone associated with those shell companies—board members, owners, those listed with the licensing offices." She paused. "Nothing."

Jillian, eager for Kara to get to the point but willing to let them have their moment, just smiled.

"Honestly, guv," Kara said, "I was about to give up, thinking I'd just imagined it, that Sarah Kolvan was just something I thought I'd seen. I mean, there were plenty of Sarahs among the list of names we've been chasing."

Kara looked over at her colleague. "Then Stacey found it."

Jillian glanced at her administrator, then back at Kara, pleased she was giving credit where credit was due. Stacey said, "The name we had seen wasn't on any member list, or board list, or licensing application." With a flourish, she handed over a sheet of paper. "It was on a check."

Jillian took the sheet, which showed a photocopy of a check. It was written to a company whose name she remembered from the long list of associated companies they were looking for. The check was signed by Sarah Kolvan.

Just then, DS Listun came in. "Boss, we've just got a call from Central," he said, referring to the main Southampton Constabulary.

Everyone turned to look at him.

"There's been an incident at the Winston estate," Listun said.

Kara was already grabbing her coat from the back of her desk chair when Jillian came out of her office and tossed her the car keys.

CHAPTER 11

The volume level was reaching a fever pitch, making it difficult for Kara Devanor to concentrate on driving through the heavy afternoon traffic. Her boss, Detective Inspector Jillian Scotte, was screaming into the phone.

"What do you mean, that's all you have in the log? I *know* what's in the log because you've repeated it to me six times. I want to know what was said on the call," Jillian said forcefully.

Kara could hear someone speaking on the other end, but couldn't make out what they were saying.

"How is it possible, in the last five minutes, that a desk sergeant can walk off shift and simply disappear into thin air? Do you lot not have the ability to communicate beyond the walls of the bloody station?" Jillian had one hand pushed up against the dashboard as Kara slalomed their car through heavy traffic. The other hand held the phone to her ear as she rolled her eyes, winced, and barked out orders.

"Have your sergeants not heard of new technology? It's called a cell phone. Ring his bloody phone, and call me back with something other than 'there's been an incident at the Winston Estate.'" Jillian said. She hung up the phone, sighed loudly, and turned to stare out the window, fuming.

Since they had left the office, she had been on the phone with Southampton Central trying to get details about what exactly an "incident" meant. Apparently, the desk sergeant who had received the call had simply written "incident at Winston estate" in the log. Because the estate had come up in their system as a VCU priority, he had relayed it to the Tof but had then gone off duty at the end of his shift.

Clearly, they were having trouble locating him to get more information, as he was apparently not answering his phone. The result was a string of expletives directed at the unsuspecting officer on duty as Jillian unleashed her frustration on the poor bloke.

Kara slowed down at an approaching red light, swerving around a moving lorry, and inching her nose into the intersection so the approaching cross traffic could hear her siren and hopefully see the flashing light on the dashboard.

Obediently, two cars coming from opposite directions slowed down long enough for Kara to speed up. She floored it across the intersection into a mostly clear section of road as they continued to make their way across the city.

Jillian's phone rang. She looked down and swiped. "Stephen," she said, speaking to Detective Sergeant Listun back at the VCU. She listened for a moment, then said, "Hang on, I'm putting you on speaker." Pressing a button to activate her speaker so Kara could hear, she said, "Go on."

"I've just gotten off the phone with the central desk sergeant who took the call."

This explained why they couldn't get a hold of him, Jillian thought. It was a credit to Stephen that he could track the man down faster than his own colleagues could.

"The call came in from Sarah Kolvan, Winston's wife," Stephen continued. "Apparently, they had a visitor who, when her husband answered the door, began shouting and causing a scene. The woman began threatening Mr. Winston with . . . and this is a quote from the wife, 'exposing him for the murder of Jinani Rasool.'"

"According to the desk sergeant, Mrs. Kolvan said her husband told her to take the children into the kitchen. And although she could hear the argument continue, she couldn't make out the words. After a few minutes, she heard the front door close. When she came out of the kitchen, her husband was gone, and she looked out the window to see him in a car with the woman as they drove away."

"Did she know who the woman was?" Jillian asked.

"No," Listun responded, "but, boss, she described her as 'a Paki with long, black hair'."

Silence filled the car. Jillian, speaking more to herself than to anyone else, said, "She said she would expose him for the murder of Jinani Rasool."

"What was that?" Listun asked. Jillian's low voice hadn't been clear over the phone. Kara shot Jillian a quick look as well, not sure where she was going with this.

Jillian, snapping out of her solitary thoughts, looked down at the phone and spoke louder. "You said that the woman said she was going to expose Winston for the murder of Jinani Rasool, is that right?"

They could hear paper rustling. They pictured Listun rummaging through his notebook before he answered, "Yes, that's right."

"She didn't say Jinani Rasool and Jonathan Blakesly," Jillian said. Then, "I think the woman might be Amelia Hamza."

Kara spoke up before Listun could. "But how would she know about the Winstons?"

Jillian gave her a look that told her all she needed to know, then said, "We need to get to that house, now."

Kara put her foot down and the car lurched forward. They turned onto a motorway leading out the other side of the city and into the country, headed for the Winston estate.

Twenty minutes later, they pulled up in the half-circle drive of the yellow brick home, just as before. This time, however, a police car with lights still flashing was parked out front and the front door was open, with a constable standing guard beside it.

Jillian and Kara approached, their warrant cards out. Jillian nodded to the constable. "Can we turn those lights off, please? Let's not draw unwanted attention from the neighbors." She wanted to add "more than we already have" but decided against it.

A female constable was sitting with Sarah Kolvan on the sofa where Jillian and Kara had sat during their last visit. Kolvan looked up as they entered the room and looked directly at Jillian.

Jillian saw her eyes flit ever so quickly over at Kara, but they returned and remained fixed on Jillian. "You have to find my husband. He's been kidnapped," she said.

Jillian sat down calmly on one of the sitting chairs opposite her. "Mrs. Kolvan. Did you see any type of weapon on the woman who came to your home?"

"Well, no, but why else would my husband leave with that . . . that . . .woman?"

Jillian wanted to reach across the coffee table and slap her, but now was not the time. Taking out her phone, she zoomed in on the image she had pulled up from the internet and held it toward Sarah Kolvan. "Is this the woman who came to your home?"

Sarah Kolvan's eyes became wide with recognition. "Yes. That's her!" she said. "Who is she? Why aren't you out arresting her? You should be getting my husband back, not here wasting time talking to me."

Ignoring both her question and her remarks, Jillian put her phone away and said calmly, "Mrs. Kolvan, we need to know where this woman and your husband have gone."

Sarah Kolvan became irate. "How should I know where she's taken him? He could be in danger and you're just sitting here as though you're waiting for a cup of tea. Well, you're not going to get one. Now get out of my house and find my husband." With that, she stood up forcefully and put her hands on her hips.

Neither Jillian nor Kara moved. The constable beside Mrs. Kolvan stayed seated but looked at Jillian for direction.

Jillian looked up at Sarah Kolvan and said, "Sit down, Mrs. Kolvan." She didn't say it maliciously, but something in Jillian's voice changed. Looking down into her eyes, Sarah Kolvan swallowed and then slowly sat back down.

"From what you reported when you called the police," Jillian said, "there is nothing to indicate that your husband was kidnapped. In fact, I would say it is quite likely that he went voluntarily."

"That's ridiculous," Mrs. Kolvan said, though much of the certainty had gone from her tone.

Jillian continued to ignore her outbursts. "I think you know exactly where they have gone."

The woman turned her head slightly away from the policewoman, sitting next to her like a petulant child.

"Tell me, Mrs. Kolvan," Jillian said, the hard edge that had been present earlier returning. "Who is in charge of Dominion."

The color from her already pale face drained, leaving her almost ghostlike.

Jillian leaned forward, her eyes boring into the frightened woman's face. "If you want me to save your husband, you have to tell me the name of the person at the head of Dominion."

Sarah Kolvan's lips moved, but the sound came out like a whisper. Had they been sitting any further apart, no one would have heard her, but the name was clear.

This time, it was Jillian's face that drained of color.

CHAPTER 12

When time stands still, it's as if the sands stop falling through the hourglass. Everything happens in slow motion.

Every light is bright; every sound seems clearer.

Then suddenly, like the crack of a whip, everything comes screaming at you all at once as time restarts.

Amelia Hamza felt everything all at once, like she'd been holding her breath underwater and had suddenly come to the surface, trying to fill her aching lungs back up.

The first thing she noticed was the smell of her own fear. The drops of perspiration at the nape of her neck.

She could hear the ticking of the clock on the wall. Each second seemed like a full minute. She wanted to look around the room, take in as much as she could in one sweep of her head.

That was not going to happen. Not with the cold blue steel of a gun pointing at her face.

Looking back, she didn't know what she had been thinking. Clearly, her mind shouted back, she hadn't been thinking at all.

When DI Scotte had told her the name Derek Winston, it hadn't taken her journalistic instincts long to kick in. She had begun digging and scoured every facet of Winston's life. Like Kara Devanor, Amelia was not a stranger to racism, and it wasn't long before she unearthed enough information about the leader of Historinaccuracy Research to know that everything pointed to her friend's murder being a hate crime.

Somewhere along the way, her mind shifted, and anger took its place over reason. The more she dug, the more certain she became that Derek Winston had killed her friend.

She couldn't sleep. She couldn't eat. The next thing she knew, she was in her car driving to the address she knew to be Winston's home. When she pulled up to the circular drive and the pristine home, she knew her suspicions were right. Everything smelled of white privilege and money.

When his wife opened the door and Amelia saw the look on her face as she took in the sight of a Muslim woman, the anger inside her boiled over.

Amelia had purposefully worn a hijab for the trip. A two-finger salute to let Winston know he wouldn't be able to push her aside. As she saw Winston's wife recoil at her appearance, Amelia didn't say a word and simply barged inside.

Derek Winston was everything she expected. Tall, reasonably fit, with a chiseled jaw, blond hair expertly cut. His shirt was pressed and, if she wasn't mistaken, the crease in his trousers had been pressed as well. His black loafers gleamed as though he had just stepped away from a shoeshine.

"Can I help you?" he asked. His expression, although not as obvious as his wife's, was equally distasteful.

Things had gone as she had hoped after that, up to a point. She had pressed Winston on the murders, telling him she had evidence and would go to the police. It was a lie, of course, but she wanted a confession. Her phone was recording everything in her purse, and she needed to get him talking.

At first, he denied everything, but eventually he told her he knew who had killed her friend and her friend's boyfriend. Something in the way Winston had said the word *boyfriend* should have tipped her off, but she was too eager to get the full story.

He agreed to get in touch and try to set up a meeting, but insisted it needed to be outside, not in his house. As they walked toward her car, he made a phone call. She waited by the car, not taking her eyes off him, but with his back turned, she couldn't hear what was going on.

After the call ended, he told her he was going to take her to someone's home who could explain everything. He said there was much more to it than she knew, and this man could give her the answers she was looking for.

When she pulled to a stop in front of the large home, her senses began to tingle. Again, looking back, she realized she should have heeded her own internal warning signals, but she was so caught up with resentment that she was blinded.

As she and Winston approached the front door, it opened for them, and a large man stood partially behind the door, beckoning them in. Winston went in first, and she blindly followed.

That's when everything changed.

***

Jillian Scotte had her phone pressed to her ear by the time they had walked out the front door after talking to Sarah Kolvan. She was asking her DS for an address.

Kara jogged ahead, sensing her boss's urgency. She got in the car, tearing out of the driveway the second Jillian was inside.

"One more thing," Jillian said into the phone. "Find out the make, model, and number plate for Amelia Hamza's car."

Hanging up, she put in the address Listun had given her into the car's satnav system.

Kara hit the lights and siren, and once again, they were speeding through traffic.

Jillian had one more call to make. She made it quickly, ending with a request for armed backup.

***

The second Amelia had crossed the threshold, the large man had pushed the front door, letting it swing shut, and placed the barrel of a pistol against the side of her head.

It was then that her self-admonitions began. All the warning signs she had missed.

The large bald man said, "Looks like you found some refuse needs taking out, eh Mr. Winston?"

The tone in the man's voice left no question as to his disdain for Amelia.

"Where is he?" was all that Winston said in reply.

"Said he'd be down in a minute. Said to take her to the library," the big man said.

Winston began walking off to the right down a hallway. The big man took his left hand and walloped the back of Amelia's head, making her stumble forward, half bent over. She felt his large foot hit her backside with such force that it almost knocked her to her knees, but she managed to stumble after Winston.

CHAPTER 13

Jillian Scotte was not the most patient of people to begin with. Her right leg was now bouncing repeatedly in the car as Kara drove around traffic in ways that certainly violated most traffic laws and bordered on recklessness.

Neither woman said anything. Kara, because all of her concentration was focused on not causing an accident, being in an accident, or in any way not getting them to their destination as fast as possible. Jillian because she was worried about Amelia Hamza and simultaneously trying to figure out how to handle the situation she was sure they were going to walk into.

The biggest challenge they faced, she knew, was that they would arrive before the armed reinforcements did.

***

Amelia Hamza, seated in a straight-backed chair, didn't hear the whip crack of the sound as it reverberated in the confined room. She did, however, feel the pain as her eye instantly swelled from the large, bald man's thunderous strike.

She saw Winston half turn his head and wince. *You should try looking at it from my end,* she thought, but her feeble attempt at internal humor did little to assuage the flash of heat and blinding pain that she felt from the blow.

The large man grabbed the back of her head and forced it back uncomfortably, his meaty hands gripping her hair and yanking.

He looked down at her like some sort of demon-possessed monster. He sneered down at her as his eyes glared wildly. "You horrid excuse of a whore. You think everyone owes you something, don't you?" he growled before hacking up a mouthful of spit and splattering her face with it.

She screwed her eyes shut, trying to keep his saliva from getting on them. She felt him let go of her head and she quickly leaned forward, raising her arm to wipe the slime from her face, but he caught her wrist in a vice-like grip.

Amelia flinched, desperate to avoid another blow to her head. Instead, she felt the sickening stench of his foul breath inches from the side of her face. She kept her eyes shut tight, feeling her body beginning to tremble.

His voice was now little more than a whisper, though no less vile. "I can't wait until it's time." He waited a moment, but she refused to open her eyes or move so much as an inch, and then he said, "Did they show you?"

Amelia wasn't sure what he meant, but as the silence dragged on, she instinctively shook her head slightly.

"No?" he said, his hand tightening even more on her wrist, which was now shaking uncontrollably. "They didn't show you what I done to your friend and her spineless pitiful excuse of a man? Well, it doesn't matter," he said with a sneer, "because what I'm going to do to you is going to be so much worse."

Despite her usual composure, she felt herself losing control. A slight whimper escaped her lips, and she felt her body begin to shake all over as tears fell down her face.

He let go of her wrist and she felt him stand up. Without warning, his open palm slapped her across the face with such force it almost knocked her out of the chair.

"That's enough, Cliff," a voice said. She knew it wasn't Winston's. Someone else had just walked into the room.

Amelia half lifted her face, and with one eye quickly swelling shut, she squinted through the other. She couldn't see clearly, but the person who had spoken was walking around behind a desk to the right of the chair she was sitting in.

"So," the voice said, "this is the journalist who threatened you?"

Winston stepped forward. His voice seemed to go up an octave and there was something in it resembling fear. "Yes sir. She came to my house and said she had proof that I killed that other Paki and . . ." His voice faltered before he said, ". . . and Blakesly."

"So, you panicked," the voice said condescendingly.

"No sir," Winston whined, but the voice cut him off.

"She can't have proof that you did it, you fool, because we all know you didn't."

"Yes, but . . ." Winston stuttered, "but she's a journalist and she found me and came to my home. My wife and kids were there . . ."

Once again, the voice cut him off. "Shut up." Then, turning his head toward Amelia, he said, "So, what exactly is this proof?"

Amelia didn't speak. Mostly out of fear, and also because she wasn't sure anything would actually come out of her mouth. She could still taste the blood from the brute's last attack on her. Her vision was getting blurrier as time went on, the effect of shock and the pain that was still ringing in her head.

"Did you search her things?" the voice said.

The bald man picked up her backpack and emptied it out onto the carpet in front of her. Grabbing her phone, he held it up, facing the other two men.

She senses more than saw the man behind the desk shaking his head.

The brute dropped the phone on the carpet. With the force of his considerable weight, he slammed his foot down onto it, instantly shattering the screen and splintering parts of the phone outward.

"I can take care of this," the big man said, an edge of hunger in his voice.

"Cliff," the voice behind the desk said, "you can't do it here."

Despite the heat from the swelling on her face, an icy shiver ran down Amelia's spine.

CHAPTER 14

Jillian and Kara almost missed the drive, which was hidden in a tight opening in a thicket of dense shrubs almost as tall as trees. Slamming on the brakes, Kara yanked the steering wheel, putting the car into a ninety-degree slide. With a quick, apologetic glance to her boss, she eased off the brake, and they slowly made their way inside the compound. At least, that's how Jillian thought of the house, hidden from sight just on the outskirts of the small village they had driven to.

In front of the home was the car that matched the information Listun had given them for Amelia Hamza. It was parked next to another vehicle, this one a white, nondescript van.

Without saying a word, both women got out of the car and closed their doors quietly.

Kara followed Jillian up the front steps to the large wooden door, which had a small window in it. Jillian stood on her toes and peered through, but the mottled glass made it difficult to see clearly. In any event, it seemed the hallway was empty.

She reached down and pressed the handle, and surprisingly, the door was unlocked. Slowly, she opened it just far enough for them to slide through.

They could hear voices inside, but not quite what was being said.

As they followed the sound of the voices down a hallway that opened to the right, they hugged the wall, now able to hear more clearly.

"Cliff," a deep voice said, "you can't do it here."

Another voice gruffly responded, "Why not? We can roll her up in the carpet. No one will know."

Kara was not prepared when Jillian suddenly stepped around the wall into the room. Holding up her warrant card, she said, "We'll know."

Kara moved belatedly to stand beside her boss and took in the scene in front of her. A man had a gun down at his side, presumably Cliff. They had seen him before. He was the man who had answered the door at Historinaccuracy Research.

He was still bald, large, and wearing clothes a size too small for his muscular bulk. This time, it was a leather jacket that couldn't possibly close around his chest. His cold, dark eyes turned in their direction and with it, the gun.

He swung the weapon in a long, slow arc. His eyes narrowed as he trained it on Jillian, but he didn't stop there, continuing to move until the gun was pointing straight at Kara. A nasty smirk settled on his face.

He was only standing a few feet away, and the gun was not that far from Kara's face. Amelia was behind him, sitting in a chair in the middle of the room, half her face black and blue.

"Easy, Clifford," a voice said.

It didn't come from Derek Winston, who was standing a few paces off to the side from Cliff. Beyond him, in front of a large desk, was the man who had spoken.

The man whose house they had driven to.

Rupert Chiswick. The Member of Parliament that Jillian had spoken briefly with on the phone with her boss.

He was tall, with dark hair parted neatly to one side. He wore gray slacks with a light-blue shirt and a white cardigan over it. If the situation weren't so dangerous, he could have been at a dinner party. Leaning his forearms on the desk, he looked across the room at the two policewomen.

"Well, well," he said. "Derek, it looks like you've led the police to our door."

There was something about his calmness that alarmed Jillian. She tried to keep her voice calm. "It's over, Mr. Chiswick. We've called for reinforcements, and I just spoke with Superintendent Sanderson. She knows we're here, and why."

"Oh, I very much doubt that," Chiswick said, a thin line of a smile spreading across his face.

Cliff motioned with his gun, prompting the women to move next to Amelia, which they slowly did. He kept the barrel pointed at Kara's chest. Kara made sure she didn't get too close to Jillian, leaving a little room between her and her boss, who was standing next to Amelia in her chair.

Jillian wanted to tell Chiswick that she wasn't bluffing, but something about his demeanor told her she'd be wasting her time. "Tell me, Mr. Chiswick," she said, keeping her voice neutral. "Did you have Clifford kill Mr. Blakesly and Ms. Rasool, or was that Derek here?"

Winston spoke for the first time, his voice cracking from stress. "I didn't do it. I wasn't even there."

"Shut up, Derek," Chiswick commanded.

Jillian turned back from Winston to face Chiswick. She considered him for a moment, then said, "You were there yourself." She said it plainly. It wasn't a question.

Chiswick stood and came around his desk, taking a step toward them. His jaw clenched and something behind his eyes shifted, leaving them devoid of any color. "He betrayed us."

"He betrayed your white supremacist club of hatred?" Jillian said, purposely baiting him. She had to keep him talking, to stall for time. She had indeed called Sanderson, and backup had been summoned, but she had no idea how long it would be before they arrived.

Chiswick sneered. "I wouldn't expect you to understand, Inspector," he said, walking up next to Winston. Then, looking from Jillian to Kara and back again, he said, "Not from someone who would hire *her*." He said the last word with unbridled contempt.

Chiswick saw his words had affected both of them. He continued, "Blakesly betrayed his race, sleeping with that whore." Then he looked down at Amelia with disgust. "How anyone could lie down with them is so revolting it doesn't bear thinking about."

To her credit, Amelia kept her composure and said nothing.

"Well," Chiswick said, "I think our little chat has gone on long enough. Cliff, I think we'll have to add two more to the carpet." Looking down at his feet, he added, "Luckily, I think it's large enough, don't you?"

Cliff smirked. He straightened his arm, his expression turning cold, and moved the gun between the three women as though trying to decide which one to shoot first.

Somewhere in the distance, a siren wailed. It was low and still some way off but getting closer.

They all heard it. Cliff turned his head, looking at Chiswick. The movement turned his shoulders, and the gun moved just a few inches. It was enough.

Kara pivoted slightly on her right foot, arcing her left foot up and striking his wrist from the outside. Simultaneously, Amelia leaped from her chair and lunged at the large man.

The gun flew out of Cliff's hand, skittering across the floor. The two women converged, knocking him to the floor.

Jillian lunged for the gun, but Chiswick reached it before her.

He saw her coming at him, but his raging anger wasn't directed at her. He turned the barrel to Cliff, Kara, and Amelia on the floor and fired a second before Jillian careened into him, knocking him backward.

Derek Winston never moved. Frozen in fear, he covered his ears from the loud retort of the gun as the blue lights of the arriving police began flickering through the window and across the walls.

Having toppled Chiswick and landed on top of him, Jillian reached back and let her fist crash down onto the man's face. She didn't know where the gun was, but the image of Jinani Rasool's and Jonathan Blakesly's bodies in the kitchen, of the look on Kara's face every time one of his minions spoke to or looked at her, and the pain they had caused Amelia suddenly surged through her body.

She kept hitting him over and over, her fist going numb as blood splattered and spread through her knuckles until a constable pulled her away.

Another group of armed police apprehended Winston and Chiswick, quickly securing the gun and just as quickly handcuffing both men.

Breathless and doubled over from exertion, Jillian looked over to where Kara was being helped to her feet. There was blood on her shirt, but she didn't appear to be injured.

Two other constables were kneeling, blocking her view. She couldn't see whose blood it actually was.

CHAPTER 15 (EPILOGUE)

The unusual lamps were the first thing Detective Inspector Jillian Scotte noticed as she entered the eclectic restaurant her boss had chosen. In fact, the entire decor had the look of something in between a modern art museum and a Dr. Seuss book.

Jillian spotted her boss, Superintendent Maryanne Sanderson, at a table for four toward the back of the room. She was on her mobile, and Jillian merely smiled and sat down, waiting for her to end the conversation.

Sanderson had made the trip down to Southampton in light of the enormity of the case and what had transpired at the home of one of England's MP's, Rupert Chiswick. She ended her call and smiled from across the table. "Hello, it's nice to see you face-to-face and not on a video call."

"You too." Jillian smiled back.

A server came over to inquire about their order. Sanderson said, "We're still waiting for someone. Could we have a pot of tea in the meantime?"

"Certainly, madam," the young man said, and turned away.

Sanderson returned her attention to her DI. "This is going to be a shit storm before it's all over."

Jillian sighed loudly.

Sanderson continued, "Mr. Chiswick is claiming police brutality from his broken nose and fractured cheekbone." She left the statement hanging in the air as Jillian looked on. What could she say? She had pummeled the man, and he'd deserved it.

Sanderson folded her napkin in her lap. "Still, considering he shot and killed someone in front of several witnesses during this, police brutality won't help his case, and the Crown don't think he has much standing on the issue."

Jillian swallowed audibly.

"I do have to ask," Sanderson said. "Is this something I should be worried about happening in the future?"

This time, Jillian took on Sanderson's full glare. Her boss's expression had turned deadly serious.

"No, boss," Jillian said. She thought about trying to explain. Trying somehow to put into words all the things that had come together in front of this smug rich white man who preyed on people's fears, who abused women, assaulted them, manipulated them, and ultimately killed them if they didn't fit his warped view of humanity. How she had seen firsthand the trauma inflicted by him and those like him in her friends and coworkers. How when he'd fired his gun into a melee that included two of those people, she had just lost all sense of control.

But no, it would not happen again. Jillian had spent much of the past week filing reports, talking to internal investigation officers, and filling in details with her boss and others at the Metropolitan Police Headquarters in London. She had spent every hour of every day imagining that her career was going to be over.

She had, in fact, assaulted a member of Parliament, despite his being the prime suspect and, without a doubt, a killer. Politics are power, and powerful people have powerful influence.

Jillian had tried to imagine what her life would be like without her job, and the answer she found was not a pleasant one. This was who she was. It was what she was incredibly good at. Without it she would be lost. She'd still have Daniella, but they both knew Jillian would not be the same if she were no longer in the police.

She half expected that this meeting—with Sanderson coming down to Southampton, not calling her up to London—to be her boss's way of letting her down easily. Perhaps she'd be taken off the VCU, demoted, reassigned.

All these thoughts flashed through her mind, but she simply stuck with her two words, "No, boss."

Sanderson, who had been staring intently at her, nodded once. "Good." Then, looking up, she said, "Ah, there you are."

Turning, Jillian stood from her chair as Amelia Hamza walked up, her left arm in a sling. Her battered eye looked almost normal now, though there was still visible bruising down her cheekbone on that side. Jillian gave her an awkward half hug, careful of her bandaged arm. Amelia returned it, but the look as their eyes met held more warmth than the hug.

"I'm Superintendent Sanderson," Jillian's boss said, holding out her hand.

Hamza shook it, and the three women sat down.

The server returned, and everyone ordered. Then, when he had retreated, Sanderson spoke. "Everything we will discuss here needs to be off the record."

Hamza nodded. "Of course."

"We are still looking into the depth and breadth of Dominion," Sanderson began, "and we continue to look into Mr. Winston's affairs, as well as the role Historinaccuracy Research played in the deaths of your friend Jinani Rasool and her boyfriend Jonathan Blakesly."

Hamza nodded slightly.

Jillian spoke up. "I'm still quite confused by that. How could a man like Blakesly, who clearly was mixed up with Chiswick and Dominion, get together with Ms. Rasool?"

Hamza seemed to have the same question, and they both looked at Sanderson. "We are still conducting our interviews with Mr. Chiswick, so I can't get into too much detail here, but what I can tell you is that it appears that he simply fell in love."

Amelia turned her head, her eyes glistening with the threat of tears.

"One cannot tell a heart who it should or should not fall in love with, no matter what the head says," Sanderson said gently.

Amelia turned back, an expression of firm resolve on her face. "What will happen to Chiswick?"

"The Crown are putting together their case for the attempted murder of yourself and Detective Constable Devanor," Sanderson said, indicating Hamza's arm, "and for the murder of Cliff Richardson."

When Chiswick had fired his gun, the bullet went straight through Amelia's arm, exiting out the back. Although it had been slowed dramatically by her body, her arm had been tightly wrapped around Richardson's head at the time. Thus, the bullet had entered his temple, killing him almost instantly.

Kara Dawson had emerged with blood covering her face and neck from the bullet's impact on Mr. Richardson, but she was otherwise unharmed.

"What about . . ." Amelia began, unable to complete the question.

"I'm afraid," Sanderson said, "that we still don't have a clear picture of what happened at your friend's flat." She looked at Amelia. There was gentleness in her voice, but her face was professional. "We may never know. It is likely that Richardson and Chiswick were both there, though he denies it. Winston says he was told by Richardson that both men were there, and that Chiswick did most of the dirty work, but it's hearsay and unlikely to hold much weight in court."

"So, he gets away with killing Jinani and Jonathan," Amelia said.

"No." Jillian spoke up this time. "He will be punished for murder. We have multiple witnesses to his killing Richardson, myself included. It may not say it was for Jinani, but the outcome will be the same."

Hamza sighed and folded her arms. "What he did to her was more than murder!" Her voice was loud, and a few other people in the restaurant looked over.

Jillian put her hand over Amelia's, but the journalist pulled away abruptly. "I'm going to damn well make sure that everyone knows what that bastard did, whether or not he gets convicted of it," she retorted.

"I don't think you should do that," Sanderson said into the silence.

Amelia exploded. "What? You can't tell me . . ." she began, but Sanderson cut her off.

"I'm not telling you anything." She waited a beat to make sure Hamza's anger wasn't preventing her from listening. "Let me explain."

Amelia took a deep breath and looked over at Jillian. Jillian smiled what she hoped was a comforting smile. They both turned to the superintendent.

"If you try to accuse him of things he has not been convicted of, his lawyers will come after you and it could very well end your career as a journalist."

Amelia started to say something, but again Sanderson cut her off, holding up one hand. "And, I'm asking you not to."

Amelia's mouth hung open. Her expression was one of disbelief.

Sanderson went on before Amelia could find her voice. "I'm asking you because we are still digging into exactly what he was involved in. We don't just want him. We want everyone and everything this evil cult had its tendrils in."

The superintendent could see that Hamza was still seething. "If you expose Chiswick and his role in Dominion, everyone else will go underground and we may never know who and what they are. We suspect there could be many more influential people involved."

Amelia looked down at her napkin, trying to take it all in.

Sanderson played her last card. "I came down here, Ms. Hamza, because I didn't want DI Scotte holding the cards on this one. I didn't want you to think she was imposing on the relationship you both have, and I wanted you to hear this from me." Again, she paused before adding, "When the time comes. When the investigation is complete. *If*—and I must say *if* because I cannot promise anything—but if there is a story to tell, you will be the one to tell it, exclusively."

Everyone was silent for a while.

Jillian broke the silence. "I know there's nothing we can say or do that brings Jinani back. I know we're asking you to sit on what you know, knowing that you may never get to tell her story, and that is not an easy thing to ask."

Amelia gave Jillian a look that spoke volumes, with tears welling up in her eyes.

Jillian continued, "But I promise you Chiswick is going to prison for the rest of his life, and if the time comes that the story can come out, you will be able to tell it." She could see Amelia wrestling with her thoughts about everything.

"Amelia," Jillian said, again reaching her hand out and covering the journalist's. This time, Amelia didn't pull it away. "This is the best we can do and it's the right thing to do. I wouldn't lie to you about that."

Tears flowed silently down Amelia Hamza's face. She made no attempt at hiding them or wiping them away. She looked from Jillian to Sanderson and back again. Then, grabbing her purse, she stood up slowly. She nodded once, then turned and walked out of the restaurant.

BOOK 2

MURDER

BY

FIRE

CHAPTER 1

Black smoke billowed into the sky like a monster belching sulfurous fumes. The smell of soot mixed with moisture in the air that, for once, wasn't from the infamous English rain but rather from the hoses of the fire and rescue services, or FRS.

Detective Inspector Jillian Scotte couldn't remember the last time she had been called as a copper to a fire scene. She and Detective Sergeant Listun climbed out of their car and looked at the chaos before them.

Hampshire Fire and Rescue Service vehicles were scattered at various angles in the street, their ladders extended, and firefighters were training hoses on the flames that licked up into the sky, scattering flickering embers into the night like confetti.

Water was pooling in the streets, casting a shimmering reflection from the flashing lights mixed with the yellowish white of the flames. The source of the fire was the last home in a row of older homes on the street. Most of the focus of the FRS was on the neighboring home, whose roof was still ablaze. The home where the fire had started was billowing black, but at least no active fire was still visible.

Jillian and Listun flashed their warrant cards when they reached the perimeter police tape. A few constables stood by, along with someone who wore a fire service uniform but was not geared up as a firefighter. Likely a community liaison. He turned as he heard the two detectives and said, "Sorry, Inspector, we're trying to keep everyone back until we get the remaining fire contained."

Jillian nodded. "Understood. We were actually called to come here, though I'm unsure who made that request."

"That would be the watch manager, mum," the fire service liaison officer said. "I'll fetch him for you now."

A moment later, he returned with another man, this one with more emblems on his jacket shoulder. He extended his hand. "I'm the watch manager, Brian Horstell."

Jillian took his hand and introduced herself and her DS, who also shook hands with the firefighter. "I believe you called us?" she said.

"Yes. I called Central, but they referred me to you," Horstell said, looking over at his shoulder and pointing to the house at the end of the row. "The fire started there, and of course spread back toward us. We thought we had managed to get the bulk of it in time, but there was a secondary explosion that happened about fifteen minutes ago, and that caused the breach to the neighboring home."

"Do you know what caused the explosion?" Jillian asked.

"Not exactly," he said, hesitating as he turned back toward her. "I haven't been in the structure myself, but I was just talking to the crew manager and the team lead that went in first, so bear in mind that this is third hand."

Jillian nodded. "Of course."

"When they first entered, they found what appeared to be a drug-mixing operation with five fatalities, either asphyxiated by smoke or"—he paused briefly—"otherwise. We think the explosion must have come from some chemical container used in the manufacturing process. The team were mostly concerned with getting the blaze under control and checking for signs of life to take too much notice of what might or might not have been in storage areas and the like."

Jillian nodded again.

"They found a similar setup on the second floor and, we believe, three more victims."

"Do you know the cause?" Jillian asked.

"We won't know that until the fire investigator can get in, but the team were fairly confident this was no accident. The acceleration and aggressiveness of the burn had to have help, and it was going on all three floors simultaneously, which wouldn't happen if it started by accident."

Listun spoke up. "Three floors?" he asked curiously, given that the home was only a two-story structure.

"It has a cellar," Horstell said grimly.

"I'm sorry, Mr. Horstell," Jillian said. "I'm still not clear why you contacted the VCU? Certainly, it's a tragic number of deaths, and while drugs and suspected arson is cause for concern, I'm not sure at this stage that it warrants my team."

"Yes," the watch manager said, taking in a deep breath, "and if that's all there was to it, I would agree with you."

Jillian's eyes narrowed. She didn't like the direction this conversation was taking.

The firefighter looked back and forth between Jillian and Listun. "There are six more fatalities," he said ominously, "in the cellar."

"Six?" Listun raised his eyebrows.

"Yes," Horstell said. "Mind you, the team didn't have time to look too closely. The flames and smoke down there made it difficult to see, but I have the same account from at least two members of the team of what they saw."

"And what did they see?" Jillian asked, knowing she would not like the answer.

"The six down in the cellar were all young teenagers," Horstell said slowly.

Listun let out a slow breath.

Jillian, seeing the look on the watch manager's face, waited.

"The thing is," he said, looking sadly at her, "they were all shackled at what appear to be rather high-end computer consoles. Lots of dual monitors, cables—it's apparently like a high-tech control room down there."

Jillian and Listun looked at each other and then back at the firefighter.

"What do you mean by shackled?" Jillian asked.

"Around their ankles. Some sort of clamp with a chain running to a pipe. That's all I can tell you at this point. Until things cool down and we're sure the structure is safe to go in, we won't know more."

Jillian looked over at her DS, who looked like he was going to be sick. The two of them looked back over at the house on the end of the street with its long billows of black smoke. Despite the heat of the blaze and the warmer-than-normal temperature in the air, a chill ran down Jillian Scotte's spine.

CHAPTER 2

Jillian had DS Listun take charge of a house-to-house canvass down both sides of the street, asking if anyone knew anything about the occupants of the house in question.

From one moment to the next, the towering flames of the neighboring house went out, and the fire service began dousing spot fires and coiling up the seemingly endless hoses that snaked about the street.

Jillian got permission to take a closer look at the house, though she had to agree to let the community liaison fire service officer accompany her for safety. Just as they were about to set off, a voice behind her inquired, "Mind if I tag along?"

Recognizing the voice, she turned around. "DS Milston, as I live and breathe."

Attired in his typical outfit of jeans and low-cut boots, he was also wearing a flannel shirt under his usual leather jacket. His cockney accent was as flowing as his dark, curly hair. "Well, you know what they say, Jills, you haven't lived until you've had a little . . ."

Jillian cut him off. "No one says that, Rob, and anyone who has said it was either drunk, under duress, or both."

Milston feigned offense and then said, "This looks like a right cock-up."

"Did you get called in from the fire service as well?" Jillian asked as they began walking toward the house. Its roof was mostly gone, and water was pouring out of where the front door would have been.

"Uhm, not exactly," Milston responded hesitantly.

Jillian looked over at him. "You already knew about this place?"

He flashed his roguish smile. "You might say that, yeah."

They got as close as the liaison was willing to let them, and as Jillian began looking at the home, she asked, "What can you tell me about it?"

"Not a lot. We know it's been getting a lot of product going in and out. It only got on our radar a few weeks ago. We've no idea who's running it, but it was turning into quite a distribution center."

Jillian walked around the corner, staying close to the sidewalk so as not to cause the liaison any angst. "The number of fatalities the watch manager mentioned doesn't seem to match it being a large operation. He said eight people involved in what looked like drug production?"

Rob followed Jillian as she surveyed the home, though she was looking around the neighborhood and at the gawkers behind the police lines more than at the house itself. Rob said, "Yeah, that's because it's nighttime, isn't it. It's at least twice that during the day, and that doesn't account for the traffic coming and going."

This was certainly SCD9's patch more than hers, Jillian thought. "What about the basement computer setup?"

"Didn't know about that until I heard you and the watch manager talking. No idea what that's about," Milston said.

"Any idea why the people working down there would need to be shackled?" she asked.

Milston now looked at the smoldering ruins of the house and then at her. His face had turned grim. "No," he said, "no idea."

***

Jillian called her boss first thing the next morning to give her an update on the previous evening's events and to ask for help in the form of technical support.

"Don't Southampton Central have a tech department?" Superintendent Sanderson asked.

"Yes, mum," Jillian responded, "but I'm not sure I'll be able to get them without a fight." After a pause, she added, "There's also something odd."

Sanderson raised her eyebrows on the video monitor.

Jillian said, "I'm no expert, but I walked all the way around that house three times. I even borrowed a torch from the fire service, and I couldn't find any indication that there was an internet connection going into the house."

"What, no cable, you mean?" Sanderson asked.

"Yes, that's right."

"Perhaps it was consumed by the fire?"

"Even if the fire damaged the cable at the connection point to the house—which, by the way, I couldn't see any sign that such a connection existed—I still should have seen a cable hanging from the lines around the alleyway, and there wasn't anything like that."

"What are you suggesting?" Sanderson asked.

"I'm not suggesting anything, mum, I'm just saying it seems rather strange for the amount of computer equipment they found in the basement. Also, given that it all sustained extensive water damage, I'm not sure Central's technical team are up to the task," Jillian said.

Sanderson said she'd see what she could do, though she told Jillian not to hold her breath. Which is why Jillian was rather surprised in the early afternoon when a young Asian man in glasses, wearing a suit and tie, was shown into her office.

"Hello, DI Scotte, my name is Thomas Redmond. Superintendent Sanderson sent me." He held out his hand, which Jillian, standing from behind her desk, shook.

"Wow, that was fast," she said truthfully.

"I caught the first train down."

Jillian filled him in on what she knew about the situation and about her inspection of the exterior of the home last night. Redmond asked if he could see the property, and Jillian called in PC Stella Dawson and asked her to take him to the site.

The rest of the day moved on the way some days do. Paperwork, phone calls, more paperwork, and more phone calls. It was one of those phone calls which came right at the end of the day that took Jillian by surprise.

"DI Scotte," she said wearily as she picked up the phone on her desk, her eyes still reading the report from the coroner's office on a recent spate of murders near the East Coast.

"Hello mum," the voice on the phone said, and it took Jillian a moment or two to realize it was the technician, Redmond.

"Oh, hello," she said.

"You were right about the lack of internet connection to the house," he began, "at least as far as a wired cable connection goes."

"Sorry?" Jillian asked, somewhat confused.

"I took a look at what was left in the basement, and it doesn't make sense that the amount of computing power down there would not have internet. Which left two possibilities." He didn't wait for Jillian to interrupt. "One was that they were stealing a wireless connection from a neighboring house, but after knocking on the four closest doors, that doesn't seem possible, as the connections at each home were nowhere near strong enough to sustain the needs of the basement setup."

"And the other possibility?" Jillian asked, her attention now fully focused on the conversation.

"That would be some type of wireless connection. An antenna of some sort. Now it could have been a wireless antenna similar to those television dishes that you see on the sides and roofs, but those also typically have cables connecting to the interior of the home."

"Mmm," Jillian said.

"While the bulk of the roof went up in flames, I still would have seen some cable somewhere in the interior of the home, and there is none, which leaves only one possibility."

Jillian waited, somewhat impatiently, for him to get past the technical explanation and get to the point.

Thomas Redmond continued, "A point-to-point antennae with a wireless signal."

"I'm not sure I follow?" Jillian said.

"Think of a dish similar to what we were just discussing, but instead of pointing up in the sky, it's pointing to another dish on another roof. The internet connection is established securely and privately between the two, with the internet coming from the dish on the other roof. In the house itself, the dish acts as a wireless router, connecting the computers in the basement without the need for wires."

Jillian signed loudly. "So, we need to look for a dish pointing toward this home from . . . what . . . how far away?"

Redmond ignored her question. "Actually, I've found it."

That made Jillian's eyes open wide. "What? Already?"

Unfazed, Redmond replied, "I began driving around the neighboring streets looking for anything pointing in that general direction and came upon an installation van. A man on a ladder was working on a dish that was just what I was looking for."

Jillian stood up. "You're joking."

"No mum," he said. "However, the technician is from a reliable firm and was removing the dish from a work order. He didn't know anything about what it connected to."

Jillian wasn't convinced. "We'll need to talk to him, and I want to know who created that work order."

"Yes, I thought you might. I have a call in to get access to their records, and I've taken down all the technician's particulars. I told him you were likely to want to speak with him yourself. I'll have everything to you in an email within the hour."

Jillian was impressed and opened her mouth to say so, but Redmond wasn't finished. "Oh, one last thing. Most of the computer equipment was damaged by the fire, and what wasn't burned through was practically underwater from the work of the fire service. There was one station, however, that looks like it might not be too far gone. We'll look at it and see what we can recover from it. Might take a day or two."

"Very good," Jillian said. "Well done. I'll look forward to your email."

Redmond said goodbye and hung up, leaving Jillian to sit down back at her desk. Despite the rapid progress Sanderson's tech man had made, it seemed Jillian now had even more questions than answers.

CHAPTER 3

Detective constable Kara Devanor was juggling multiple cases like everyone else at the VCU, but this new one involving children shackled to a steel pipe had everyone on edge.

The morning briefing started off normally. But it was interrupted when one of the police constables answered the bell in the front lobby and then leaned over Kara to whisper that she was needed.

Catching DI Scotte's eye briefly, Kara left the incident room. The door to the lobby clicked as she scanned her ID on the badge reader, and she walked in.

A woman in full fire-service uniform stood with her cap tucked under her left arm.

"Hello," Kara said, "I'm detective constable Devanor. How can I help?"

Shaking her hand, the woman said, "I'm Inspector Holly McGowan with the Hampshire and Isle of Wight fire investigations division." She handed Kara a business card with her contact information, then said, "I was told to come and give you an update as quickly as possible."

Kara decided it would be better for Jillian to hear this firsthand, so she took McGowan back to her boss's office and grabbed her from the briefing. After introductions, Jillian said, "What can you tell us, Inspector?"

"We won't have a full report for a few days yet, but I can tell you that this fire did not start by accident. Accelerant was used in multiple spots throughout the house and likely thrown down the stairs to the basement," she said.

"Sorry," Jillian interrupted, "what do you mean, *thrown*?"

"The splatter pattern of the accelerant shows that some type of container, perhaps a petrol can or something similar, was tossed down the stairs and then ignited."

Jillian shuddered, but motioned for the fire inspector to continue.

"At this point, that's all I can really tell you. However, I can send you a list of known arsonists in Hampshire that we have in our database that we would consider a mass arsonist."

Kara spoke up this time. "What does that mean? Mass arsonist?"

"Sorry," McGowan said. "That's someone who sets three or more fires at the same location at the same time."

"That would be very helpful, thank you," Jillian said.

The fire inspector promised to send the list as soon as she got back to her office, as well as the full report once they were finished with their investigation.

As she was leaving, McGowan passed DS Rob Milston, who stepped back to give her space and then continued to look at her as she walked toward the exit. After that, he turned and entered Jillian's office.

Both Jillian and Kara were looking at him.

"What?" he said, holding his arms out. "There's no harm in looking."

"Could you be more blatantly sexist, Rob?" Jillian asked, shaking her head.

"I mean, if I tried exceptionally hard, I'm sure I could come up with . . ." he began. Again, he held his palms up and shrugged sheepishly.

Kara just rolled her eyes and left to return to her desk.

"What's up?" Jillian asked.

Evading the question, Milston said, "Anything interesting from the fire service?" He motioned to the hallway where the inspector had just left.

"Only that they're fairly certain the fire was started intentionally," Jillian said. "What they call a mass arsonist."

"Look," Milston said, his expression turning serious, "there are some things I can't go into, even with you." He was referring to the long-standing history they had and the trust they'd built up over the years. "SCD9 have been working on something for a while now, and this may or may not play into it."

"What kind of thing?" Jillian asked.

"That's what I can't get into," he responded. "But I can tell you that part of it involves some new super-strength street drugs. They're called nitazenes, which are a type of synthetic opioids more powerful than heroin and fentanyl."

"Christ!" Jillian exclaimed.

"Yeah," Milston agreed, "we think they're mostly being manufactured in labs outside the UK, mostly in China, and then imported. The problem, aside from the obvious, is that it's a new market of drug that is incredibly lucrative."

"Are there specific players you have in mind?" Jillian asked.

"That's part of the problem. Everyone is getting in on it, though some big players are more established than others. It's also attracting some OC heavy hitters here and in Europe."

"Great, just what we need, an organized crime gang war," Jillian said.

Milston just pursed his lips and nodded. "Just thought you ought to know what you might be up against here."

"Thanks," Jillian said, meaning it. "I appreciate the heads up." Then, leaning forward on her desk, she added, "And this other thing you can't tell me about, everything going okay?"

"It's . . ." Milston began, then looking wistful, he said, "It's fine, it's all good."

Jillian didn't believe him for a second, but knew better than to push him. Just then, DS Listun knocked on her door and she motioned for him to come in. "Sorry to interrupt, guv," he said, "but you've got a visitor in the lobby."

Jillian frowned. The VCU was not like a local nick and rarely had visitors. Between the fire service and DS Milston, they'd already had their complement of visitors for a typical week. Milston stood up to leave, and Jillian clicked on her computer monitor to show the CCTV they had installed in the lobby. Sitting peacefully in one of the waiting chairs and smiling at the camera was Sebastian Hughes.

Jillian rolled her eyes and sighed more loudly than she had intended. There was no way to avoid Milston seeing him, so she needed to act as if there was nothing to it. "Show him in, Stephen," she said to her DS and then added to Milston, "Thanks again, Rob. I'll let you know if we come across anything."

Milston feigned a salute. Instead of heading toward the exit, however, he approached DC Devanor's desk and perched himself on the corner, leaning over to speak to her.

Sebastian Hughes walked into Jillian's office, briefly looking at Milston before turning his attention to Jillian. "Thank you for seeing me."

"People are going to start talking if you keep spending all your free time at the Violent Crimes Unit," Jillian said from the chair behind her desk.

Hughes took the chair Milston had just been sitting in. Whereas DS Milston had the casual air of a motorcycle rider, with jeans, boots, and a leather jacket, Sebastian Hughes looked, as always, like he had just stepped out of a tailor on Savile Row. He wore a black suit with very faint pin stripes, a white shirt complete with cuff links, and a gold tie with a black diamond pattern.

He straightened his pant leg as he crossed one leg over the other. His black loafers gleamed with polish. Jillian looked on silently, waiting for him to begin.

"I came to ask for a favor," he said.

Jillian's eyebrows rose.

Hughes continued, "It's about the house fire."

Jillian thought she, at some point, would stop being surprised at the number of things Hughes knew seemingly out of the blue, but that day wasn't today. "And what do you know about the house fire, and why come to me?" she said.

Hughes spoke as if he hadn't heard her questions. "I believe you will find that the operation in the basement had to do with cryptocurrency," he began. "Specifically involving video games where cryptocurrency is earned as players succeed in the games."

"How could you possible know that?" Jillian asked, crossing her arms as her jaw tensed.

Hughes inspected something on his shoe, then looked up at her. "I don't know for certain, and no, before you ask, I did not know about the uhm . . . conditions that the players were working under," Hughes said.

"Are you branching out into cryptocurrency?" she asked.

Hughes smiled. "No. My interest has to do with a new form of online gambling that has grown alongside the cryptocurrency craze." After a pause, he continued, "Punters, as you probably know, will place a bet on anything and everything. Like all addictions, there is an endless supply of excuses to support the habit."

Jillian couldn't help herself. "And you are happy to profit."

Hughes expression didn't change and yet something in the air shifted. "I'm a businessman, that's all. The point is they will bet on everything— from which elevator is going to arrive first in a business office to whether the next person to hail a cab will be a man or a woman. It's not just the horses and card games."

Jillian leaned back in her chair and nodded for him to continue.

"Once the crypto movement ventured into video games, it created a side benefit, if you will, with the emergence of online voyeurism," Hughes said.

Jillian frowned. "How do you mean?"

"Believe it or not, there's a whole community of people who will pay to watch other people play video games."

Jillian had heard of this, but knew little about it.

"The natural extension, when it comes to cryptocurrencies and the video games people play to earn that currency, is that now people will bet on who will win, or who will complete a particular level first, or who will be eliminated first, et cetera, et cetera," Hughes explained.

"And are you expanding into this online gambling craze?" Jillian asked.

"No," Hughes said seriously, "but someone else is."

CHAPTER 4

It was getting late in the day. Jillian Scotte sat in her office with Detective Sergeant Listun and Detective Constable Devanor.

"Where are we?" Jillian asked.

DS Listun spoke first. "We're going through the list of probable mass arsonists we received from the fire service, mum. Admin and uniforms are contacting them either in person or via phone and establishing if they had alibis."

Jillian nodded. "How many?"

"Seventeen in the immediate area. The list grows as we widen the scope," Listun said.

Jillian sighed and looked over at Kara, who was frowning. "Something troubling you?"

"Well," she began, "it doesn't make much sense, does it? I mean, if you're known to the fire service, and likely the local police as well, would you target a home that has people in it, and especially a home that is a known drug location?"

"Maybe they didn't know?" Listun probed.

Kara lifted up her notepad in his direction. "If SCD9 know about it, I'm betting everyone in the community knew as well."

Jillian nodded. "I agree. Coppers are usually the last to know, and Kara has a point."

"So, if not a known arsonist, are we looking at a new one?" Listun asked.

"We need to start thinking about motive," Jillian said. "Let's start with possible drug gangs in the area. Kara, get on to SCD9 and find out what they know about rival drug operations with this new synthetic—what's it called?"

"Nitazenes. Yes guv," Kara said.

Turning back to Listun, Jillian said, "There's also this cryptocurrency gambling angle. Let's see if we can find out more about who might want to see something like that stopped."

"You mean other than someone like Hughes?" Listun said, raising an eyebrow.

"Mmm," Jillian pondered, tapping her lips with a pen. "Seems unlikely that he would come and alert us to it if he was the one who did it though, does it?"

Listun looked unsure what to say to that, so he kept quiet. They went over a few other details on the team's workload and then called it a night.

***

The next morning, the team was back at it, chasing down various leads and reviewing potential witness statements from neighbors of the burned-down house, when DS Milston walked into Jillian's office.

He leaned against the frame of her doorway, dressed in his usual jeans and boots, this time with a matching-colored denim shirt under his brown leather jacket. His roguish smile present as ever, he said, "Mornin', DI Scotte,"

Jillian looked up from her pile of papers, and despite herself, smiled back. "Good morning, DS Milston. To what do I owe this unexpected pleasure?"

He looked over his shoulder in the direction of Kara's desk before turning back and saying, "That pretty little DC of yours called over asking about possible drug-related gangs that you should take a look at. Thought I'd deliver the list personally."

Jillian stood up from her desk and walked around it, coming to a stop directly in front of Milston. She was no longer smiling. "That *pretty little DC*"—Jillian used air quotes as she repeated his words—"has a name, which you know all too well."

Milston opened his mouth to answer, but Jillian cut him off. "Your swagger may play well in the men's club of SCD9, but I don't want it here. Do I make myself clear?"

Milston stopped smiling and tilted his head slightly in apology. "Sorry, I didn't mean . . ."

Once again, Jillian cut him off. She walked around him out of her office, but as she passed, she said, "Oh and Rob, she is *way* out of your league."

Jillian called for Kara and DS Listun to come into her office.

Milston and the two detectives said hello politely. Jillian walked back around and stood behind her desk. "DS Milston was just about to discuss his list of possible drug gangs we should take a look at."

Clearing his throat, Milston took some folded papers from inside his jacket and laid them out on the front of Jillian's desk. Everyone leaned over beside him to look. There were some names and descriptions, covering two pages. Three of them had been circled. "These," he said, pointing to the circled ones, "I can't help you with because . . .uhm . . . I'm somewhat of a known quantity."

Jillian assumed he meant he was working undercover with them, but kept it to herself.

He went on describing one or two that he thought had the most to gain by attacking the house.

Kara spoke up. "Aren't any of these the ones who actually ran that house?"

Milston straightened up from the list. "We're not sure, but we don't think so. The crew going in and out are mostly unknown to us, and remember, we had just been putting this house under surveillance, so we don't have a lot of intel on the operation itself."

"Rob," Jillian said, "are any of these gangs using cryptocurrency?"

Milston shook his head slowly. "No, not that I know of. They want cash quickly, not some digital money they have to convert or whatever. Most drug trade is cash only. I supposed they could consider washing the money through cryptocurrencies, though I don't have any idea how that would work or even if it's possible."

DS Milston took his leave at that point, saying he was due for a briefing on an upcoming operation they were working on.

Jillian and her team began looking through the list he had left. Jillian told Kara to keep working on the cryptocurrency angle to see what they could find out. She and Listun then put together a plan for talking to a couple of the most promising gangs from Milston's list. Only two really made any sense, and one of them was a long shot. Listun announced he wanted to see that one today, given that not that far away.

Jillian agreed. "Take a PC with you," she said. "We'll figure out a visit to the other one." That one was nearer London, and they would need to tread lightly. Although they were part of the Met, the local police wouldn't take kindly to have them nosing about on their patch.

***

Stephen Listun and PC Peter Gursey soon found themselves in one of the unit's marked cars on their way to the longshot drug outfit. PC Gursey was more than a little nervous driving his DS to this interview. He was excited, to be sure, but being new to the team, he hadn't had a lot of time to get to know everyone.

DS Listun looked out at the passing streets of Southampton and then at the coastal scenery as they made their way over to Chichester. His mind, initially on the task at hand, quickly moved on during the thirty-mile journey.

He was thinking of his wife, Deborah, and of their newborn baby, Lizzy, named after his grandmother and her mother's sister.

Listun knew he was a lucky man. He had a lovely wife, a beautiful daughter. Well, at least he and Deborah thought so. He knew all parents were partial to their children being beautiful babies, but he'd seen some ugly ones in his day, and he knew Lizzy was an angel. The fact that she already had her father wrapped around her tiny little finger was not lost on him, and the thought made him smile.

DS Stephen Listun also loved his job. He'd been excited to join the VCU. He'd heard all about DI Scotte, and he wanted to learn from her. He had ignored some rumors because the people who kept harping on about them were, in his opinion, not the type of coppers he could learn anything from.

Now, after all the cases they had worked on together, he knew he'd made the right decision. Life was good. Never mind that he barely got any sleep, what with Lizzy's colic and the late nights he sometimes worked. It was all part of the package.

Listun's daydreaming quickly faded as they approached the address they were looking for. PC Gursey found a no-parking area halfway down the block and parked the marked car visibly in it. The pair walked down to the kabob restaurant and walked in.

CHAPTER 5

As a restaurant, the King of Kabob wasn't much to look at. It was just clean enough to pass a health inspection, but only just.

DS Listun and PC Gursey looked at each other after walking in the front door. Neither would be placing an order to go. Listun flashed his warrant card to the woman who greeted them and said he needed to see Jimmy Tang.

"Don't know anyone by that name," the woman said. She was maybe twenty, with blond hair that looked dyed. She had multiple piercings up and down both ears and one in her nose.

Listun sighed. "Look, we can play this game and I'll have health and safety crawling all over this place within the hour, which I doubt your boss will like. Or you can tell him we need to speak to him and keep things quiet." He didn't raise his voice to try to sound intimidating. In fact, he did the opposite and purposefully sounded bored.

It worked. She told them to "wait here" and disappeared into the kitchen. A few minutes later, she returned with a tall, thin man who wore a suit with a button-down shirt but no tie. He motioned for them to follow.

They made their way to the back of the building and into a smoke-filled room. Two men played cards on a table and another sat on a worn sofa against the wall. The man on the sofa said, "I'm Jimmy Tang."

He was thin, with greasy black hair and stained teeth. Gursey looked over at Listun and back again, surprised to see that the man was white. Listun, looking at the two men playing cards, said, "Could we have a word in private, Mr. Tang?"

Tang snapped his fingers and the room cleared out, including the tall man in the suit.

"If you're here for more bangers and mash, you can piss off, man. I already paid this month," Tang said. He wore a white T-shirt over a pair of gray slacks. A matching gray suit coat was lying over the arm of the sofa. He spoke with a heavy Cockney accent.

Listun knew that bangers and mash was Cockney slang—rhyming words to signify a different meaning. In this case, bangers and mash meant cash.

"What do you mean, you already paid?" Listun asked.

"Same as every month, innit?" Tang said. "You lot send the old geezer with his putrid breath up to collect, and we pay."

Listun's eyes narrowed. That description fit someone he knew. "The old geezer got a name, then?"

Tang furrowed his brow. "What's this about?"

"I want to know the geezer's name," Listun said.

"If you don't know his name, I'm not going to be the one to tell you. I'm sure you can find him if you follow that horrible breath or his equally putrid aftershave," Tang said.

"What do you know about a house fire two days ago?" Listun asked, giving him the address.

Tang waited a bit before answering, "I don't know noffin' 'bout that."

"And where were you that night?"

"I was here till closin', then I was home with my girl," Tang said as he stood up from the sofa.

Listun didn't move even as Tang walked up into his space. "And you were there all night?"

Tang smiled, his yellow-stained and crooked teeth showing. "Yeah mate. All. Night. Long." He punctuated each word with a suggestive thrust of his hips.

Listun asked Tang to give PC Gursey his home address and the name of his girlfriend. Gursey tore a piece of paper from his notebook and handed it to the drug dealer.

Tang snatched it out of his hands, and taking the offered pen the same way, he leaned down on the table the men had been playing cards at and scribbled the information.

"Look," he said, throwing down the pen on the piece of paper for Gursey to pick up, "we pay a lot of money so we don't get harassed by the likes of you." He pointed his finger at Listun.

Listun half smiled. "Yeah, well," he said, nodding to Gursey for them to leave. "I'm not the old geezer, am I?"

***

The following day, Jillian took Kara with her as they headed up toward London. Given that this wasn't their "patch," she didn't want anyone from the London Met giving her DS a difficult time. She was less likely to be admonished, and just to cover her backside, she'd arranged to have drinks and possibly dinner with Superintendent Sanderson.

This most promising of Milston's possible suspects owned a courier business in Slough, west of Heathrow Airport. The two detectives pulled into a visitor's parking space and looked around as they got out of their vehicle.

Several cars were parked in what Jillian assumed were employee parking spaces, but one stood out. A lime-green Lamborghini. Perhaps the owner—and drug dealer, according to Milston—thought it symbolized how quickly the courier service could deliver their packages.

It was midafternoon, and the traffic hadn't been too difficult. Still, the drive up from Southampton was tiring, and Jillian was in no mood to be messed about. She walked in and announced herself, flashing her warrant card by way of greeting to the nearest woman behind the counter.

"We'd like to speak to Jeremy Spinner," Jillian said.

The automatic smile that had been plastered on the woman's face faded as quickly as it had appeared. She half sneered before turning and walking through a door at the back.

A minute later, a short, fat man in a tan suit with brown tie walked back with her, as confident as a rooster in his henhouse.

"I'm Spinner. What's this all about?" he asked.

"I'm Detective Inspector Scotte, and this is Detective Constable Devanor," Jillian said. She once again flashed her badge, which had the added benefit of getting everyone in the room to look over. "Perhaps we could go somewhere a little more private to talk?"

Spinner wanted to throw his considerable weight around and push back. She could see the indecision on his face. The problem was that employees and customers alike were half listening or blatantly looking at them, and he didn't yet know what the conversation could entail.

Sighing loudly, he nodded toward the back door. "Come on then, let's get this over with." Then he added loudly for the benefit of his customers, "All our paperwork is in order, you know. We just passed our annual customs review last month."

Once they had walked back through the usual cubicle hallway and into his corner office, Spinner walked around a large standing desk and pressed a button, lowering the desk down to its sitting level. He took a seat in a large, high-backed black leather chair. It was so tall that his head was positioned in the middle of the chair back, with the rest of it towering over his thinning hair.

As Jillian and Kara sat down in his stiff and unremarkable "client" chairs, she glanced at Kara and saw her suppressing a smile at how ridiculous Spinner looked sitting in what he clearly thought of as his throne.

"Let's cut to the chase, shall we, Mr. Spinner," Jillian began. Her tone was professional and had a hint of authority to it. "We both know that we're not here to look at paperwork and that the purpose of our visit has to do with the . . . shall we say, product distribution side of your business."

Spinner smiled a twisted smile and opened his hands with palms facing upward. "I haven't the faintest idea what you're talking about, Detective Inspector."

"Is that your Lamborghini outside?" Jillian said.

The change of questioning threw him. He turned his head slightly, frowning. "Yes," he said cautiously, then after a moment's pause, he said, "Why? Did you want to take a ride?"

Jillian allowed her own thin smile to cross her lips and thought that his Napoleon complex must be in full force for him to need such a flashy car to counterbalance the insecurity about his short stature. "No, it's just a rather expensive car for a manager of a courier company."

"Owner, actually," he said defensively.

Changing course again, Jillian said, "What can you tell me about the fire that burned down a drug-operation home in Southampton a few days ago?"

Spinner laughed loudly. "You must be joking," he said. "What could I possible know about a house fire in Southampton?"

"That's what we'd like to know," Jillian said.

"Look. Inspector," Spinner said, placing his elbows on his desk and leaning forward. "I don't know what you've been told, but I am quite a busy man. I couldn't tell you about the latest home in London to catch fire, let alone homes in other parts of England. You might as well be asking me about a house that caught fire at the end of a street in Australia."

"I never said the home was at the end of a street," Jillian shot back.

Spinner wiped the incredulous look from his face and glared across at Jillian. He spoke with a slow, steady cadence, and his expression was no longer friendly, if it ever was in the first place. "I don't know anything about any house fire. I have, in fact, been in London for the past three weeks. He held up one of his hands with the palm facing outward. "And yes, before you ask, I have plenty of people who will corroborate that for me."

At that point, he reached over and pressed a button on his phone, but said nothing. He simply stood as the door to his office opened and two men walked in. Both men were dressed in suits that were too large for them, likely to conceal weapons.

"My associates will see you out. I have work to do," Spinner said, and pushed the button on his desk that began raising it to a standing position again.

***

"What did you think?" Jillian asked Kara as they returned to their car.

Kara visibly shook as though she had just been blasted with cold air. "He's slimy," she said, "and he definitely knew about the fire."

"Mmm," Jillian agreed.

"Though, to be fair," Kara said, "Milston said word was spreading like wildfire—sorry, pun not intended—throughout the drug world because of the nitazenes they were mixing with and on account of no one being clear who was running the house."

"Yes," Jillian said, agreeing again, "but it could also be because it was one of his houses."

Kara nodded.

"Let's keep digging and see if we can come up with a connection between the house and Spinner or even this courier business. There has to be something that will point us in the right direction."

"Yes, mum," Kara said.

CHAPTER 6

The restaurant Jillian and Kara sat in later that day had an old-world feel to it. All dark brown wood and actual paintings on the walls, no prints. The waitstaff were dressed in dark trousers and starched white shirts, with maroon aprons tied around their waists.

Superintendent Maryanne Sanderson was, as usual, late. Though this time she didn't arrive bustling through the front door but appeared from a set of French doors at the back of the restaurant. She was dressed in her full uniform. Carrying her hat, she walked up to the table, and catching the server, she said, "I'll have a gin and tonic please, and make it a double."

She put her bag and hat on one of the chairs between Jillian and Kara and turned toward Jillian, who stood up and gave her a hug.

"Sorry I'm late," Sanderson said. "That seems to be a constant refrain of mine, I'm afraid."

Jillian indicated Kara, who was also standing. "You remember DC Devanor?"

Sanderson reached out her hand. "Of course I remember Kara. How are you?"

Kara shook the offered hand and said she was doing well. Everyone settled back down into their chairs, and Sanderson said, "I know we were meeting for drinks and possibly dinner, and I hope you'll join me for food. I've been in a strategy meeting all day, and although they fed us lunch, it was hours ago and I'm famished."

With that, they ordered meals and a bottle of wine, as Sanderson was already halfway through her G&T. They were just bringing her up to speed on the investigation when the French doors opened once again and several more uniformed police officers spilled out.

Jillian, whose seat was facing the back of the restaurant, recognized the Metropolitan police commissioner, the highest position within the force. He had announced his retirement several months ago and couldn't have much time left.

As the group milled about, he and a few others began walking toward the front of the restaurant. Passing their table, the commissioner stopped, and the three women stood up. The commissioner, tall, broad shouldered, with thinning gray hair, fluttered his arms out quickly, saying, "Please sit . . . sit." Then, looking at Sanderson, he said, "Maryanne, I just wanted to thank you for your insights today. You made some excellent points and I very much appreciate your perspective."

"Thank you, sir," Sanderson replied. "I don't believe you've met Detective Inspector Jillian Scotte from one of our Violent Crime Units."

Turning to Jillian, the commissioner said, "I have not." Then, extending his hand, he added, "Though I am, of course, aware of who you are. Your unit is down on the coast, is it not?"

"Yes sir," Jillian said, shaking his hand.

"Excellent work. Maryanne has told me all about you, of course," he said, smiling.

Jillian half nodded, then indicated across the table, "This is DC Devanor. She's one of the best we've got."

The commissioner made his way around the table to shake Kara's hand. Kara clearly wasn't sure if she should stay seated or stand and ended up in an awkward half up–half down position. The commissioner, seemingly not noticing, simply said, "Well, if you're at this table you must have earned it. It's nice to meet you, Detective."

One of his aides cleared his throat in a not-so-subtle way, and the commissioner said, "Yes, yes, I'm coming." Then, looking at Sanderson, he said, "I mean it, Maryanne, don't let them bully you in those meetings. Keep speaking up. What you have to say is valuable." And then he turned and walked on with his group.

Everyone reached for their glasses almost simultaneously. Jillian said, "He seemed nice," with a half-smile on her lips before drinking some wine.

Putting her glass back down on the table, Sanderson said, "Mmm." Then she added, "He also wants something. Tomorrow, I'm sure I will receive a call or a summons."

The server arrived with their food, and soon the conversation turned back to the investigation.

After Jillian and Kara had finished catching her up on their progress, Sanderson said, "I actually have something for you."

This caught both Jillian's and Kara's attention.

"I received a message from Thomas Redmond today," she said.

Jillian looked over at Kara. "He's the one who found that network connection dish on the other house."

Kara nodded her understanding.

"Yes, well," Sanderson said, "he's been able to track down a bit more information, all having to do with technical details around internet routers and switches and service providers, and honestly, I get lost in all the jargon. It's like a completely different language."

The other two women nodded understandingly.

"The thing is, he said the scope of data being collected by that antennae he saw being removed was far too much for a single point of collection, and as it turned out, this particular building was being used as a sort of hub with multiple other antennae.

"The bad news is that he wasn't able to get a lot of trackable data from the antennae company," Sanderson continued, "but he did manage to track down one path which led to another point, and then another, and then"—here she paused for effect—"he was able to track down an end point belonging to a real estate firm in Essex."

Jillian and Kara looked at each other, then Jillian turned back to her boss. "I'm not sure I quite understand, mum?"

"Yes, that's because I haven't told you the last bit." Here again Sanderson paused, though it seemed more for thought than for effect. Eventually she said, "This particular firm has ties to a man called Damien Onslow."

Here Sanderson stopped and looked at both women to see if the name rang a bell. It didn't.

"He is one of the biggest—well, certainly the fastest-growing—organized crime figures in the UK," Sanderson said.

Jillian raised her eyebrows. Kara reached into her handbag and brought out her notebook.

Sanderson lifted her hands slightly. "I know. But before you get too excited, I need to warn you. This is not your ordinary OC gang member. From what I gather, he is as nasty as they come."

"And," she added, "he's intelligent. He's fairly new, within the last five to ten years, they believe." She didn't have to say who "they" were, since organized crime fell to SCD9's branch of the Met.

"He starts slowly, apparently, finding untapped opportunities and then taking over anyone and anything that stands in his way." Sanderson looked at Jillian now, her eyes demanding her attention. "You do *not* want to take him on on your own, do you understand?"

"Yes, I think so," Jillian said. "Do you think your Mr. Redmond will be able to get us anything further?"

"He's working on it, but Jillian?" Sanderson said forcefully, "I mean it. Don't underestimate this man. He is more dangerous than anyone we've encountered, and that's saying something."

***

The next morning, Jillian and Kara met with DS Listun and Chief Inspector Alan Dobson of SCD9's southern unit, as well as his DS, Rob Milston, around a long table in the VCU incident room.

"What do we know?" Jillian asked.

Dobson cleared his throat. "Well, I reached out to our counterparts up north after I got your call yesterday. They sent me some background on Mr. Onslow this morning."

Everyone gave him their full attention. "He's originally from Cambridge, if you can believe it. Apparently quite intelligent and was destined to go to the city's namesake uni, but his parents were killed in a . . . wait for it," he said provocatively, ". . . house fire."

He looked around the room before continuing. "That's when things began going off the rails. Seems our Mr. Onslow left secondary school just months before finishing. Took his younger sister with him." Dobson flipped through some notes and then said, "She's six years younger. Would've been eleven or twelve at that point. Name's Lucile. They head up to Leicester, where his criminal activities take root."

DS Milston spoke up. "He did 'ave a few run-ins back in Cambridge, but just the usual juvenile stuff, nothing serious as far as we can tell."

"How long ago was this?" Kara asked.

"His move to Leicester, you mean?" Dobson asked. Kara nodded. "About eight years ago, which puts him at just twenty-six or twenty-seven. Quite young for someone in OC with his stature."

"And just what is his stature?" Jillian asked.

"The next Tony Soprano, if you believe the OC unit in London," Milston said just as his boss opened his mouth.

"Well," Dobson said, giving Milston a stern look, "that might be exaggerating a bit." But then Dobson turned to the three VCU detectives. "Although I will say he's got quite the reputation and none of it good."

"Such as?" DS Listun asked.

"Read for yourself," Dobson said, sliding some papers across the table.

Listun began reading the notes and passing a page at a time to Kara, who then passed them on to Jillian. The room was quiet while they read, save for the noises of disgust and shock.

"This bit about his sister—is that true?" Kara asked, looking up.

"Some of what you've got is fact, some of it is reputation," Milston said. "I talked to a mate of mine up in the Manchester SCD9 unit. He says that part is true, but how he knows, I couldn't tell you."

"What is it?" Jillian asked, having not read that page yet.

Kara hesitated, then said, "It says he turned her out as a prostitute when she was thirteen."

Listun grimaced. "His own sister? That's disgusting."

"Never mind that she was a child," Kara added.

"There's much worse in those pages," Dobson said, "and that's just what they were willing to share with us on short notice." He leaned forward and spoke to Jillian. "This man is as evil as they come, DI Scotte. You don't want to go messing about with him."

"Mmm," Jillian said, still reading the page in her hands. Everyone, including Dobson, could hear in her voice she was thinking of doing that very thing.

"I'm not joking, Inspector!" Dobson said sternly.

That made Jillian look up. She held his gaze for several seconds. "I can see that, sir," she said. "I cannot, however, ignore the strongest lead we have in this case just because this up-and-coming crime boss has a fetish for doing nasty things to people."

"That's not what I'm suggesting," Dobson said, then lowering his voice as if that would prevent the rest of the room hearing, he added, "I just . . .you have a reputation . . ." Realizing that everyone was looking at him, he said, "I'm just saying there is a right way and a wrong way to handle this, that's all."

Jillian opened her mouth to reply, but he cut her off. "And," he said, pointing his finger at her, "you will be taking DS Listun and DS Milston with you when you do."

Jillian could see he wasn't going to budge, and she didn't really mind having them with her, though two seemed excessive. Still, she simply nodded her assent.

CHAPTER 7

DS Listun parked the car in the seashell-laden driveway outside the home of Damien Onslow and turned off the engine. Beside him, Jillian craned her neck to look out the windshield at the two-story home that in another part of the country would be called a manor house. DS Milston was already getting out of the back seat.

As the trio approached the double-door entry, the right door opened, and two men stepped out. The first was a broad-shouldered, dark-skinned man. His voice was very low when he said, "Mr. Onslow is a busy man. He would like to know what this is about?"

Rob Milston flashed his warrant card. "This is about us having a conversation with Mr. Onslow." He looked up at the facade of the large house before letting his gaze fall back to the security goon. "We can either do it here, or back at the nick." Milston smiled broadly.

The big man took a deep breath in, expanding his chest, and opened his mouth to speak, but the man behind him stepped around and cut him off, saying, "If I'm not mistaken, Detective Sergeant, that warrant card is from Southampton. Not exactly local, are you?"

Sensing a shift, Jillian now stepped forward with her own warrant card on display. "Not exactly, but we're attached to the Met, so, as DS Milston said, here or there?" Jillian did not smile and nor did the man before her.

He was European, not English. He had dark hair neatly trimmed, with equally black eyes, and his skin suggested Spanish or perhaps Italian. His accent, however, was definitely British. Jillian said, "May I ask who you are?"

A brief smile crossed his face before he said, "I am Mr. Onslow's business partner"—he held out his hand—"Tom Figaro."

Italian, Jillian thought as she shook the offered hand.

Figaro turned. "Please, follow me," he said, walking back up the four steps into the entrance of Damien Onslow's palatial home.

They walked through a foyer that had an open ceiling all the way to the second floor. Listun almost whistled, but caught himself as Jillian fixed him with a gaze that left no doubt as to his best course of action.

They followed Figaro into a large living room—or at least what might pass as one. It was easily three to four times the size of any living room the three detectives had ever lived in.

"Wait here," Figaro said, pointing to the floor beside him, and then he turned to the right and went down another hallway.

Sitting on a leather sofa just to their left were two young ladies, nineteen or twenty, if Jillian had to guess. They were painting their toenails, with a large assortment of nail polish bottles, remover, and magazines spread out before them. It seemed they were trying to copy a design from the magazine.

The one closest to where the trio stood was blond and had bright red lipstick on. She was wearing white shorts and a plain orange T-shirt over her thin figure.

"I like the color," Jillian said, pointing to her feet. The young woman was carefully brushing a light-blue polish with sparkles mixed in over her big toenail. She looked up and met Jillian's eyes, but then quickly looked back down.

Just then a booming voice said, "Fucks' sake, Lucy, how many times have I told you not to do that in here? That stuff smells something awful."

Jillian, Listun, and Milston all turned. The man approaching them was broad-shouldered and wore an open-necked white button-down shirt with two large gold chains showing and dark blue slacks. Figaro was walking behind him.

"The infamous Damien Onslow," Jillian heard Milston whisper out of the corner of his mouth.

As he approached, he bellowed, "Go on, piss off upstairs to your rooms. That's why you have them. Christ, that stuff smells." Then, shooting a glance toward the detectives, he added, "I'll be with you in a minute." He and Figaro returned to the foyer and closed the door behind them.

The young blonde named Lucy had closed the lid and brush to her polish bottle and put it back in a large plastic container that easily held over thirty bottles. The other girl was moving things around, apparently looking for some missing item. Suddenly, she stopped and looked over at Lucy. "Shit."

"What?" Lucy said, not bothering to look away from packing up the rest of their supplies.

"I left the cotton balls upstairs."

That made Lucy look, sighing loudly, her shoulders dropping exaggeratedly. "Mandi, I told you not to forget them." Then, pointing to her toes, she said, "How the hell am I supposed to get up there before he gets back without ruining these?"

Jillian reached into her purse and pulled out several of her business cards. Holding them out, she said, "Here, tear these in half and then bend them over. You can stick them between your toes and they'll help you keep the nails dry till you get upstairs."

Lucy hesitated. Taking a look around to make sure no one else was watching, she reached out and grabbed the cards. "Thanks," she said.

"No problem," Jillian replied.

Doing as Jillian suggested, Lucy walked carefully, with Mandi holding the supplies as they crossed the room. They had just walked through a door at the back when Onslow and Figaro returned.

"Right," Onslow said, sitting down in an armchair close to an unlit electric fire. "Let's get to it. I haven't got all day."

Since he had not offered them a seat, the trio stood in front of him as Figaro took another armchair next to his business partner's.

Before Jillian could start, Onslow said, "Tom tells me you lot are from Southampton. Why are you bothering me all the way up here? The bizzies not have enough manpower . . . uhm . . . woman power, whatever, in London that they have to scrape the barrel down south?"

Jillian wondered how much time he'd spent in Liverpool to use their slang police term, *bizzies*, and decided she would have someone look into it. Focusing her attention back to the present, she said, "Mr. Onslow, are you aware of a house fire that took place a week ago in Southampton?"

She could see his face pull back and knew he was going to scoff at her, so she quickly added, "Before you answer, I should tell you that the home was purchased by a real estate holding firm which is owned by your company."

Onslow stared at her, his gaze heavy and not at all friendly. "Detective . . ." Frowning, he turned to Figaro. "What's her name?" he asked.

Figaro opened his mouth to speak, but Jillian interrupted. "I'm Detective Inspector Scotte."

"Well, Detective Inspector," Onslow said with more than a trace of sarcasm, "I own a great deal of properties and can't be expected to know what happens to each one. Perhaps you could be more specific."

"Specifically," Listun said, not caring for the tone Onslow was taking with his boss, "it was a drug house with a basement full of teenagers working on an elaborate computer system playing games to earn cryptocurrency."

Damien Onslow slowly turned his head toward DS Listun, and the look he gave him was enough to make Jillian take a deep breath. Listun simply stared back unflinchingly. After a tense few moments, Onslow said, "Tom here is the wizard with our technology." Then, turning to face Figaro, "You know anything about a fire starting on the top floor of one of our houses?"

This time it was Milston who spoke. "We didn't say anything about the fire starting on the top floor."

Onslow turned to face the detectives, but said nothing. Figaro spread his hands out and said, "Presumably when you said something about teenagers in the basement but nothing about the fire, we assumed it started above."

"There is that thing about assuming," Milston said.

Figaro's eyes narrowed, though his expression didn't change. "As Mr. Onslow said, our business holdings are vast and varied. Whatever happened to this home, I'm sure our insurance will cover the damages."

Milston replied, "Not sure insurance can bring back the dead though, can it?"

Jillian, focusing her attention back on Figaro, said, "What can you tell us about the drug and cryptocurrency operation?"

Figaro flashed the same quick grin he had earlier. "I'm sure we know nothing about those dealings, Detective. Mr. Onslow and I run an honest business."

Milston actually laughed out loud, with Jillian shooting him a quick look, though she doubted he noticed.

"Right," Onslow said, standing up, "we're done here. The next time you want to waste my time and barge into my home unannounced, you can call my solicitor."

CHAPTER 8

Jillian Scotte was not pleased with the start of her morning. She had received an email the evening before from her boss, Superintendent Maryanne Sanderson, informing her she was to be on a video call at half-past six in the morning and that the assistant commissioner of the Metropolitan police force would be on the call.

The AC was third in line to the throne, as it were, behind only the commissioner and deputy commissioner in the police hierarchy. The assistant commissioner, a man called James Bellingham, was someone Jillian knew by sight, though they had never actually met.

Among the many varied duties the AC performed, his job also included liaising with external stakeholders and representing the police force at high-profile events. This put him in front of the camera more often than the commissioner, and thus almost everyone knew who the AC of the Met Police was if they happened upon him in the street.

Normally, Jillian could take a video call from her boss early in the morning at home. She had a secure laptop connection via the virtual private network device the Met had installed for her just for such a purpose. However, a call that included the AC meant she needed to be at her desk, and most annoyingly, in her uniform. Protocol and all that, the email from Sanderson had said.

She set down her coat and bag and just had enough time to make herself a cup of tea before signing in to the secure video connection. Sanderson and Bellingham were already there, talking to each other when she "beeped" into the call.

"Ah, here we are," Sanderson said as though Jillian were late, even though she was right on time. "Good morning, DI Scotte. Thank you for joining us at this early hour."

"Of course, mum," Jillian said, following her boss's lead with a formal tone.

"Assistant Commissioner Bellingham, I don't know if you've met DI Scotte? She heads up one of our VCUs down in Southampton," Sanderson said.

James Bellingham was a man of medium height, with gray hair and dark blue eyes. He was somewhere in his late fifties and had spent his entire career in the Metropolitan Police. "No, I don't think we've met, though I do know of her exploits," he said, then added, "It's nice to finally see you face-to-face, DI Scotte."

"Likewise, sir," Jillian said.

"Look," he said, leaning forward with his arms on his desk, "I'll get right to it, as I'm sure we've all got a lot on our collective plates. Superintendent Sanderson was kind enough to arrange this call at the last moment, because what I need to discuss with you is of a sensitive nature."

Jillian restrained herself from an eye roll at the "kind enough to arrange" comment, knowing that her boss had no choice in the matter. When someone with the rank of AC asks, the answer is always yes.

Bellingham continued, "It's come to my attention that you paid a visit to the home of Damien Onslow yesterday. Is that correct?"

It always bothered Jillian when those above her asked questions they knew the answer to. Nevertheless, she played the game. "Yes, sir, his organization is tied to a case we're working on down here."

"Tied how?" he asked.

Jillian filled him in on the case. At one point, Superintendent Sanderson jumped in with additional details that Jillian didn't know she knew, though it was a good addition to the conversation.

Bellingham looked as though he weren't really paying attention, but once they had finished, he said, "Yes, I see. Well, here's the thing, Scotte." Jillian noted the fact that he had dropped her rank, meaning he was now asserting himself in the pecking order. "Organized Crime have been keeping their eyes on Mr. Onslow for some time, and we need to tread very carefully here because there is a lot more at stake than a few dead bodies in a home in the south of England."

Jillian wasn't sure what she was supposed to say. Luckily, Sanderson stepped in. "Assistant Commissioner, I think DI Scotte needs to investigate the connection to her case and the murder victims. Surely you're not suggesting that she ignore that?"

It was all Jillian could do not to smile. She was also surprised at how forcefully Sanderson was pushing back. The AC was not someone you wanted on your bad side if you wanted your career in the Met to continue, which Sanderson most certainly did.

Bellingham made a face as though he'd just heard something unpleasant. "No, Maryanne, of course not. We must always follow a case where the evidence points us. That is the job," he said, as though this were new information. Then he said, "All I'm saying is tread carefully where Mr. Onslow is concerned. Make sure you have solid evidence you can prove before taking any action. In fact," he continued, beginning to shuffle papers on his desk, clearly nearing the end of the time he wanted to spend on the call, "I would say avoid going anywhere near the man unless you absolutely must do so. I will also add that anything that involves Mr. Onslow ought to be coordinated, if not handled, by SCD9 branch. Now, I have another meeting I must get to. Maryanne, keep me apprised of any developments."

And with that, he ended the call, not even saying goodbye or acknowledging Jillian further.

Sanderson sighed loudly, and although she didn't exactly roll her eyes, she opened them wide enough to convey her displeasure at what had happened on the call. She and Jillian spent a few more minutes catching up, and then the call ended.

Jillian already felt a headache coming on, and it wasn't even seven o'clock in the morning yet.

By the time the rest of the team had arrived, gotten settled, and assembled in the incident room, Jillian was already on her second cup of tea. She noted the updated board at the front of the room, and she thanked DS Listun for having stayed late last night to get everything up-to-date.

"Right," she said, "where are we this morning?"

DS Listun flicked through his notebook and said, "We paid a visit to Damien Onslow's residence yesterday and he was predictably unhelpful. His business associate"—he flipped a page on his notebook forward, then back again—"name of Tom Figaro was there as well and equally unhelpful. They did, however, confirm that they do have real estate holding companies, so that still puts them on the board as possibles." He finished by pointing to their photos, now up on the incident board with lines connecting Onslow to the real estate company, and the company to the crime scene house photo.

Jillian nodded and then said, "Kara, where are we on the tech side of things?"

DC Devanor, who was also holding a notebook, stood up and walked to the front near the whiteboard. She took a magnetic disk from the lower corner and used it to hold up a sheet of paper. "This is an executive summary of what the techies have been able to recover from one of the computer's hard drives that was the least damaged from the fire or subsequent deluge of water from the fire brigade.

"As we suspected, they were primarily playing video games to earn cryptocurrency, which doesn't help us much. However, there was something interesting," she said. "Mr. Redmond said that between the internet connection router, or whatever it's called, and the hard drive, they noticed that an account, other than that of the various players, connected from time to time when the cryptocurrency was in transfer."

That got Jillian's attention. "What did he mean by *connected from time to time*?"

"I didn't get the details, guv," Kara replied, "but the gist, as I understand it, is that this account would connect sometimes, but not all the time, when the cryptocurrency the gamers had earned was being transferred from the house network to the wireless hub he was tracing at the other house."

"Then what happened?" Jillian asked.

"They don't know yet, but he suspects that this account might have been skimming off some of the money in transfer," Kara said.

"What do we know about the account?" DS Listun asked.

"Not much as yet, sarge," Kara said. "The dark web isn't apparently easy to pull information from, but Redmond said they're still working on it. What we have is the username and avatar of the account." Grabbing the remote controller, she switched the input on the incident room mounted television screen to her computer, which she had set up to feed it. On the screen now was a blown-up image of a user account image, or avatar, and a name underneath it.

The image was of a high-end sports car, bright yellow, spinning around and around. The name underneath was "Motora Gif."

Listun walked up to the screen. "A GIF is an animated icon," he said. Then, pointing to the spinning car, he added, "Like that."

"Yes," Kara added, "and *motora* is Spanish for motor."

Jillian looked at her two detectives as they turned to face her. Then she said, "And who do we know likes fancy motorcars?"

Kara and Stephen answered at the same time, "Jeremy Spinner!"

CHAPTER 9

Later that afternoon, Jillian and Kara visited Southampton General Hospital off Tremona road. They walked through the main entrance on level C, then walked down two flights of stairs to level A, not wanting to wait for the lifts. Turning left, they walked to the end of the hall, made a right-hand turn, and walked into the mortuary.

Dr. Daniella Morales, Chief Pathologist with HM Coroner's Service in Hampshire, Portsmouth, and Southampton met them at the front desk. Smiling warmly at Jillian, she took her hand briefly and squeezed before moving over and giving Kara a hug. Sweeping her hand behind her, she said, "Welcome to my humble abode."

Both detectives had been to the mortuary before, of course, but not since Daniella had taken over as the chief pathologist. Her boss, Senior Coroner Michael Thorsby, was nearing retirement and now worked almost exclusively out of the official coroner's office on Castle Hill in Winchester. This left Daniella doing much of the pathology work on high-profile cases.

As they walked back to her office, Daniella turned to look at the two detectives. "I take it you've seen the report from the fire service investigator?"

Jillian nodded. "I took a quick look, but Kara spent a little more time with it."

"She got most of it right," Daniella said. "I'll try to fill in the blanks."

Once everyone was seated in the cramped space Daniella used as her office, she punched some keys on her computer keyboard and brought up the files she was looking for. "Right," she began, "there were fourteen victims in all. Five female adults aged late thirties to mid-fifties, three male adults aged late twenties to mid-thirties, and six young adults, all males, aged mid- to late teens."

Kara chimed in to get her boss up to speed on the postmortem and fire service report. "The five women were on the second floor processing the drugs. The three men would have likely been made up of two guards and one supervisor, who would have constantly been up to check on the women as well as down to check on the boys in the basement."

Jillian nodded and turned her attention back to Daniella, who continued, "The cause of death for the five women was primarily from gunshot wounds, each with a differing number and placement. The three men also received GSWs, mostly to the chest and abdomen. However, their cause of death was most likely a follow-up shot at point blank to the front or back of the head."

As she paused to look up, Jillian asked, "You said the GSWs were the primary cause of death for the women?"

"Yes," Daniella answered. "Two of them died from their wounds almost instantly, though it's important to point out that none of the women received the point-blank shots to the head. Three of them, however, had smoke inhalation in their lungs indicating that they were still alive when the fire was started."

Jillian nodded her understanding, looking over at Kara more as a habit than anything, knowing that her DC was taking meticulous notes.

Daniella continued, "That leaves the six boys in the basement." Here she paused, taking a deep breath. "None of them received any gunshot wounds. They all died of smoke inhalation and asphyxiation. There were marks on a few of them that showed the extent to which they tried to escape from their bonds." She looked up and took off her reading glasses, setting them on the desk before adding, "It was a horrible way to die."

Kara, having stopped with her pen in mid-sentence on her notepad, swallowed hard and said, "Were they . . . did they . . ."

Daniella nodded, cutting her off. "They were dead before the fire consumed their bodies. Well, four of them anyway. The other two mercifully didn't get ravaged by the fire, as the fire service's water saved their surviving family members that atrocity."

Jillian considered this for a moment. "So, do we think the killers simply couldn't shoot the boys, or were they not aware of them?" she asked.

Kara spoke up this time. "According to the fire service report, there was no accelerant spread around in the basement, only on the main and upper levels. The only accelerant in the basement came from what they assume was a gas canister thrown down the stairs. I think this, combined with the lack of GSWs, means it's unlikely they even knew about the boys in the basement."

Daniella nodded in agreement.

Jillian, however, wasn't convinced. "I've seen boys playing video games. They're not the quietest children on the planet."

"True," Kara said, "but if you were shackled to a computer and forced to play those games all day, it would hardly be something fun to laugh and joke about, would it?"

Jillian pursed her lips, nodding. "Good point." Then, looking back at Daniella, she asked, "Is there anything else you can tell us?"

"Not much, I'm afraid. The fire destroyed a lot of things we would normally look at. I can tell you one thing though," she said, and Jillian raised her eyebrows slightly. "Preliminary DNA results from two of the women match with two of the juvenile boys."

Jillian and Kara looked at each other. Kara finally voiced their shared thought: "The mothers were forced to work on the drugs while their children were shackled in the basement working on cryptocurrency video games."

Daniella added, "Whoever set up this house is not someone who has a conscience. And whoever did the killing wanted to destroy everything in sight. They just didn't know they were destroying more than a drug den."

***

Back at the Tof, Jillian filled the team in on what they had learned from the postmortem.

"Guv?" Police Constable Stella Dawson asked. "Wouldn't whoever did this already know what was going on inside the house? I mean it stands to reason they would've had a purpose for attacking this particular house. Surely they must've known what was going on inside?"

Jillian considered this. Then DS Listun spoke up. "What if they weren't the ones that wanted the house shut down?"

Jillian turned to her sergeant. "Meaning?" she asked.

"Meaning," Listun responded, "what if someone put them up to it? Gave them the information, or maybe just enough of the information to get them to want to do it, without telling them about the cryptocurrency bit?"

Now Kara chimed in. "It would make sense, wouldn't it? If someone else wanted in on the cryptocurrency part of the operation, they tell Spinner about the drugs trying to take hold on his patch and hatch the plan for them to burn it down."

Jillian let the team banter back and forth for a bit, throwing out pros and cons to the arguments, positing more theories, until she spoke up to rein them in. "All right, all right, everyone quiet down. What we need to do is start eliminating some of these theories. And we can start by doing what we often do. Chasing the money."

"But guv," Listun said, "we don't have a lead on the cryptocurrency money from the house. That bloke, what's-his-name from Sanderson's team, is working on it, but we have nothing to chase yet."

Jillian nodded. "You're right, but what we *can* do is start with Spinner and see about his money. That spinning car isn't exactly subtle. If he's involved in skimming money, then it has to show up somewhere."

Now she addressed the entire team. "I want to know every part of his finances. Where he shops, where he banks, how much he spends at his local and how often. I want to know how much money he has coming and going on a personal level. This isn't about his sham of a business to cover his money-laundering. Let's find out exactly how our Mr. Spinner funds his hobby of driving luxury cars."

And with that, Jillian brought the meeting to a close and went back to her office. She was tired. It felt like they were chasing their tail on this case, and the killer—or killers—were always one step ahead of them at every turn. It was like chasing a shadow: The minute they reached out to grab it, it drifted away.

It also felt like they were fighting with one arm tied behind their backs. She was fairly certain that Damien Onslow and Jeremy Spinner were somehow tied to this, but they had precious little to go on. Her admonishment from up high that she couldn't even approach Onslow without hard evidence felt out of sorts. She couldn't quite put her finger on it, but something wasn't right.

She shut down her laptop and put it into her messenger bag, knowing she would be up later in the evening catching up on reports and email.

CHAPTER 10

Jillian walked into the Tof still exhausted, having stayed up much too late to catch up on the endless administrative work that never made it into the books and television shows about policing.

Although she was somewhat earlier than usual, determined to get a head start on her day, she noticed much of the team was already working. She passed DS Listun on his way to the gents, and as she approached her office door, her cell phone rang.

Looking at the caller ID, she saw it was DS Rob Milston from SCD9. "Hello Rob, how are you this dreary morning?"

Milston, usually the one always willing to go a few rounds of banter, instead said bluntly, "You need to get down to the house straightaway."

Given his involvement in the case, she didn't need to ask which house he was referring to, though she was curious what anyone could have done to the burned-out shell that would warrant her immediate presence. "Look, Rob, can't you just tell me what's going on? I've got a full plate at the moment, and I really don't have the time."

Milston's usually chipper voice lowered an octave. "Damien Onslow is standing outside looking at it right in front of me."

Jillian was stunned. She told DS Milston she was on her way. Looking around for Listun, she realized he was still in the loo, so she called out to Kara, and the two women set off.

With Kara driving, Jillian could focus on what she should do. Clearly, she had been warned off Onslow, but he was now on her patch. Surely they couldn't fault her for investigating why?

She was also more than a little nervous. She didn't like to admit it, but she wished she had Listun with her—though at least Milston would be there. Men like Onslow respected male authority far more than female, and given the profile she had on him, she wasn't sure what she should expect.

They pulled up behind Milston's car. It was parked a little way up Manse Road, which formed a T with the house at the end of Bryn Road. Manse Road was also on a hill, so they were effectively looking down on the crime scene.

DS Milston, in his ever-present leather motorcycle jacket, got out in the light, drizzling rain and made his way into the back of their car. "Morning. What brings you lovely ladies out on this beautiful morning?" Clearly, his bravado was back.

Jillian, maintaining her view of the burned-out shell of a house and the group of three people standing in front of it, said, "What's going on there?"

"Well," Milston answered, "you've got your run-of-the-mill OC boss Onslow and his lapdog Figaro, with a third man who looks to me to be an estate agent."

Kara turned halfway toward the back and then indicated the two cars parked in front of the house, one of which had a firm's estate agent placard magnetized to the door. "They teach you how to deduce that in sergeant's school, did they?" she teased.

Milston tapped his temple with his index finger. "Noffin' gets by me, love."

Jillian sighed and then opened her door. "Come on, let's get this over with."

As the trio began walking down the hill toward the house, Milston said, "They know I'm here. Figaro spotted me and nudged his boss, who turned and gave me a rather unpleasant gesture with two fingers."

As the detectives approached, the trio of men turned toward them.

Damien Onslow, dressed in a long black coat that looked like it could have been made of cashmere, scowled. "Well, if it isn't the plod squad. Am I going to have to report you for harassment, Detective Inspector?"

"We're conducting a murder inquiry, Mr. Onslow, as you well know. Your unannounced presence here was cause for our interest," Jillian said.

The estate agent, trying to earn his keep, spoke up. "Inspector, surely there is nothing illegal in the owner of a home inspecting the damage from vandalism."

Milston visibly laughed before trying to put a straight face back on.

Ignoring the agent, Jillian addressed Onslow again. "I thought you said this home was simply one of many managed by your holding company?"

Figaro answered her. "Regardless of which of Mr. Onslow's businesses are on the *legal* sale paperwork"—he emphasized the word *legal*—"Mr. Onslow is still the ultimate owner and, as Mr. Jenkins pointed out, there is no crime in reviewing his investment."

There was a moment of silence as everyone considered this.

Milston, clearly enjoying himself, said, "Odd though, isn't it, for you to come down all this way and stand out in the rain to look at a home you said you didn't even know you owned? Unless, of course, there was something of value you lost during the uhm . . . how did you put it, Mr. Jenkins . . . vandalism?"

Figaro opened his mouth to respond, but Jillian cut him off. "Especially considering that fifteen lives were lost as a result."

Onslow took a step forward, getting right up into Jillian's face.

Milston was instantly by her side, which caused Figaro to step up as well. Everyone froze for a moment. Kara looked a bit out of place, with her and the estate agent Jenkins the only ones not actively involved in the face-off.

"I don't like your insinuations," Onslow said angrily, his spittle hitting Jillian in the face.

She didn't flinch or even move, standing her ground and looking him straight in the eye. Trying desperately not to show the fear rising up inside of her and keeping her voice even, she said, "I'm not insinuating anything, Mr. Onslow, merely stating the facts."

Jenkins, seemingly wanting to de-escalate the tension, spoke up. "Inspector, if there's nothing else you need, perhaps my client and I can continue our conversation in private?"

The intensifying rain seemed deafening in the silence. Jillian finally looked over at Milston and nodded behind them towards the car, suggesting that they leave. There was nothing to be gained by annoying Onslow any more than they already had.

As she began walking away, she turned back, acting as though a thought had just occurred to her, though of course it hadn't. "Oh, just one more thing. Do you know anything about an online account skimming money from the crypto transfers called Motora Gif?"

Onslow frowned. A look of confusion crossed his face quickly and just as quickly disappeared, replaced by his scowl. "As I've told you before, Inspector, we merely owned the property as an investment. The inhabitants and whatever they were up to were not something I was privy to."

The detectives turned and began walking back to their cars.

Milston spoke up as they approached his car. "I don't think they were too happy to see us," he said cheekily.

"You laughing didn't help," Kara said.

"Yeah, but, come on. Vandalism?" he responded with an incredulous expression.

Jillian punched him gently on the shoulder. "Thanks for the heads-up, Rob."

"All part of the service," he said, and got in his car.

As they approached their car, Kara was pulling out her key fob to open the doors when Jillian, looking up the road behind them, suddenly said, "What the bloody hell . . ." Then she began walking up the sidewalk to the next intersecting street.

Kara, looking in that direction but not quite understanding the problem, quickly caught up with her boss. As they approached the next street, she took more notice of the dark sedan parked with its motor running.

Jillian, with Kara in tow, approached the passenger side just as the window lowered silently.

Sitting inside was Sebastian Hughes. "Good morning, Detectives. Fancy meeting you both here."

"Don't give me that," Jillian responded testily. "What are you doing here?"

Hughes's smile didn't waver. "Would you believe we just stopped to drink our coffees?" he said, indicating two cups in the cupholders between him and his driver.

"No," Jillian said flatly.

Sebastian didn't respond immediately, and Jillian and Kara simply stood waiting. They were getting good and properly soaked now as the rain intensified, and if Hughes was bothered by the water hitting his car interior through the open windows, he didn't show it. Finally, he said, "I heard Damien Onslow was in town and wanted to see why. It pays to keep an eye on the . . . ahh . . . competition."

"I wasn't aware Onslow was your competition," Jillian said.

After a pause, Hughes answered, "Let's just say he seems to be dabbling."

"Also," Kara spoke up now, "how did you know he was here?"

Jillian nodded and looked back at Hughes, making a mental note to ask Milston the same question later.

Something flashed in Sebastian Hughes's eyes, but Jillian couldn't put her finger on what it was. His countenance never changed, but there was something. Something indescribable that could only be felt. His voice still calm and even, he said simply, "I make it my business to know."

Jillian sighed loudly, recognizing that this was getting them nowhere. Turning to Kara, she said, "Come on," and they both turned to go.

"Jillian," Hughes said. His tone and the use of her first name caused her to stop and turn around. She looked straight into his eyes as he said, "Be careful." Then, as he reached down to press the button and raise his window, he added, "Whatever you've heard about Onslow, he's ten times worse than that."

Jillian shuddered so visibly that Kara could feel it, and it caused her to shudder as well. They had both been standing in front of the man minutes earlier, and what Hughes was saying felt all too real to them.

They approached their respective sides of the car, and this time Kara pressed the key fob to open the doors. Jillian, with her door open, glanced down once again at the burned-out remains of the house. Looking over the roof of the car, she said, "When I asked him about the online account, what did you think?"

Kara thought for a moment as they both climbed into the car, where she pressed the button to start the engine and get the heat going. Then she said, "It was news to him. That was the first time he'd heard of it."

Jillian nodded, thinking the same thing.

CHAPTER 11

It was getting on toward the end of the day, and Jillian had been restless ever since she and Kara had returned from their morning visit to the house.

It wasn't just her confrontation with Onslow or that Sebastian Hughes had been lurking up the street—there was something else. She was tired of not having answers.

She had been deliberating stirring the pot a bit, but wasn't sure if she should do it or not.

Since the day of the fire, the police had purposefully kept the information about the boys in the cellar to themselves, which had not been easy. Every faction that had been on the scene knew that if a leak came out, it would be a small group and could be tracked back, and so Jillian was confident in her fellow officers. There was also the fire service, but they were typically a tight-lipped bunch.

The bigger issue had been, of all things, Daniella. Being newish to the hospital, certainly as the lead pathologist, she didn't yet have a good handle on everyone in her department. Add to that the normal flow of people in and around the A level of the hospital, and any one of them might learn something that could leak.

Daniella had kept her circle small and threatened them with their jobs if anyone found out about the six young corpses attached to that fire. Somehow, it had all worked.

And now, Jillian was considering undoing it all, which is why she was restless all afternoon.

Even DS Listun had noticed, at one point, sticking his head into her office. "Guv?" he inquired. "Is there anything I can do to help you?"

She had, of course, told him it was just lack of sleep, though she wasn't sure he believed her.

As members of her team began to slowly head home for the day, she finally decided and picked up her mobile, typing in the first few letters of the person she needed to reach.

Amelia Hamza—journalist for the digital startup Daily Coast—picked up on the second ring.

"Hello," Amelia said.

"Hi," Jillian responded, "it's me. Do you have a few minutes?"

"Only just," she said. "I'm working on my piece for the digital top story tomorrow morning."

"Good," Jillian said, "because I have something you'll want to put there instead."

Amelia paused briefly, then said, "It better be good."

Jillian asked if she remembered the drug house that had burned down, killing nine people, and Amelia said she did.

"It was more than nine. There were fifteen fatalities. Six young men between the ages of fourteen and seventeen were kept in the cellar and also died in the fire."

After another brief pause, Amelia asked, "What do you mean by kept?"

As she often was, Jillian was impressed with how quickly Amelia picked up on the details. "They were shackled to an iron pipe."

By the deep intake of air she heard down the phone, Jillian knew the journalist's interest was piqued.

"Why were they shackled in the cellar?" she asked.

"I can't say," Jillian said.

Amelia waited, thinking before she asked, "Why wasn't this information released earlier?"

"We had to wait to notify next of kin for all of them, given their ages," Jillian said. This was a stretch of sorts, but one that she doubted Amelia would care much about.

They spent the next ten minutes going back and forth: Jillian giving Amelia minor details, but nothing that would compromise the case, and Amelia trying to get more out of her and rarely succeeding.

"Well," Hamza said, "you're right."

"About?" Jillian responded.

"I will be writing about this for tomorrow morning." And with that, the two said goodnight and ended the call.

***

The team were all buzzing when Jillian came into the incident room for the morning briefing. Clearly, they had read Hamza's piece, and everyone was a little on edge as to how the information was leaked. Everyone knew of Jillian's relationship with Amelia, so she was going to have to put on a show lest they connect the dots too easily.

"All right," she said sharply as everyone quieted down and took a seat or perched on the edge of a table. "Obviously, someone leaked this information to the press about the bodies in the basement. Thankfully, other than the basic information, there isn't anything that compromises our investigation." Here, she paused and looked around the room. "Whoever is responsible for this better pray I never find out."

You could hear a pin drop, and the only sound was the whirring of the air vent in the ceiling.

DS Listun, ever the placater and always looking out for his team, said, "Mum, to be fair, it's a miracle the information stayed quiet this long given the number of people privy to various aspects of this case, many of whom are outside of the VCU."

"Yes, well," Jillian said, feigning acquiescence, "that's as may be, but we keep certain information from cases away from the press and public for a reason. Now, our bloody phones are going to be ringing off the hook from the public demanding results, not to mention the calls from every parent in the country who has a missing child, thinking theirs might be one of the victims."

Listun nodded, but everyone acknowledged he had diffused the boss a little.

Jillian asked for updates, and the morning brief began.

As various members of her team began reporting, Jillian felt a pang of guilt for doing what she had done. What she had said was true, and it wasn't lost on her that she was the one responsible for increasing the workload of her team. Ultimately, it was her call, and she stood by what she did. That, however, did very little to assuage her guilt.

Her focus snapped back as she heard Listun asking Kara about finances.

"Sorry, sarge," Kara said. "We haven't been able to get much because SCD9 have locked down most of it, given that they have Spinner on their watch list."

"Do I need to make some calls?" Jillian asked.

"I tried calling DS Milston, mum, and he told me it would take someone at the Met who oversees all the SCD units across the UK to grant us permission to get to his bank records."

Jillian didn't like the answer. It meant that even Superintendent Sanderson would have trouble getting them access, given what little actual evidence they had to go on. Which made her decision for her.

"Right," she said. "Kara, you and the team keep working and see if there's anything else you can dig up on Mr. Spinner." Then she turned and said, "DS Listun, you and I are going to pay him another visit and see if we can shake loose anything from the tree itself."

***

DS Listun pulled up once again in the visitor parking area of Spinner's courier service building, and the two detectives walked inside with purpose.

Unlike their prior visit, they didn't mess about, and within ninety seconds they were shown into Jeremy Spinner's office. He was on the phone and briskly said, "I'll have to call you back," before slamming the cradle down. "What is it now?" he snapped.

Jillian walked casually around one of the client chairs in front of his desk and sat down, with Listun choosing to stand just to her left. "Mr. Spinner, as we told you on our prior visit, we are investigating a rather brutal multiple murder, and we have had some new information come to light that we would like to explore with you."

"Oh yeah?" he jeered. "And what's that exactly?"

"Are you familiar with an online profile called Motora Gif?" Jillian asked.

"No, why? Should I be?"

"Well Mr. Spinner, you see, this particular profile has a connection to our case, and the . . ." At that point, she looked over at DS Listun.

Listun, taking his cue, said, "The animated gif, mum."

"Yes, that's it. The animated gif of this profile is one of a rather sporty looking car, not unlike the one you drive, Mr. Spinner." She paused here for effect and then added, "And the thing is, that this gif, this animated gif, is spinning around in circles." She indicated a spinning motion with her index finger as she emphasized the word that was his namesake.

Spinner looked from Jillian to Listun and back, his mouth agape. "You must be joking?" he said. "That's it. That's your *new* evidence." Taking a cue from Jillian, he used his fingers to draw air quotes around the word *new*. Continuing, he said, "You've come all the way here to harass me because you found an online profile on the dark web of some geezer with the word *motora* and an animation of a car turning in circles?"

Spinner was enjoying himself, laughing with his assistant who was standing by the door, adding, "You lot must be really grasping at straws now."

"I don't recall saying we found this profile on the dark web," Jillian said, wiping the smile from his face, then adding, "This is hardly a laughing matter, Mr. Spinner."

"No, Inspector, it isn't," Spinner said, "and neither is your harassment of me and my place of business. You can be sure I'll be reporting this to the

London Met the minute your backsides have gone out the door. Honestly, with all the problems the bloody police could be spending your time on, you choose the death of nine drug-dealing criminals to focus on. There are our taxes being put to good use, I tell you," he lamented.

Getting up from her chair, Jillian said, "Oh, didn't you see the news today?" She waited until she had turned toward the door before pausing and looking back. "We had to hold the information back until the families had been notified, but it was more than nine people. There were six young children in the basement who were also killed."

Listun and Jillian both knew the children were related to the women on the second floor, but Spinner didn't. The look on his face told them all they needed to know.

***

Back in the car, Listun started the engine and began heading for the motorway back to the office.

"What do you think?" Jillian asked.

"He did it," Listun declared.

"Mmm," Jillian said, agreeing. "He had no idea about the children. Did you see the blood literally drain from his face?"

Listun nodded. "And he slipped on the dark web bit with the profile."

Jillian's brow furrowed, and she bit her lower lip in thought.

Listun, catching a quick glance, said, "What you thinkin', guv?"

Jillian shook her head slowly. "I dunno. Something's just not right. I mean, if he's the one on the profile, and I grant you it certainly seems like it, then how did he not know about the children in the basement if he knew there was a crypto money scheme coming from the house?"

Listun opened his mouth to reply, only to realize he didn't have an answer.

CHAPTER 12

Jillian was in her office later that afternoon when her mobile rang. The caller ID was Daniella.

"Hello love," she said, holding the phone up to her ear as she typed away on her keyboard.

"Hello," Daniella said. "Look, there's no way that leak came from us. I've spoken to everyone on my team, and they swear it wasn't them and . . . Jills, I believe them." Daniella didn't pause for breath. "I mean, I suppose it could've been someone else in the hospital, but honestly, we've been very careful about the bodies and locking the door when we're working."

Jillian tried to interrupt, but Daniella talked over her. "I promise you. I *promise*. It wasn't someone from my team, I just know it wasn't, and . . ."

This time, Jillian was the one talking louder. "Dani, stop! It's okay. I know it wasn't you or your team."

"You do?"

"Yes," Jillian said, and before Daniella could ask, she added, "It was me, Dani. I'm the one who leaked it to Hamza."

"Wait. But I thought—" Daniella stammered.

"I know. Look, it's rather complicated, and Daniella, I really need you to keep this between us, okay?"

"Yes, yes, of course, but . . ." Daniella began.

"I can't talk right now, but I promise I'll explain everything tonight when I get home," Jillian said.

Jillian could hear a sigh of relief over the phone. "Look, I'm sorry I didn't tell you and that you were worried. I know you're working very hard down there to build rapport with your team, and I'm sure this wasn't what you needed."

"No, it's okay, really," Daniella answered.

"No, it's really not, and I'm sorry," Jillian said. "There's just so much going on. I wasn't thinking about how this would affect you. I'm really sorry for worrying you."

There was a pause. "Thank you," Daniella said, "and it's fine, it really is. I'm just glad to know what happened, so I don't have to worry about something that isn't there, you know?"

"Yes, I do. Look, I must run, but I'll tell you all about it later, okay?"

"Yes, of course," Daniella said. "I'll see you tonight."

"Absolutely, I love you."

"I love you too," Daniella said, and the call disconnected.

As she was setting down her mobile, it rang almost immediately, and this call was from DS Rob Milston at SCD9.

"DI Scotte," she said.

"It's Rob," DS Milston said.

"Hello Rob, what's up?"

She could hear him moving, the sound of a door opening and shutting behind him, perhaps. "What did you do yesterday with Spinner?"

She paused ever so slightly, then said, "Nothing. We're just following up a lead that put him square in the frame." Then she added, "Why?"

This time she could hear the *ding ding ding* of his car and the slam of his door. Milston's voice returned to normal. "Well, your visit was logged by the peeping plods," he began.

Jillian smiled despite herself at his oft-used expression for the clandestine surveillance police that he thought were paid just to spy on people, not that he was too far off the mark.

Milston continued, "And not long after you left, lots of activity started happening."

"What sort of activity?"

"That's not the important bit. Late last night, his longtime girlfriend booked a passage on Eurostar and caught the last train out," Milston said.

"Okay," Jillian said slowly, shaking her head and trying to understand what was so important about that.

"Yeah, well, she booked another ticket at the same time for her brother, only this one is a private jet that leaves in less than an hour," Milston said.

"Look, Rob, I still don't understand what this has to do with Spinner or my visit with him yesterday!" Jillian exclaimed.

"The girlfriend doesn't have a brother," Milston replied.

Jillian felt a chill come over her. "Shit!"

"I'm headed to Southampton International now. The flight was booked through a site called PrivateFly and the jet is chartered to Milan."

Motioning for Listun and Kara to follow, she quickly headed out to their car park. As they approached the car, she tossed her keys to Listun and, holding her phone away briefly, said, "Airport. Now!"

Once inside the car, she put the phone on speaker. "Rob, how sure are we that it's Spinner?"

"The peeps lost track of him two hours ago and haven't been able to reacquire him," was Milston's response. He gave them the hanger and other flight information he had, which Kara busily wrote down in the back seat.

Milston said he was coming down from Winchester and there was heavy traffic putting him about twenty or twenty-five minutes out. The way Listun was taking corners, they would be there well before him.

They had to ask an airport worker for directions once they were on the airport grounds, but they soon pulled up beside a private jet that was clearly being prepared to leave. Serendipitously, a black saloon had just pulled up as they approached. The driver came round to open the door for none other than Jeremy Spinner.

Spinner didn't give the approaching car much more than a glance and simply buttoned his suit coat and turned toward the waiting stairs of the jet.

Listun brought the car to a screeching halt, which caused Spinner to turn. As the three detectives began climbing out of the car, Spinner's eyes widened in recognition.

"Police," DS Listun said loudly. "Jeremy Spinner, we would like a word."

Spinner turned on his heel and, pushing the driver to the ground, made his way round the front of the saloon and climbed into the driver's seat.

Without saying a word, all three detectives climbed back into their car, and the chase was on.

CHAPTER 13

It was clear that Spinner had no idea where he was going. Likely because he'd never paid much attention when his driver entered the airport. Instead of going back the way they would have likely come, he drove further into the airport grounds.

Jillian had instructed Kara to contact airport police for backup. She was in the back seat trying to hold onto the handrail with one hand and her phone with the other as Listun followed Spinner's winding and reckless getaway attempt.

More than once, airport personnel had to dive out of the way as Spinner revved his dark saloon in their direction.

Jillian was giving Listun directions, while simultaneously trying to look at the surrounding layout of the airport and keep their target in sight. For his part, Listun was just attempting to keep Spinner in view without further obstructing the airport services.

"God help us if he heads out toward the runways," Jillian said.

"I don't think he knows where he's going," Listun said, then swore loudly as a cart full of luggage overturned in front of them, having swerved to get out of Spinner's rapidly approaching car. Luggage was now spread out across the concrete, and Listun was swerving like a slalom skier trying to avoid them.

"They're going to set up a block if he goes round at the end of this hanger," Kara announced from the back, her phone pressed tightly to one ear.

Which is exactly what Spinner did. The back end of his saloon fishtailed wildly as he took the turn faster than caution allowed. As Listun followed, slowing only just enough not to completely lose control, they found themselves running a gauntlet.

Spinner was speeding straight ahead. To their right was a large chain-link fence separating them from one of the runways. To their left, a row of hangars and airport buildings. Ahead were two police vehicles with lights flashing, parked horizontally and effectively blocking the only way out.

If the detectives expected Spinner to slow down, they were sadly disappointed. In fact, if anything, he seemed to increase speed. They could see the two police officers ahead looking at each other nervously from behind their respective vehicles.

Suddenly, Spinner's car swerved to the left, the boot fishtailing wildly once more, and then it shot forward toward one of the hangers, into the small gap left by a partially closed door.

Listun followed suit, this time without slowing down, and both female detectives hung on to whatever they could find purchase with as the car lurched sideways, then forward.

The hangar was filled with smaller propeller aircraft and, more frighteningly, lots of people and equipment. Mobile toolboxes and racks of varying sizes all suddenly broke apart or spun out of the way as Spinner simply crashed through them. At least one person careened off the bumper of Spinner's saloon as he pressed on.

Jillian could hear Kara telling whomever she had on the phone that an ambulance was needed inside the hangar.

Having careened through the hangar, Spinner exited once more out the other end and sped off as aircraft of varying sizes taxied by.

Spinner continued trying to find a way off the airport grounds, weaving in and around buildings. Airport police had now joined the chase behind Listun, and the procession of cars was rapidly headed toward the main entrance. Suddenly a group of police vehicles, including one large truck, appeared up ahead and effectively blocked the way.

Taking the only option available to him, Spinner turned in to a large parking structure.

Perhaps, Jillian thought, he hoped to go out through another exit, but that was now being blocked, and so the convoy followed him as he began climbing the parking ramps.

With each floor, Spinner's car lurched forward, causing Listun to accelerate as well. As they approached the last ramp leading to the roof, Spinner narrowly avoided a blue Vauxhall on its way down. The car, swerving wildly, tried to correct itself, but the driver lost control and as the back end swerved around, it smashed into the front driver's side of the detectives' car.

The crash effectively blocked the ramp. Listun's airbag had deployed, but Jillian's had not. Her head, having been banged about in the carriage, was still ringing as she emerged. Looking back at Listun, who was moving slowly, and then at Kara, who was climbing out, she said, "Stay with him."

She heard Kara shouting after her, "Mum, wait," but Jillian was already heading up the ramp.

She reached the top and looked around for Spinner's car. She found him around the corner, having come to a stop once he realized there was no way out. The driver door was open, and Spinner was walking in circles in a panic.

"Spinner," Jillian called out, one hand pressed to the side of her aching head, "it's over. Stay where you are."

Instead, Spinner began backing away toward the corner of the car park. "Stay away from me. Just stay away." When he reached the corner, he turned and looked over the edge, then back toward Jillian. Slowly he climbed onto the concrete wall.

"Jeremy," Jillian yelled, coming within about ten feet of him before she stopped. "Jeremy, listen to me."

"Shut up!" Spinner yelled. "I'm not going back to prison. I can't go back."

"We can work something out," Jillian began, catching her breath. "Let's just talk it through."

"I didn't know," Spinner said, looking at her, his arms flailing as he tried to keep his balance on the precarious edge.

"What?" Jillian asked. "What didn't you know, Jeremy?"

He looked back over the edge. For a moment Jillian thought he was going to lose his balance, but he steadied himself. "Don't come closer," he warned.

Jillian held her hands up, palms facing outward. "Okay, I'll stay right here. Tell me, what was it you didn't know?"

Spinner looked her straight in the eye. What she saw was the look of a frightened little boy, not that of a drug-dealing adult. "I didn't know about the boys in the basement."

Jillian waited a moment. "I believe you," Jillian said.

Spinner, as if life had suddenly left him, began to collapse, and his body leaned backward.

Jillian lurched forward and stretched out her arm, her hand closing tightly around his right wrist. She instinctively bent her knees and tried to lower her center of gravity as the weight of his body going over the edge slammed him forcibly against the outside of the garage. Her upper body simultaneously slammed against the side of the concrete wall, his weight partially pulling her over.

Jillian's breath left her body as her abdomen was crushed against the top of the wall. Her knees were pressed as much as she could manage against the inside of the wall, trying desperately to keep the rest of her from going over the edge.

Spinner's instincts had also kicked in, and his hand was now grasping Jillian's wrist as much as she was grasping his. She wanted to reach down with her other hand and tighten her grip on him, but her free hand was gripping the edge of the wall and was the only thing preventing her from letting his weight pull her over.

"Hold on," she managed to get enough air in her lungs to say, but she could already feel her grip on his wrist loosening.

Spinners' eyes were looking frantically from the ground to the sky and back. Then they settled on Jillian and once again locked onto hers. "He never told me about the basement," he said.

Jillian grunted trying to solidify her grip unsuccessfully. "Who? Who didn't tell you?" she pleaded.

Spinner stopped struggling, as though accepting his fate.

Jillian could hear footsteps behind her. "Hang on, Jeremy, they're coming."

Spinner, looking at her, said, "Motora Gif," and then smiled a sad, anguished smile and let go of her wrist.

She tried to hang on, but his weight was too much, and his hand just slipped through hers.

Spinner fell just as two police officers appeared on either side of her. They each grabbed hold of her, but she fought back, keeping her eyes locked on Jeremy Spinner as he plummeted to his death.

***

It was nearing midnight as Jillian sat with her back against Daniella on their small back porch overlooking the city and coast in the distance. The sky was dark, and the city lights twinkled. Daniella had a large blanket around her shoulders and was wrapping it around Jillian in front of her. Nearly empty wine glasses sat on a small outdoor café-style table.

"I couldn't hold on," Jillian said, her voice barely above a whisper, tears falling slowly down her cheeks.

"I know," Daniella said softly, kissing the back of Jillian's head. "I know."

"I tried," Jillian said.

"Shhh," Daniella said, planting more kisses. "Don't, love. Don't dwell on what you could or couldn't have done."

Jillian wiped the tears from her eyes and took a deep breath. "I know he wasn't a good man, Dani, I know that," she said, half turning her head to look at Daniella.

Daniella just nodded, gently stroking the side of Jillian's face.

"But the look in his eyes," Jillian said. "I can't explain it." Jillian turned back toward the night. "I watched his face all the way down." A shudder ran through her body and Daniella hugged her even tighter.

After a little while, they disentangled and got up from the porch. As they turned to go in, Jillian's voice seemed tiny in the night. "I just don't understand why I care about someone who killed so many other people."

Daniella stopped as they stepped back into their cottage. Turning, she set down the wine glasses and stood facing Jillian. Taking her head gently into her hands, she said, "You care because you watched a man die. You were there. You were the last person he saw on earth. That is not an insignificant thing, Jills. The fact that you care about people, good people and bad people, is what makes you, *you*. It's why you're so good at what you do." Daniella smiled a warm smile. "It's part of why I love you so much."

Daniella leaned forward and kissed Jillian's forehead, then wrapped her arms around her, holding her tight as Jillian's body shook and the mournful sounds of her sobbing filled the room.

CHAPTER 14

The dark gray clouds and steady drizzle were a perfect fit for Jillian's mood as she sat down behind her desk and looked at the pile of work still vying for her attention. She pushed her laptop into the docking station and flipped up the screen, waiting for the connections to establish. Having gotten very little sleep, she was in early again.

Listun and Kara approached her office quietly. Looking up, Jillian waved them in.

"How you doin', guv?" Listun asked. He took up his usual perch, leaning against the credenza along the far side wall of her office. Kara also took her usual seat in one of the visitors' chairs.

"Tired," Jillian said as thunder boomed outside the office. The sky was growing ever darker, along with her mood.

The trio covered the status of varying cases before getting to the issue at hand.

"Do you think he was talking about himself?" Kara asked.

They were discussing Spinner's last word before he fell. "I honestly don't know," Jillian said. "I've been up most of the night thinking about it. I keep going back and forth on it. Was he answering my question or admitting that he was Motora Gif?" She shrugged. "We'll never know."

Jillian had pulled up the spinning car graphic of the online profile and was just staring at it.

"If you think back," Kara asked warily, "what was your immediate thought? Your gut instinct when he said it?"

Jillian's answer surprised even herself, because she answered almost immediately. "He was answering my question."

"It makes the most sense, given the conversation before he, uhm . . ." Listun said awkwardly.

Jillian got up from her desk and turned around, looking out the window at the gathering storm. There was a sudden crack as lighting struck nearby, and the rain pelted her windows. No one spoke. The power inside the Tof went out and the office was engulfed in darkness, save for light from Jillian's laptop.

It was only out for three or four seconds before everything flickered back on.

It was in those brief seconds that Jillian cried out, "Bloody hell!"

Listun and Kara exchanged looks. Jillian turned around quickly as the lights flickered back on in the office. She placed both palms on her desk and leaned in close to her laptop, staring intently.

"Guv?" Listun asked.

Jillian looked up at her two detectives. Then, walking around her desk, she approached the small markerboard on the wall of her office. She cleaned off the existing notes and picked up a black marker.

When the power had gone out a moment ago and the office went dark, her eyes had been drawn to the reflection of her laptop screen against the window.

Taking the marker, she wrote "MOTORAGIF" in big, bold letters on the board.

Then, she drew a line from the *I* in *GIF* down below the *F* and placed the *I* below it.

M O T O R A G I F
                                    I

Then she continued to add one letter at a time below the *I*.

M O T O R A G I F
                                    I
                                    G
                                    A
                                    R
                                    O
                                    T
                                    O
                                    M

When Jillian had looked at the reflection of her laptop, it had been reversed in the window's reflection.

"You're joking!" Listun said, straightening up from his perch.

"Oh my God!" Kara exclaimed.

***

DI Jillian Scotte, along with her two detectives, DS Stephen Listun and DC Kara Devanor, were speeding along the M3 with lights flashing. Where traffic was lighter, Listun would shut off the siren, only to turn it back on again when the inevitable congestion loomed.

The downpour of rain and the poor visibility didn't help.

Jillian was becoming more frustrated by the minute. As soon as they got in the car, she had tried calling her boss, Superintendent Maryanne Sanderson, only to be told that "the superintendent is in an executive meeting with both the chief superintendent and commander of the Met and cannot be disturbed."

Since both her bosses' boss and his own boss were in that meeting, she was forced to climb higher up the ladder. She was finally able to get through to the deputy assistant commissioner, a woman by the name of Minu Singh. Which was a relief because given how her last call had gone with the assistant commissioner himself, she wanted as much as possible to avoid calling him.

DAC Singh's gatekeeper took some convincing before they finally connected the call. After Jillian explained the situation as succinctly as possible, the silent pause had been so lengthy that she thought they had dropped the call. Eventually, in her strong British Indian accent, Singh said she would need to make some calls and get back to her. That had been almost thirty minutes ago.

Startled by her phone's ring, Jillian punched the speakerphone and said, "DI Scotte, how can I help?"

"DI Scotte, this is Deputy Assistant Commissioner Minu Singh calling you back."

"Yes mum," Jillian answered formally.

"It has come to my attention, DI Scotte, that you were told by Assistant Commissioner Bellingham very specifically to stay away from Mr. Onslow. Is that correct?"

"Yes mum," Jillian said, "and I have done so. We have no intention of causing Mr. Onslow any more disturbance than necessary. We are only interested in his associate Mr. Figaro, who, unfortunately, lists his address at the same location as Mr. Onslow."

After another lengthy pause, Singh said, "I have been advised by SCD9 Main Branch that Mr. Onslow left the country three days ago for a conference in Berlin."

Listun looked over at his boss with a scowl. Jillian just held up a hand and spoke into the phone, "Does SCD9 know if Figaro went with him?"

"They say Onslow went alone," Singh said, then almost as an afterthought added, "They have not had contact with Figaro for over two days."

By "contact," Jillian knew she meant the surveillance team had not seen him, though she expected the team wasn't large enough to keep every member of Onslow's organization under constant observation. "Mum," she said, leaning toward the phone, "it stands to reason that his not going to Berlin means he stayed behind to run Onslow's business, and that means he's probably inside Onslow's estate."

After another lengthy pause, Singh said, "I'll call you back," and before Jillian could say anything, the call ended.

Jillian shouted an expletive and pounded her fist on the dashboard.

"What the hell was all that about Onslow if they knew he was out of the country?" Listun asked, sounding equally frustrated.

Jillian, looking out the side window at the traffic going by, said, "The AC just wanted me to know he had been made aware of what I'm doing, and he doesn't like it."

They had transitioned to the M25, and while traffic was still annoyingly heavy, it wasn't as bad as the motorways heading straight into London.

They were within fifteen minutes of their destination when Jillian's phone rang.

"DI Scotte," Jillian said gruffly.

"DI Scotte, DAC Singh." The deputy assistant commissioner was equally brusque. "I am to tell you that you have been granted permission to make inquiries regarding Mr. Figaro at Mr. Onslow's estate. However, as you will not have a search warrant and there is no time to obtain one, you will not enter the premises uninvited. Is that clear?"

Jillian heard Kara mutter under her breath, "There would've been time if you hadn't messed us about."

Jillian bit her lip to keep a smile from forming. Voice steady, she said, "Understood, mum."

"Please keep me apprised on the outcome of your inquiry."

"Yes mum," Jillian said, and once again the line went dead.

***

Listun pulled up to the estate gate and lowered his side window. Reaching out, he pressed the button on the small metal speaker box mounted above a black post in the ground.

"How can I help you?" a distant voice said through the box.

"Detective Inspector Jillian Scotte to see Mr. Figaro," Listun said, looking up at the CCTV camera mounted over one of the brick gateposts.

The box replied, "Mr. Figaro isn't here at the moment."

"When do you expect his return?" asked Listun. "We can wait."

There was a pause, and then the box said, "He won't be returning today."

Jillian leaned across the car as Listun leaned back hard in his seat to make room for her. "We need to speak to Mr. Figaro urgently. Do you have a number for him or an address where we can find him?"

There was a longer pause, after which a new voice, this one lower and more authoritative, said, "We are not at liberty to divulge Mr. Figaro's personal information, Inspector. If you do not leave these premises immediately, we will be forced to call our solicitor and report you for harassment."

As Jillian leaned back, the gates of the estate opened and a dark green Mercedes appeared round the bend. As it passed through the gates, it stopped next to Jillian's side of the car, and the driver's side window slid down.

Behind the wheel was the woman they had encountered on their last visit. Onslow's sister, Lucile. Two other girls were in the car with her.

"Hello," she said, frowning. "What brings you back? My brother isn't here, you know?"

"Yes, so I've been told," Jillian said pleasantly. "Actually, we aren't here to see him. We wanted a word with Mr. Figaro."

"Tommy?" Lucile asked. "What for?"

"I'm sorry. I'm not at liberty to say," Jillian said. "Do you know where he is?"

Lucile shook her head. "No, he and Damien got into a huge row a couple of days ago and Tommy stormed off. Hasn't been back since." The expression on the young woman's face looked forlorn.

"Headed somewhere fun?" Jillian asked, just to be saying something and to prolong the conversation.

Lucile's face perked up. "We're going shopping." Then with a finger to her lips, she said, "Shhh, don't tell anyone."

Jillian smiled and made a motion with her thumb and forefinger across her mouth in the universal "my lips are sealed" gesture.

As she was raising her window, Lucile called out, "If you talk to Tommy, please tell him to call me."

Jillian smiled and nodded, and Lucile put the Mercedes in gear and drove off.

While they sat in the car contemplating what they should do next, Jillian's phone rang.

Picking it up and looking at the caller ID, Jillian saw it was DS Milston. "Hello Rob," she said.

"What are you doing at Onslow's estate?" Milston said, loud enough that Jillian pulled the phone away from her ear.

"We're not here for Onslow. We're looking for his partner, Tom Figaro," she answered exasperatedly.

"Well 'e's not there, is 'e?" Milston said.

"No, well I know that now, don't I?" Jillian said heatedly, then frowning, she said, "Hang on, how do you know he's not here?"

"Because I'm lookin' right at 'im" came the reply.

***

The ride back from Onslow's estate was quiet.

The trio of detectives pulled up Bryn Road behind Milston's car outside the burned-out house. Police tape that had once been secured around the building now flapped in the wind, having been torn in two. Several other police vehicles with lights flashing were parked up and down the street.

Listun handed Jillian one umbrella and grabbed the other as they all got out of the car. Kara huddled under Listun's umbrella as they walked behind Jillian toward the house. The rain was still coming down in buckets, but thankfully, the lightning and thunder had stopped.

They found Milston inside on the main floor, just near where the door to the cellar had been.

There, on the floor with a bullet hole in the back of his head, was Tom Figaro.

Everyone looked on quietly as the rain cascaded down through the open roof.

"Shit," Jillian said forcefully.

"Well put." Milston said.

CHAPTER 15
EPILOGUE

Jillian walked into the restaurant late. It was the first time that she could remember being late for a meeting with her boss. It was still early for the breakfast crowd since it was the weekend, and it didn't take her long to spot Superintendent Maryanne Sanderson sitting by the window.

"Sorry I'm late," Jillian apologized, sitting down.

Sanderson had been taking a sip of what looked like a mimosa. She put the glass down and said, "Don't be. I'm just glad it wasn't me this time." She smiled and cocked her head a little to one side. "What's wrong?"

"What?" Jillian deflected. "Nothing, just traffic."

"I'm not talking about the time. I can see it in your face," Sanderson said.

As usual, Maryanne Sanderson was dressed to suit. Even though it was early morning on a Saturday, she wore a gray skirt with a cream-colored button-down blouse. Her nails were manicured, and the pumps she wore matched her skirt.

Although Jillian was appropriately dressed in her dark blue slacks and matching jacket over a light-blue shirt, she felt somehow underdressed. But it wasn't the wrinkles in her clothes or the fact that her shoes didn't quite match the outfit, Jillian knew, that caused her boss's inquiry.

It was the bags under her eyes, the droopiness of her shoulders, and the unstyled untidiness of her mess of hair. She looked like she felt. Beaten.

"I'm just—" Jillian began, but she simply stared off out the window, unable to find the words. "I'm just tired," she said, hoping the old standby excuse would be enough.

Fat chance.

"You're still fixated on the fire case and Figaro's murder, aren't you?" Sanderson said.

"He was executed." Jillian said. "One shot to the back of the head, clean exit. It was a hit, and the fact that it was done in the house where he orchestrated the fire was not an accident."

Sanderson nodded. "No argument from me," she said.

"It had to be Onslow," Jillian said forcefully.

"You don't know that," Sanderson responded. "Besides, he was out of the country when it happened."

"That doesn't mean he didn't order it, and besides, who else would it have been?"

"I'm only saying, just because you want it to be true, doesn't mean it is," Sanderson said.

"Why is everyone trying to protect that vile piece of . . ." Jillian never finished the sentence because Sanderson held up her hand.

"I'm not trying to protect anyone, Jillian," she said.

"Well, what is it then? From the off, I've been told to stay away from this guy, and now I'm not even allowed to investigate a murder he's clearly behind!" Jillian practically shouted, though she quickly lowered her voice.

Sanderson leaned forward, her wrists on the edge of the table. "Look, I don't know why SCD9 Main Branch are so insistent that we stay clear of Onslow. But you and I both know you don't have a shred of evidence to pursue him with. The execution was clean, no fingerprints, no DNA, no clues of any kind left behind. And with the storms that were raging for the two days he was missing, anything that might have been there had washed away long before you arrived."

Jillian tried looking away but knew she shouldn't, so she looked directly into Sanderson's eyes.

"What I'm saying, Jillian, is that you know as well as I do that sometimes you win and sometimes you lose. That's the way it goes in this business."

Jillian opened her mouth to speak, but Sanderson cut her off. "No one, least of all me, is saying you're wrong. But this case? This murder? With nothing to go on, it's just a waste of your time and talents and will only serve to annoy people you have already gotten off on the wrong foot with."

She wasn't finished. "I've got three levels of Met brass banging on my door, demanding that I reprimand you."

Jillian leaned back in her chair, though her gaze never left Sanderson's. "What do you need me to do?" she said resignedly.

"Nothing," Sanderson answered. "They're my problem, not yours. It's my job to manage them. My point is that nothing good can come from you fixating and digging your heels in on this one. Let it go. I know it stings and—" Here she lowered her head a little, ensuring that Jillian was paying attention. "I know you don't like letting things go. But I'm asking you to." Then she said something that made Jillian tilt her head ever so slightly. "For now."

"What does that mean?" she asked.

"It means what I said," Sanderson replied. "Let it go, for now. There will come a time with Onslow, believe you me, and we will both be there when it does."

The server came over, and they both looked over the menu and placed their orders. The conversation changed to the usual things. Life, work, more work, a little more life, then work again.

Sanderson, bringing the conversation back, said, "Were you ever able to fit some of the pieces together on why Figaro did what he did?"

Jillian sighed loudly. "No."

Maryanne Sanderson took another sip of her drink. "Is that why this feels like you failed on this case?"

Jillian's head snapped up. It was uncanny how her boss knew what she was thinking even when she didn't say it.

"Look," Sanderson said gently, "I made some calls to SCD9 Branch, and while they are not happy with how things happened, I did manage to learn that Figaro and Onslow's sister might have . . ." she let the sentence linger.

"Really?" Jillian said, surprised.

"It's nothing concrete," Sanderson clarified, "but the collective opinion from the peepers and one of the people I talked to at SCD9 is that there was something between them."

"So, what, this had something to do with Lucile?" Jillian asked.

Sanderson shrugged and lifted both hands, palms facing up.

Jillian sat in thought for a moment, her brow furrowed.

"The peepers weren't well situated to catch everything when Onslow and Figaro had the fight Lucile mentioned to you," Sanderson said, "but one of the few words they did manage to capture was Figaro shouting her name back at Onslow."

"So maybe this was, what, about love?" Jillian posited.

Sanderson shrugged again. "You know what they say. It's either money, power, or sex."

As they were finishing and Sanderson had paid for the check, she stood up and took hold of Jillian's hand. "I know it's difficult, and I know you don't like it, but I need you to refocus away from Damien Onslow for the time being. Figaro's death going unsolved is not the end of the world. There's more to be done, and you will be far more effective doing it if you're not losing sleep and spending energy on someone who doesn't deserve to be given the time of day." She leaned in and gave Jillian a hug, taking her hand and looking straight into her eyes to make sure she understood.

Jillian nodded, squeezed her hand, and turned as they headed for the door.

Sanderson was right, of course. She was especially right about one thing.

Jillian would do as she asked and let it go because she respected her boss immensely, but she didn't have to like it.

THE CONTAINER MURDERS

CHAPTER 1

The sun wrestled with the clouds to crest the horizon as Detective Inspector Jillian Scotte reached for her vibrating phone on the nightstand.

A call this early in the morning was never good news. She slipped out of bed, trying not to wake Daniella, and walked, yawning, into the kitchen before swiping the green circle to answer her phone.

Looking out at the first rays of the sun over the Channel from their small cottage up on the hill, she said, "Hello Listun," addressing her detective sergeant.

"Mornin' guv," Listun said, his voice sounding a little sleepy as well. "Sorry to wake you, but you're needed down at the docks."

Jillian ran her right hand through her rumpled light brown hair. "I thought Kara was on duty this weekend?" she said, referring to Detective Constable Kara Devanor.

"She was," Listun replied, "but she did me a favor last month when Lizzy wasn't feeling well, so I swapped shifts."

Lizzy was DS Listun's baby girl, and she kept him and his wife up most nights.

"What have we got?"

"Multiple homicide."

Jillian yawned. "How many?"

"Eight."

Jillian's weary body suddenly straightened to her full height. "Eight?" she said. "Bloody hell, what happened?"

There was a pause, then Listun said, "Boss, it'll be easier if you come see it for yourself."

Not liking the cryptic nature of his response, Jillian was already on her way to the bedroom closet to pull out clothes. Daniella stirred and, with her eyes half closed, dreamily said, "What time is it?"

Speaking into the phone, Jillian said, "I'm on my way," and hung up. Turning, she went to the bed, leaned down, and kissed Daniella on the forehead. "Go back to sleep. I have to go to work. Multiple homicide down by the docks."

Daniella groaned and pulled the covers over her head as Jillian started getting dressed.

***

Kara Devanor was in that blissful space between sleep and awakening. That moment of realization that though she is beginning to wake up, she doesn't have to. Which then leads to the blissful notion that the comforting duvet and soft pillow are hers for however long she wished.

That luxurious thought was short-lived, however, as she came out of her half sleep to full consciousness.

She knew where she was.

In her bed.

She knew it was Saturday and that she had switched her shift with Listun, so she didn't have to cover the desk this weekend.

So why did she have a gnawing feeling in the pit of her stomach?

She was suddenly wide awake; her eyes flew open, and she knew exactly why.

Last night.

Of all the foolhardy things she had done in her life, this one might top them all.

She didn't want to move her head for fear that she would be proven right.

Kara tried not to move at all. She didn't want to wake *him*. Part of her didn't want to believe *he* was still there, but of course *he* was. She could hear *him* snoring softly. This was definitely not a dream.

She wished, however foolishly, that if she went back to sleep it would all be a dream, and she would wake up alone in her flat the way she always did.

Then her phone began to ring.

***

Jillian pulled up and parked her car next to several emergency response vehicles with their lights flashing.

She didn't need to flash her badge as she ducked under the police tape held up by a constable. Southampton's finest knew her well now.

DS Listun saw her approaching and turned away from the small group of people he had been talking to. "Morning, guv."

Jillian handed him one of the two cups of coffee she had grabbed quickly on the way.

"Bless you," Listun said.

"So," she said, "what's the big mystery?"

Listun indicated a large lorry, a flatbed loaded with a rust-colored shipping container. "That container was supposed to be loaded for the crossing, but when it was inspected, they found the eight victims."

The pair began walking toward the lorry, which now had four work lights shining on the back. The container doors were wide open. Jillian wanted to say something, knowing there had to be more to it than her DS had just told her, but she waited for him to get to it—whatever "it" was.

"The thing is, mum," Listun said, stopping just shy of the back of the open container and off to the side, forcing Jillian to stop and turn toward him, "they've all been chopped up."

Jillian frowned, her head turning slightly to the side. "What do you mean, *chopped up?*"

"Arms. Legs. Heads."

Jillian turned and walked the remaining few feet, looking around and into the back of the container. She slowly walked around the open door where the SOCO team were working. One of them, clad in his head-to-toe blue jumpsuit, turned and, upon seeing her, stepped to one side to give her a clear view.

She rather wished he hadn't.

It was a gruesome sight. Limbs, heads, and torsos were heaped in a pile. There were dark pools around the parts on the bottom. Looking at the SOCO man in white, she asked, "Is that blood?"

"Not exactly," he answered. "It is a mix of blood and water. They were covered with bags of ice." He indicated bags of half-melted ice that had been stacked for evidence inside a nearby tent erected for that purpose.

"Probably to keep the stench from getting too bad," Listun chimed in.

Jillian wasn't dressed in protective gear and so she didn't step inside. Not that she thought she would see anything SOCO would miss. She would have to wait for their report.

Moving away from the crime scene to let the technicians do their work, she turned to Listun. "Has the medical examiner been yet?"

"On his way," her DS answered. "Had to wake him up, and he said he was an hour away."

"An hour?"

Listun just raised his hands in defense.

Jillian looked around the docks. Listun had done an excellent job of securing the area, though she could already see several dockworkers standing around, watching. It wouldn't be long before some supervisor was yelling and screaming about needing to get the ships loaded and on their way.

This was going to be a right mess. More than it was already, she thought.

"We're going to need to bring the team in," she said, looking at Listun, who nodded. Then she tapped her phone and dialed Kara's number.

***

So much for her dream, Kara thought as her phone buzzed.

She reached for it quickly, hoping not to disturb *him* lying next to her. Looking at the caller's name, she cursed inwardly.

A call this early from her boss could only mean one thing.

It also meant she was going to have to deal with the man in her bed sooner rather than later.

This was not how she had planned to start her weekend off.

CHAPTER 2

The book fell off the nightstand as Kara tried to sit up in bed, missing her phone and hitting it instead. The phone was still vibrating noisily in the stillness of the morning.

She got up as quietly as she could and padded barefoot out into the kitchen, grabbing her nightgown off the back of her bedroom door as she went.

"Hello," she said, half yawning into the phone.

"Hi Kara," her boss said. "Listen, I know Stephen's covering your shift this weekend, but something's come up. We've got eight bodies."

Kara let out a deep breath she hadn't been aware she was holding. "Christ," she said.

Jillian didn't give her time to process. "I need you down here as soon as," she said, "but I also need you to start the call chain. We'll need everyone back at the Tof straight away."

"Yes, boss," Kara said. The call ended.

Sighing, Kara opened the call chain file on her phone and hit "dial" on the number next on the list. Luckily, PC Stella Dawson answered groggily straightaway. Kara explained what she knew and told Stella to continue the call chain, then hung up.

Walking back slowly into her room, she hoped the man in her bed might be still asleep.

No such luck.

Propped up on one elbow, his hair ruffled and a smile on his face, he said, "Good morning."

Kara leaned against the bedroom doorjamb and looked back at the man in her bed.

Sebastian Hughes.

How the hell had she gotten herself into this?

***

THREE WEEKS EARLIER

Kara walked out of her flat and looked up at the dreary sky. It was looking like another wet English morning as she repositioned her bike and got ready for her ride to work. She had started riding as soon as the temperature warmed up, despite the almost daily threat of rain. She wasn't as fond of riding as her boss, and hers wasn't a racing bike, just a simple, go-to-the-shops sort of bicycle.

Just as she placed a foot on one pedal to start her ride to work, a black Mercedes with tinted windows pulled up and the passenger side window slid down smoothly.

Looking inside, Kara saw Sebastian Hughes smiling out at her. "Good morning, Detective," he said, his dark blue eyes sparkling as much as his teeth.

Kara stared back, surprised to find him on her doorstep. "Mr. Hughes," she said, nodding slightly.

"I was wondering if I could entice you to join me for a cup of coffee?" he asked. "Malcom can put your bicycle in the boot, and we can drop you by your office afterwards."

She heard the car's boot open with a click, and the driver-side door opened. A man the size of a small tank got out and walked around the car toward her.

Not feeling like she was being given much of a choice, she handed her bike over to the tank and climbed into the back of the car. They drove several blocks to a coffee shop she didn't know was there, and the driver dropped them off just in front, seemingly oblivious to the honking horns of the cars waiting behind them.

Sebastian Hughes, dressed in a dark suit, white shirt, light-green tie, and dark, gleaming shoes, opened the door for her, and they walked in.

An older man with a thick foreign accent looked up from wiping a table. "Mr. Sebastian, it is good to see you."

"Good morning, Serge."

"I assume you would like your usual?" the man asked. "And for your lady friend?"

Sebastian turned to Kara. "What would you like?"

Turning to the older man, she gave him her order. He said, "Of course," and Sebastian led them to a table by the window in the corner. Helping her out of her coat, he held out the chair facing the wall for her to sit in, and he took the chair in the corner, facing the room.

As they waited, Kara said, "So, what can I do for you, Mr. Hughes?"

"First of all," he said, "please call me Sebastian."

After a pause, Kara said, "And second?" She sounded slightly annoyed, because she was. She had things to do.

"Second, nothing. I just wanted to have coffee with you."

Kara's eyes narrowed.

Just then, Serge arrived with a tray holding two cups of coffee and two croissants. "I thought you might like something to eat, with the English rain washing the outside of my windows," he said. His accent was thick, but not difficult to understand.

"Thank you, Serge, that's kind of you," Hughes said.

Kara noticed Serge didn't ask for, and Sebastian didn't offer, any payment.

After taking a sip of his coffee, Sebastian looked up at her. His dark brown hair looked like a barber had attended to it that very morning. His dark blue eyes had a hint of something she couldn't quite put her finger on. "So, Kara—is it all right if I call you Kara? Tell me about you. When did you decide you wanted to join the police?"

Kara held her cup in both her hands, the chill of the morning still lingering. "Is this a joke?" she asked.

"No," he said, his smile broadening as he sat back in his chair.

Sure. There was definitely something else going on, so Kara went along with the chitchat, waiting for the other shoe to drop.

Except it never did.

After thirty minutes, Sebastian looked at his watch, which cost more than Kara's entire wardrobe. "Well, we'd better get you off to work or your boss will wonder where you've gotten to." He stood up, dropping two large banknotes onto the table.

Kara pulled out her phone and, seeing the time, cursed under her breath and stood up.

Sebastian held up her coat for her. Was it her imagination, or had his hands lingered just a little too long as he helped her shrug into it?

"Kara," he said, as she turned back to face him, "would you like to have dinner with me? This weekend, I mean."

She stood for a moment, wondering if she had heard him correctly. After what seemed like an impossibly long pause, she opened her mouth, but then closed it. Opening it again, she started to say something, but nothing came out. Finally, she said, "Are you serious? I mean . . ." She struggled again. ". . . you must be joking. You. And I. Dinner, as in *dinner* dinner?"

He smiled a soft laugh that made crinkles appear at the side of his eyes. *Why am I noticing that?* Kara thought.

"Yes," Sebastian said, "as in a date, Kara. I am asking you out to dinner on a date."

They were walking out to the car now, the clouds looking ever ominous, and Kara felt a pang of gratitude at not having to bike all the way to work in the rain that would start any minute.

She was aware that she hadn't answered him. The car glided to a halt just as they approached the road. Hughes bent down and opened the back door for her. Her mind fleetingly took in the fact that she had not seen him text his driver to let him know they were coming.

She looked at him then, their faces close to each other. "I'm not sure that's a very good idea."

He didn't seem fazed at all. "It's just dinner. I promise not to ask for the secret police handshake or the code to steal the Crown Jewels."

Despite herself, Kara laughed aloud. "They don't trust me with the code, and even I don't know the secret handshake." *Damn it, Kara*, she chided herself, *did you really just flirt with him?*

"I'll text you, then," Sebastian said, closing the door as she settled in the back seat.

They dropped her off two blocks from her work, and she was biking the last of it in a light sprinkle when it occurred to her she had not given him her number. Yet somehow she knew he would text her later the next day, which, in fact, he did.

The next three weeks were a mixture of surprises and anxiety for Kara. She went back and forth all that first day after the coffee, trying to decide whether to tell Jillian about it.

She could not, for the life of her, understand why she didn't tell her boss. All day she perseverated, and at one point late in the afternoon she had half decided to tell her. But when she turned to get up and go into her bosses' office, Jillian was leaving with her coat, saying she would see everyone tomorrow.

And that was that.

Having not told her the first day, it seemed harder and harder each day after. As the weeks passed, it became easier to avoid saying anything.

That weekend, she had dinner with Sebastian. The food was lovely. He was incredibly charming. They didn't talk about work. It was, as he had said, just a date.

The fourth "date" had been last night.

Kara had been determined to get it all out. This was ridiculous on so many levels.

"Look, Sebastian," she had begun, after fortifying herself with half a glass of wine, "we can't keep doing this."

"Why not?" he asked.

"You *know* why not." Kara answered, raising her voice, then lowering it as she leaned onto the table. "I'm a bloody police officer and you are a . . ."

Having faltered in finishing her sentence she repeated, "You are a . . ." but once again couldn't quite bring herself to say it.

"I'm a criminal," Sebastian said, sparing her.

Sighing loudly, Kara said, "Yes, I mean . . . but . . . yes, exactly."

Now Sebastian leaned his forearms on the table. His tone became profoundly serious, but not in the way she had seen on other occasions when it was business. This was different, and the look in his eyes, although no longer mischievous, was intense in the most nonthreatening way.

"Look," he said, "I like you. A lot. I find you attractive in every possible way. I want to get to know you, I want to spend time with you. This has nothing to do with my work or your work. It has everything to do with the fact that since the first time I saw you, I haven't been able to stop thinking about you."

Kara was speechless. Not a common occurrence for her. She realized her mouth had dropped open and quickly closed it.

"But," she said, trying to find the words again, "I mean . . . it's just that . . . Damn it!" she said slamming her wine glass down on the table.

Sebastian said nothing, simply looking at her quietly with those deep blue eyes of his.

Kara folded her arms as though, somehow, they would protect her from his gaze.

She tried again. "What if . . . let's just say . . . what would happen if we . . . how would I . . ." Then she threw her hands up exasperatedly and dropped them on the table.

Sebastian reached over and gently placed both of his hands on top of hers. "Let's just take it one day at a time. No promises. No demands. No expectations."

The way he looked at her made her insides wobbly, and Kara could swear that there was electricity in his touch.

That was earlier last night.

Now, here she was, having spent the night with him in her bed, with her boss calling her in on her weekend off for eight corpses in God knows what kind of murder case they were about to take on, and she was looking at him from the frame of her doorway.

"You have to go," he said.

"Yes." She sighed heavily.

"It's all right," he said. He started getting out of bed, but looking back at her, he added, "Unless it can wait for a few more minutes?" This time, there was most definitely mischief in his eyes.

CHAPTER 3

The endless tide had a rhythm that Jillian Scotte had always felt connected to. Standing on the edge of the concrete dock looking into the water, she couldn't see the incoming tide the same way she could when standing on a beach, but she knew it was there, nonetheless.

Eight victims.

The state of the victims, the dismemberment, had not been lost on her. How could she forget the case the papers had dubbed the Lumberjack Murders? Body parts had been strewn all over the UK to discredit Jillian as a detective by her former boss.

Jillian shuddered in the early-morning chill. She was past the point of wondering what was wrong with people and why they did what they did. Why, it seemed to her, was a question too late. Let the psychologists and profilers worry about why. Her job was not to understand why people killed, but to find them, bring them to justice, and make her streets just a bit safer for the people who lived on them.

She turned back, away from the harbor, in time to see the chief coroner, Michael Thorsby, climbing out of his car. He looked harried, as usual.

An hour later, Jillian walked into the Tof, threw her coat onto one of the "client" chairs in her office, and went straight into the incident room, having called ahead and asked Kara to get everyone ready. She had left DS Listun at the scene until SOCO finished and the bodies were removed.

"Right," she said, walking up to the front of the smallish room. Everyone was either in a chair or perched on the edge of a table. The whiteboard behind Jillian was clean, ready to be filled with the various details of the case. "I'm sorry to call you all back, but as you've no doubt heard, we have eight victims on our hands. We won't know much about the victims for a while. SOCO have their hands full, and Thorsby was already grumbling when I left."

The last remark elicited a few smiles, but everyone was all too aware of the grievous nature of the crime, having been filled in via calls and emails from DS Listun.

"Kara, why don't you fill us in?" Jillian said.

Kara stood up with her notebook and two printouts from her email. "All we have to go on at present is the lorry and driver." Looking at her notes, she continued, "A man named Ahmal Buggeri. Central uniforms are bringing him down now."

Jillian spoke up. "Kara, you and PC Dawson take his statement." Then, in a question that seemed like an afterthought, she added, "Has he asked for a solicitor yet?"

"No, mum."

"Okay," Jillian said, then turning to their chief administrator, Stacey Alston, she said, "Stacey, while they talk to him, I want you to find out everything you can about Mr. Buggeri."

"Yes boss," Stacey said.

"The rest of you," Jillian said, taking center stage again, "while we wait for SOCO and the coroner's office, I want you to dig into this lorry's route, where it originated, where it went, how many stops it made, how much petrol Mr. Buggeri purchased and when—the lot."

There was a murmur and nodding of heads as the team dispersed to begin their assignments.

Getting back to her office, Jillian saw she had a message on her mobile and blinking lights on her desk phone. She checked her private message first.

It was from Daniella. "Hiya, it's me. Michael just called me in. He hasn't told me anything, just told me he needed me to get to the office. Says it's one of yours. Call me."

Jillian hit redial, and Daniella picked up on the second ring.

"Hi, what's going on?" Daniella said, getting right down to business. It was one thing Jillian loved about her. She understood that when Jillian was at work, she had little time. She never complained about it, just got to the point and waited for her to come home if she wanted to discuss it more.

"Eight victims," Jillian said.

"Eight!" Daniella said, almost shouting.

"All in a transport container."

"Oh God," Daniella said, her voice softening. "Were they immigrants?"

"We don't know yet. And listen, Dani . . ." Jillian's voice trailed off.

There was a pause. Daniella now sounded concerned. "Jills, what is it?"

"They're all . . ." Jillian paused. She couldn't quite bring herself to say it.

"They're all what?"

Jillian swallowed. "They've all been cut up. Dismembered. Arms, legs, heads."

Now it was Daniella's turn to pause. "Look, he can't be involved," she began. "It doesn't mean it has anything to do with . . ."

"I know," Jillian said, taking in a deep breath.

"I'm sorry. I'll let you know as soon as I can what we have."

"Thank you."

"I love you," Daniella said.

"I love you too."

They disconnected and Jillian stood staring out the window of her office. There was no way Paul Davies could be involved in this, she thought. He was safely behind bars. Well, maybe not safely; police do not do all that well in prison.

Last she had heard, he was trying to keep his head down and stay alive, though it was very unlikely he would ever leave prison.

Either way, she couldn't believe he had any pull to orchestrate something like this, no matter her fears.

So then, if not her former nemesis, who? And what was it all about?

Right now, they had loads of questions and precious few answers. What she knew was that eight human beings had lost their lives on her patch.

If the killer, or killers, could have looked into the window of her office as she stared out at the rainy morning, they would have gotten a chill themselves from the look in her eyes.

CHAPTER 4

Doughnuts. Apparently Detective Sergeant Listun had recently binged some American crime show and felt compelled to bring in some jam-filled cake doughnuts from his local baker.

Jillian looked at the box and hesitated only slightly before grabbing one for herself on the way to the incident room. It had been a long day, and she needed the sugar rush if she was going to stay awake.

Everyone looked weary as she made her way to the front of the room. The general hubbub quieted down as Jillian stood in front of the whiteboard. She looked at her DS and asked, "What've we got?"

DS Listun nodded toward Detective Constable Kara Devanor, who consulted her notebook. "PC Dawson and I interviewed the lorry driver, Ahmal Buggeri. He seemed quite upset about what had happened. Says he had no idea there were dead bodies in the back."

Kara looked over at PC Dawson, who chimed in, "His paperwork checks through. His lorry has all its registrations. According to Mr. Buggeri, he was called in early because there've been massive road works on the M6. He took alternate roads trying to get around them but apparently so did everyone else, and it took him much longer than he expected just to get down near Coventry." Flipping a page on her notebook, she continued, "He was finally able to get on the M6 south of the road works and eventually onto the M40. However, he was nearly past his four-and-a-half-hours-without-a-break drive time, so he pulled into a large service station just north of Oxford."

Listun spoke up. "Stacey, what can you tell us?"

Stacey Alston was the unit's chief administrator and all-around wizard with background searches. Putting down one of the doughnuts, she said, "He works out of Manchester, mostly as a driver for hire. Has some regular routes, regular employers who use his services, but he doesn't have much in the way of consistent routes. Married, two kids, both in school. Finances seem about average. They're not well off, but not strugglin' either. Wife works at a local school, though not the one their children go to. She's been there about six years."

"Who hired him for this trip?" Jillian asked.

"He says he was hired by a Manchester firm called Central UK Imports, Ltd.," Kara answered. "He's done work for them before."

"And where did he pick up the container?"

Alston replied, "Port in Liverpool."

Jillian looked at her team with no small amount of confusion on her face. "Let me make sure I've got this right. An import firm in Manchester hired a lorry driver to go to Liverpool, pick up a container, and drive it all the way down to Southampton to put it on a ship bound for France?"

Listun smiled. "That's right, guv. And here's the best bit . . ."

"I can't wait to hear it," Jillian said.

"I spoke to the port harbormaster. Apparently, Mr. Buggeri's lorry was flagged for a routine inspection while it was in line for loading."

Sensing there was more to the story, Jillian merely waited. Listun had paused for effect before he continued, "While the inspection of lorry cargo is routine, it's not common to have it done in the loading line, as that can cause delays and backups. The inspections are normally done prior to the loading line when the lorry drivers check in at the dock."

"So, who ordered this unusual inspection?" Jillian asked.

"That's just it, mum, no one knows."

"What do you mean, no one knows?"

"The paperwork has an illegible signature that doesn't match any of their port employees. I've got someone going down tomorrow morning to ask the a.m. crews if they recognize it, but it looks like someone flagged that lorry and then disappeared," Listun said.

Jillian thought about it for a moment. "Someone wanted that lorry searched. It was never intended to go all the way to France."

Murmurs around the incident room agreed.

"Anything else?" Jillian asked.

"We're still waiting on victim identifications. Coroners are working on it, but it's slow going, as you can imagine," Listun said.

"Okay," Jillian said, finishing her doughnut, "we need to find out where that container came from, what happened while it was in Liverpool, what this import company in Manchester is all about, and who flagged the container at the port."

DS Listun began giving out assignments based on that list, and then everyone got up. Jillian called out, "Hang on."

Everyone stopped amid whatever state they were in and turned back to face her.

"It's been an early start and a long day. Everyone go home, get some rest, and come back tomorrow ready to dig in."

There was a general murmur of thanks around the room as everyone went to their desks to shut down their computers, grab their belongings, and head home.

After returning to her office, Jillian had just sat down at her desk when her phone rang.

"DI Scotte," she said, picking up the receiver.

"It's me," Daniella said.

"Hi," Jillian said with a sigh.

"I don't have much for you yet, I'm afraid. This is going to take most of the night and probably into tomorrow."

"I understand," Jillian said. Both women were professional when they were at work, and their voices, though keeping in that professionalism, were always laced with something else. Something unspoken in the slight pauses after each sentence.

"What we do know is that the victims were all Eastern European, all in their thirties. We don't have positive IDs yet, but we're running everything through Interpol."

Jillian took in the information, making notes on a pad of paper. "Were they . . ." she began, then asked, "How did they die?"

"We're quite sure they were dead before they were dismembered," Daniella said. Jillian closed her eyes, thankful for small mercies.

"But," Daniella began. Something in her voice made the hairs on the back of Jillian's neck stand up. "We're still running some tests, mind, but we think they were beaten to death."

There was a noise in the background on the phone and Daniella said, "Look, I've got to go. We should know more in the morning."

"Yes, of course," Jillian said. "Thank you for calling."

"No problem. Get some rest for me, will you?"

"I'll miss you."

"I know, me too. Gotta run," Daniella said.

Jillian tried to say "Love you," but the phone had already gone dead. She looked down at her notes and tried to make some sense of what she knew, but her brain was too tired. There was simply too much they didn't know.

Looking up, she saw Kara walk by the windows in her office, then suddenly jerk to a stop. The look on her face was odd, and Jillian was trying to place what it was when she saw one of her officers bringing in a visitor.

The officer knocked on the frame of her open door. "Man wants to see you, guv."

"Thank you," Jillian said as she rose from her chair.

Into her office walked Sebastian Hughes.

CHAPTER 5

S hoes maketh the man or something like that, Jillian Scotte thought as Sebastian Hughes sat down in one of the two chairs facing her desk and crossed his legs.

He was wearing a blue pinstriped suit with a light-blue shirt and gray tie. His shoes looked to her to be Italian leather and likely cost more than her entire wardrobe.

It had already been a long day and Jillian wanted to head home, but she was, as always, curious about the somewhat mysterious Mr. Hughes, and even more so about what prompted him to come in to see her.

"To what do I owe this pleasure?" she asked.

"I heard about the container," he began. "I thought I might be of assistance."

That made Jillian's eyebrows go up. She simply fixed him with her questioning look. She had found that saying nothing often elicited more information than asking questions.

Sebastian Hughes was not one to be rushed, and he took his time. "My information tells me you have eight bodies of foreign nationality that, uhm . . . perished . . . in the container."

Again, Jillian said nothing and simply looked on.

"Having originated in Liverpool, this likely means that the people in the container were illegally smuggled into the country."

"You do seem to be well informed, Mr. Hughes," Jillian said.

Sebastian Hughes simply smiled his charming and often disarming smile.

Jillian decided to get to the point. "What does this have to do with Southern England's gambling king?

Hughes chuckled and looked down at his hands, apparently deciding there was nothing to see there and looking back up. "I would hardly consider myself king," he said, "but I do know a thing or two about immigrant imports."

"You mean human trafficking," Jillian said bluntly.

Hughes' face did that thing where nothing really changed and yet his demeanor shifted. Jillian had seen it happen more than once, and she still couldn't put her finger on what it was exactly that happened. Something in his eyes? A slight dip in the wattage of his smile, perhaps? Maybe it was just a feeling. Whatever the case, she knew he had suddenly become more serious, even though he still wore the same expression as before.

"There is a man in Manchester whom you might call . . ." He seemed to be searching for the right word. ". . . England's human-trafficking king."

"And who might that be?"

"His name is Laghari," he said. "Raj Laghari."

"Laghari," Jillian said. "How do you spell that?"

Hughes spelled it out.

"Is that Pakistani?" she asked.

"Indian I believe," Hughes replied. Then, as though it had just occurred to him, he added, "Do you know that Raj in Hindi means 'King'?"

Jillian looked up from her notebook and thought, not for the first time, how much of a dichotomy Sebastian Hughes was. His impeccable taste in clothes and a seemingly unending trove of odd knowledge bespoke someone highly educated, yet here he was running his former boss's gambling empire. "And what is it you know about this Mr. Laghari, exactly?" she asked.

"I know that when it comes to the import of . . . human trafficking," he corrected, "he knows anything and everything there is to know. If foreign nationals are brought into this country illegally, you can bet that Raj Laghari has something to do with it."

"What exactly is Mr. Laghari's business?"

"He runs an import–export company in Manchester," Hughes said, "but his primary source of income is prostitution and pornography."

Jillian made a note in her book. "Well, thank you for bringing this to my attention, Mr. Hughes. I'm not sure how relevant it is given that these victims were older than your average tart, and certainly not the teenagers one usually finds being imported for the likes of someone like this Mr. Laghari."

Sensing his cue that the meeting was over, Sebastian got to his feet. "Your victims were in a shipping container. Their ethnicity suggests that they were foreign nationals, and I'm willing to bet you won't find them registered in any UK database." Hughes turned toward the door, but as he reached for the handle, he turned back around.

"Jillian," he said, his blue eyes now staring straight at her with piercing intensity. "Raj Laghari is not a nice man."

There was something in his voice. Something in the way he said it that gave Jillian goosebumps.

Hughes wasn't finished. "If your victims were illegals, Laghari either has something to do with it, or knows something about it."

"Sebastian, these women didn't fit the profile of prostitutes." Jillian closed her eyes briefly as the images of the dismembered bodies flashed before her eyes. "From their ages according to the medical examiner's report, they seemed more . . . average. If they weren't part of Laghari's stable, then who else might have brought them in?"

Hughes stared at her with his dark blue eyes that seemed to penetrate through her. "There is a couple, Victor and Liddya Crommel. They run a string of cleaning services all along the coast. They are known to use primarily East European workers. You might start there."

Jillian made another note in her book.

Sebastian opened the door, though he continued looking at Jillian. She glanced up from her book and met his gaze. "If you decide to talk to Laghari," he said, his voice low but cold, "call me first."

He turned, not waiting for a reply, and left her office.

***

The next morning, Kara Devanor got to the office earlier than usual, having spent a somewhat restless night alone in her bed.

When Sebastian had shown up unannounced at the Tof late the previous day, she had almost dropped the files she'd been carrying. It had taken every ounce of strength she had left to act normal while he met with her boss.

Desperate to know what was being said, she found every excuse to get up from her desk and wander about the room to catch glimpses into the office. Since her desk faced away from her boss's office, sitting down at it gave her little clue as to what they were talking about.

Her imagination had run wild with thoughts of Sebastian telling Jillian about their . . . their what? Relationship? Just the thought of him telling her made her sick to her stomach.

She imagined that as soon as the meeting was over Jillian would call her into her office to sack her, but that didn't happen. Her boss saw Sebastian out, returned for her coat, and with another admonishment for everyone to go home, left.

And so, Kara had spent the night tossing and turning and wondering what the next day might bring. Agonizing over how to tell her boss she was seeing, and sleeping with, one of Southampton's most prominent criminals.

***

Jillian Scotte walked into her office, deposited her coat on the coat rack, and hurried into the incident room where her team now waited.

Everyone seemed more refreshed from a good night's sleep as Jillian began going over what they did and did not know. The coroner's office promised a preliminary report by midday.

After the meeting, she called DS Listun and DC Devanor into her office. Stephen Listun, she noticed, was rubbing his eyes, still seemingly not quite awake. Though, given that he had a young baby at home, this didn't come as a surprise.

Kara, normally bright-eyed and eager, seemed off somehow. She was sitting in one of the two chairs with her notepad at the ready, but she was looking down, her posture slightly slouched.

"All right?" Jillian asked, looking at them both.

Listun nodded, "Yeah, good, baby was up on and off," he said.

There was a silence in which both Listun and Jillian looked over at Kara. As if sensing this, Kara looked up bewilderedly and said, "Yeah, fine," before looking back at her notepad.

Jillian's eyes narrowed a little, but she decided whatever was going on would have to wait; they had work to do. "Right," she said, "Sebastian Hughes came in yesterday."

Jillian sensed more than saw something in Kara stiffen, but when she looked, her DC was sitting with pen in hand, looking up at her with an odd expression. Pausing slightly, Jillian continued, "He had some information which may be relevant to this case that we need to pursue.

"Stephen, I want you to look into a Mr. and Mrs. Crommel. Victor and Liddya Crommel." She spelled their names out for him. "They run some sort of cleaning services company. Find out whatever you can, and then you and I are going to pay them a visit. Preferably this afternoon."

"Right, guv," Listun said, making notes in his notepad.

"Kara, I want you to call Manchester's Criminal Investigations Department and see what they have on a Mr. Raj Laghari." Again she spelled the name, looking down at her own notes. "It should be extensive, as apparently, he's the current man of the hour when it comes to tarts and pornography up there."

"What's that got to do with this case, guv?" Listun asked.

"Maybe nothing," Jillian said, "but Hughes says he's also the king of human trafficking in all of the British Isles."

Listun and Devanor looked at each other, and then they each wrote more notes on their notepads.

***

Back at her desk, Kara tried to focus on the task at hand, but her mind wouldn't let her. Just when she was beginning to fall into a groove, her phone buzzed, and she saw a text from Sebastian asking if she was free tonight.

What was she doing? The thought kept banging around inside her head. A police officer going out with a known criminal element just wasn't on. She knew she had to tell Jillian, but the mere thought of it terrified her.

She went back and forth for the better part of the morning as her mind and heart played tug-of-war. She went to the toilet and splashed water on her face, admonishing herself for the mess she now found herself in. She had to do something. Staring at herself in the mirror, she met her reflection and looked straight into her own eyes.

It was time to talk to her boss. Whatever the consequences, she deserved to know, and Kara needed to unburden herself. She dried her hands and headed down the hall to Jillian Scotte's office.

CHAPTER 6

"Are you out of your bloody mind?" The shout came out of Jillian's mouth before she could stop it.

DC Kara Devanor looked crestfallen sitting in front of Jillian's desk, her hands in her lap. She had knocked on the door, then entered her boss's office, closing the door behind her, which was unusual for Kara.

Jillian had put down the paperwork she'd been trying to focus on and given the young detective her full attention, assuming she had something important but discreet to discuss about the case.

It was, perhaps, the complete non sequitur from where her mind was that had resulted in her explosive question.

Kara had said it with no preamble, as though she were holding her breath and had to expel it all at once or she would explode. "I'm seeing Sebastian Hughes," she had said, then, as though seeing the need to clarify it, she added, "I'm sleeping with him."

Jillian's question came out so loud that no doubt it penetrated the thin walls of her office windows and was audible in the squad room, because several heads turned to look. She could feel the anger rising and suddenly stood up, sending her chair careening back into the half wall beneath the windows behind her. She marched around her desk and past Kara to her door, which she yanked open. "Get back to work and mind your own bloody business!" she yelled, before slamming the door hard enough to rattle the windows of her office.

She stormed back behind her desk, but she didn't sit down. She looked briefly out her window at the gray clouds of another rainy English day and took a deep breath. She needed to calm down. Turning around, she looked down at her DC, who sat in her chair completely deflated, as though all the energy had left her body.

Her voice only somewhat toned down, she asked, "What the hell were you thinking?"

Kara looked like she might be on the verge of tears. She swallowed audibly before answering, "I didn't plan it, if that's what you're asking."

"Do you have any idea how bad this is?" Jillian asked. Kara nodded, looking down before raising her eyes again and meeting Jillian's. Jillian paused for a moment; there was something about the way Kara was looking at her. There was pain in her eyes, certainly. Perhaps even shame, but there was also something else.

Jillian shook her head slightly, as though trying to clear the thoughts away. "Just by telling me, you've not only thrown your career away, but now you've jeopardized mine."

Kara's eyes grew wider. "But this isn't anything to do with you . . ." she began.

"Kara!" Jillian said in exasperation, throwing up her arms. "You are one of my team. It has *everything* to do with me. By telling me, you've put me in an impossible situation."

Just then, there was a knock on the door.

"What?" Jillian barked before even looking at the door.

DS Listun opened the door gently. "I'm sorry to interrupt, guv," he said sheepishly, trying to balance on the tightrope between interrupting his boss in what was clearly a sensitive time and needing to do so. "You said we'd need to leave now if we're going to make it by five." He was referring to a meeting he and Jillian had set up, the reminder of which did nothing to improve her mood.

Jillian looked at him with a stare that would have made a weaker man's knees buckle. To Listun's credit, he simply said nothing and waited for her response.

"Two minutes," was all Jillian said.

Kara, wanting to salvage what was left of her career, her now-more-than-fragile friendship, her life, said, "I'm really, really, sorry. I didn't mean to do this to you. I didn't . . . I wasn't . . . it just . . ." She couldn't find the words.

Jillian turned to her, cold faced, her voice hard, "It just what, Kara?"

Kara was now completely dejected. Tears were falling from her eyes. Her voice was barely a whisper. "It just happened," she said, her body language reflecting her complete despondency.

"We're not finished," Jillian said as she picked up her coat and bag. Stopping at the door, she turned briefly before walking out. "Get back to work. We'll discuss this later."

***

As DS Listun drove, he tried to find the right moment. The tension in the car was more than palpable—it felt like an electric charge about to ignite if he so much as hit a bump in the road. He debated what to say, how to say it, whether to say anything at all. Finally, after what seemed like the hundredth time in his head, he actually said out loud, "Boss, do you want to tell me what that was all about back there with you and DC Devanor?"

Jillian turned her head slowly toward him, and Listun made the mistake of taking his eye off the road to look over at her. The look she gave him told him all he needed to know, but while she had his attention, she said, "No, Stephen, I don't. If I think you need to know something, I'll tell you."

Listun pulled the car over and parked. They had arrived.

Victor and Liddya Crommel's offices were housed out of what looked like an old video shop, the name still emblazoned above the door where the letters used to be. Victor Crommel was a short man with thinning hair and a dark mustache. His wife Liddya was plump with glasses. She seemed content to sit with her hands in her lap and let her husband do the talking.

Listun went through the motions with them, asking the basics, until he finally got to the point. "Can you tell us about your dealings with a man called Raj Laghari?"

Victor Crommel looked at his wife. He spoke to her in a what Jillian thought might be Croatian or perhaps Slovenian. His wife responded more strongly than her appearance suggested her capable of.

Victor looked back at Listun. "I do not know this man Laghari, but my wife tells me he is the man who owns the shipping company we sometimes use, Central UK Imports."

Listun looked at his boss, but Jillian simply stared at the couple saying nothing. Taking his cue from her, Listun simply looked back and said nothing.

Victor Crommel looked uncomfortable, finally saying, "We use Central UK Imports to get cleaning supplies from Asia. The prices are more . . . how you say . . . affordable."

Listun continued his line of questioning for another ten or fifteen minutes, but the Crommels had little of value to offer. They used various companies for shipping, all from different ports depending on the products they needed.

Listun asked them what their hiring practices were, and they said they advertised online.

Back in the car, he put the key in the ignition. Jillian looked over at him. "What do you think?"

Pausing with his hands on the keys, Listun said, "I dunno. There was something odd about them."

Jillian nodded. "I agree. The wife seemed odd, and Victor was definitely hiding something."

Listun nodded. "Yeah, he seemed quite nervous talking about Laghari. Was a bit more comfortable talking about the company itself, but he still seemed unsettled."

Jillian grabbed her safety belt and drew it across her body. "Let's get into the Crommels and their cleaning business. Find out everything we can about who they are and what they do."

Listun started the car. "Yes boss."

CHAPTER 7

Jillian Scotte was up before dawn. She hadn't slept well at all. Daniella had been asleep when she got home. As part of Southampton's coroner team, Daniella had been working most of the last two days on the multiple autopsies of the women in the container.

Jillian, having attended a late meeting at Southampton Central, didn't get home until after nine. Although exhausted, she had been unable to sleep, her mind playing ping-pong between the case and the predicament Kara had placed them both in.

Grabbing her bike, she set off at a blistering pace in the predawn light, working through her frustration and anger. Her legs churned with increasing speed as she wound her way in and around the still quiet streets of Southampton's outskirts.

By the time she got back home she was drenched, not from the early mist and moisture-filled air of what promised to be another wet day in southern Britain, but because she had worked up a sweat that left her clothes clinging to her like limpets.

She took a shower, made some coffee, and brought a cup over to Daniella, who was just stirring awake. Smiling, Jillian sat on the edge of the bed and set the coffee on the nightstand.

Daniella opened her eyes, "Coffee, oh my God, I love you."

"Is that me you love, or the coffee?" Jillian said.

Daniella took in a long breath through her nose as she got up on one elbow, her long black hair, tangled and messy, falling around her shoulders. "Both," she said, smiling.

Jillian leaned down and kissed her. "I've got to go, just wanted to say good morning."

Coming fully awake, Daniella looked up at her. "You're not going to ask me more about the report?"

"No," Jillian said, "I'll read it more carefully when I get in and call you if I need to."

Daniella sat up fully now. "Jills, what's wrong?"

Jillian smiled ruefully. Daniella knew her too well. "It's complicated. I'll tell you about it later. I just need to get in, that's all."

***

DS Listun had made it a point to arrive early, wanting to beat both his boss and his team in, but DC Devanor was already there, working silently at her desk. She looked like she might have been there all night, though she wasn't wearing the same clothes as the day before. It didn't, however, appear she had slept.

Leaning against her desk, he looked down and chose his words carefully. "Kara. Is there anything you want to talk about? Anything I can do to help?"

"Thanks, sarge, but no. This is something I have to deal with myself. I appreciate the concern, though." Then looking up at him, she added, "I really do."

Listun nodded, biting his lip slightly. "Right, well, let me know if you change your mind."

Hearing something, he turned and looked out the row of windows behind them. "Boss is here. We'd better give her an update."

Kara's shoulders slumped, but she gathered her notebook and she and Listun walked into Jillian's office shortly after the boss had hung up her coat.

Jillian didn't start off with pleasantries. "What have we got?" she said bluntly as her two best officers came in.

Listun took up his position, leaning against her credenza, while Kara sat down on one of the chairs facing Jillian's desk.

DS Listun began, "We still don't have much on the lorry or the driver, Ahmal Buggeri. He thought he was driving a shipment down to Amsterdam that he picked up in Liverpool. The container was packed and checked at the depot. He simply hooked up to it and set off on his route."

Jillian looked up from her desk. "Didn't he bother to check the container before he left?"

"No," Listun said, "apparently that's quite common for drivers who work for hire. They do this day in and day out, so they simply pick up the container, paperwork is all ready for them, they deliver the container, get the paperwork signed, and back they go to do it again. It's all routine."

Jillian sighed. "Where are we at with the Crommels?"

"Victor and Liddya Crommel own a business cleaning service that employs mostly Eastern European immigrants and a few local Britons looking for daytime work. There aren't any major infractions on record, though there were a few queries from the Immigration Service in recent months, but nothing came of them," Listun said.

"What were the queries related to?" Jillian asked.

"Doesn't say," Listun said. "I've left a message with IS in London, waiting to hear back." Looking down at his notes, he continued, "They often use various shipping companies coming through local ports. Southampton mostly, but also Immingham, London, and Liverpool."

"Isn't that a lot?" Jillian asked.

Listun shrugged. "Apparently they have clients in London as well as here in the South, so they ship supplies and what have you based on location."

Jillian pursed her lips, thinking. "Doesn't it seem odd to you that a business with that kind of trade, and clients all over, would run out of such a small office?"

"Yeah," Listun said, nodding, "I thought that as well."

Jillian nodded thoughtfully and turned to Kara.

Kara took a deep breath and said, "We looked into Raj Laghari. He runs Central UK Imports out of Manchester. Aside from your basic import–export business, he also runs an extensive lorry service that goes up and down the UK and into Europe."

Consulting her notes, she said, "Lots of inquiries over the years. Mr. Laghari isn't a stranger to the courts and has both won and lost various cases involving a few run-ins with tax and license, but nothing serious. I called up to GMP," she said, referring to Greater Manchester Police. "They certainly knew of Mr. Laghari, saying he's been on their radar for quite some time, but they've never been able to make anything stick. Apparently, he's a well-known figure in organized crime, but the Met hasn't been able to get anything on him either."

"Perhaps we should pay him a visit," Jillian said, looking over at Listun.

"That's just it," Kara said. "I called their offices to inquire about that, and they said that he's been out of the country for most of the month."

Jillian looked back at her DC. "Out of the country?"

"That's what they said," Kara responded blankly.

Jillian sat back in her chair as her phone rang. Looking down at the display, she rolled her eyes, knowing she'd have to take the call. "All right. Stephen, keep digging into the Crommels." Turning back to Kara, she added, "Keep looking at Central UK Imports and how they fit into all of this."

She wanted to feel proud about the fact that Kara was, as always, one step ahead of her, but that thought was fleeting given the circumstances.

Looking up at both her detectives as she picked up the phone, she said, "And let's dig into the lorry itself. Someone somewhere put those bodies into what was supposed to be a load of something else. Find out who." Then she said into the phone, "Jillian Scotte, how can I help, sir?"

***

Kara spent most of the day glued to her desk, trying her best to do her job. Every time she got up and walked past Jillian's office, she wanted to go inside, to talk to her boss, her friend, but she couldn't. Not just because Jillian spent most of the day in video conferences and on the phone, but because she didn't know what to say.

Part of her wanted to get it over with. To have Jillian call her in and fire her. To yell at her. Something. Anything. She wanted to apologize and tell her she hadn't meant for any of it to happen.

And what about Sebastian? Try as she might, she couldn't stop thinking about him. He'd texted her several times and called to leave messages as well. She'd been ignoring him, and she felt awful about that.

Her whole life seemed to be falling apart around her, and she felt increasingly alone and isolated.

She could tell Listun was attuned to how she was acting. He almost tiptoed around her, fielding off other officers who approached her desk with normal requests and taking them on himself. She was grateful for his help and simultaneously angry with him for doing it.

In short, Kara was a mess.

As she left the Tof, uncharacteristically before the rest of the team, she thought about grabbing a bottle of wine and going back to her flat to drown her sorrows.

Her phone buzzed as she made her way through the jostling crowds of workers calling it a day.

She looked at the number and her heart sank.

She didn't want to answer, but knew she should. Sliding her finger over, she lifted the phone to her ear and said, "Hello."

CHAPTER 8

Detective Inspector Jillian Scotte felt her anger building as she drove. The closer she got to her destination, the more her anger grew.

She had been on her way to work when she got the call. Sebastian Hughes, asking her to meet him.

Oh, she'd be happy to meet him, she'd told him, the sarcasm purposefully present in her voice. She had more than one or two things to say to him.

She pulled into the parking lot near a row of food vans. The hawkers were selling their early-morning wares to lines of Southampton's business-district workers on their way to work.

She saw Hughes's gleaming black sedan parked among a few other cars, but found herself a spot further down. Getting out of her car, she spotted Hughes walking away from a coffee van holding two cups.

He was, as ever, dressed like he was in a magazine. Today, he was wearing a dark blue suit with a matching shirt and a light-green tie. His shoes seemed to gleam as though he'd spent the entire night shining them, though more likely he had someone doing it for him.

"Good morning," he said, smiling, and handed one cup of coffee over.

Jillian did not smile back. She took the coffee without saying thank you. Instead, she said, "I've half a mind to smack that smile off your face."

Hughes half nodded as if to himself and then steered them over to the railing that overlooked the river Itchen. A few tourists were busily taking photos of the early-morning light on the water, but they were a ways off and out of hearing range.

Sebastian Hughes took a sip of his coffee, leaned an elbow on the railing, and looked over at Jillian. His smile was no longer bright, but he looked on pleasantly.

Jillian turned to face him. "What the bloody hell are you playing at?"

Hughes tilted his head slightly, his eyes narrowing a bit, questioningly.

"Is this some sort of game to get inside my team? So you can keep up with what we're doing? Get your own inside track on the coppers?" Jillian asked pointedly.

She didn't give him a chance to answer. "Because if it is, you've barked up the wrong bloody tree, I can tell you that!" She used the hand holding her coffee cup to gesture at him, causing some coffee to spill out the small opening in the lid. Switching hands, she shook the coffee off angrily before she continued, "Did you really think you could seduce one of my female officers and I wouldn't know? Are you so bloody arrogant that you think your charms and good looks give you carte blanche to do whatever you want?

"Our . . ." Jillian struggled for the right word, finally settling on, ". . . history . . . does not entitle you to a damn thing, Sebastian. Whatever games you're playing, I am fed up with them!" Then, as if an afterthought, she added, "And they stop right now!"

She kept her eyes fixed on his, anger seething out of every part of her.

Sebastian Hughes stared back. He hadn't flinched or even averted his gaze the entire time. He simply stood, looked directly into her eyes, and listened to her. Finally, after a moment's pause, he said, "Are you finished?"

His stoic calm was infuriating, but Jillian swallowed her anger and merely nodded. "For now."

"What I am doing," Sebastian said, his dark blue eyes fixed hard on hers, "is not a game. I am not, in fact, trying to *do* anything." He looked around briefly, his eyes seeming to take in everything and nothing all at once.

Jillian knew that if she asked him, he could tell her details about their surroundings that she likely would not have seen had she looked around. Sebastian Hughes never missed anything.

His voice brought her out of her briefly meandering thoughts. "I care very deeply about Kara. It is nothing more or less than that."

Jillian couldn't help herself. "Do you have *any* idea what your actions have done to her career? Can't you see that her consorting with you is the end of any hope of a future she has in the police?"

"Consorting," Hughes said. "Interesting choice of words."

"Well, what would *you* call it?" Jillian said in exasperation. Sighing loudly, she turned and looked out over the river, taking a drink of her coffee. "Damn it, Sebastian!" she said, pounding her fist on the railing.

"Jillian," he said. His voice was still calm, and yet somehow there was a strength to it at the same time. It was said in a way that demanded she turn to look at him, which she did. Hughes dropped his head slightly, making sure she could see he was making complete eye contact with her before he said, "I promise you. I am not trying to hurt her, or you, or jeopardize anything. I have simply fallen for someone who happens to be a brilliant detective on your team."

"Oh, so you're now an expert on brilliant detectives, are you?" The words came out of Jillian's mouth before she could stop them. She took a breath. "You do not seem to understand the enormity of what this means."

Hughes opened his mouth to speak, but Jillian cut him off. "Simply by her telling me, I am duty-bound to report her to the IOPC," she said, referring to the Independent Office for Police Conduct. "Once I do that, everything is out of my hands and her career is over."

She saw him open his mouth, and she said quickly, "Before you even suggest it, if I don't report her, I am equally culpable once this comes out, which could cost me *my* job. And believe you me, it will come out." Now she threw up her hands. "Don't you think the Met have been watching you? They're probably watching this meeting right now. You're the head of one of the largest gambling operations in England, for fuck's sake. Of *course* this is going to come out."

Hughes simply looked at her with his infuriatingly calm expression, waiting for her to finish.

When she said nothing more, he said, "You should do whatever you think you have to do . . ."

"Aren't you listening to me?" she shouted, drawing a look or two from some of the closer tourists, who turned and began walking in the opposite direction. "What I have to do, as you blithely put it, will probably ruin her career." Then, without thinking, she added, "You're not the only one who cares about Kara, pal."

At last, Hughes' face changed, though the slight smile that crossed his lips did nothing to soothe Jillian's anger.

"Perhaps there's a perspective you're not considering," he began. "Perhaps, they might see it as having someone from your team keeping a close eye on—how did you put it?—'the head of one of the largest gambling operations in England, for fuck's sake'?"

Jillian stood still, speechless.

Hughes's smile widened. "It's simply the other side of the coin."

"You have got to be joking," she said.

"Why not?" he replied. "Why is it possible that I'm trying to get in on the VCU, but you're not trying to get in on my business?"

Jillian crossed her arms, careful not to spill her coffee. "Are you suggesting that I put Kara up to this?"

Hughes almost laughed. "No. I was the one who approached Kara, not the other way around. What I'm saying is that you could claim, should it *come out*"—he used air quotes with his index fingers—"that she was going undercover, if you'll pardon the pun."

Jillian winced, not wanting that image in her head.

"All I'm saying is that there is more than one way to look at this, and I want to reiterate that *this*"—he drew a large circle in front of him as he said the word—"is nothing at all nefarious. I truly do care about Kara." Then, after a pause, he added, "A lot." Those two simple words held a power in them that Jillian could not define, but she felt it, as if jolted by an electric current.

Jillian, her arms still crossed, could feel the beginning of a migraine coming on and closed her eyes, hoping to ward it off.

Hughes's voice intruded on her mindfulness moment.

"You didn't have a chance to hear from Kara last night on her research into Raj Laghari," he said.

Jillian's eyes flew open. That Hughes knew Kara was looking into Mr. Laghari meant that he and Kara had spoken about it, which further reinforced her fear about this whole thing.

Sensing her alarm, Hughes held up a hand. "Yes, I talked to Kara last night. After her conversation with you, she needed someone to talk to, and before you judge her, or me, hear me out."

If Jillian bit her tongue any harder, she feared she might cut it in half.

Hughes continued, "She did her due diligence on Laghari, but when she tried to track him down, she ran into a dead end."

Jillian knew that much, as Kara had said, Laghari was out of the country for weeks.

"Only I know Laghari is, in fact, in Manchester as we speak."

This got Jillian's attention.

"Kara did everything right, Jillian," Hughes said. "She used all the proper channels and what she was told about Laghari being out of the country is exactly what everyone, including the plods up in Manchester, believe."

Jillian let the slang insult go.

"In fact," Hughes continued, "it's what Laghari himself wants everyone to believe."

This was getting more and more interesting, Jillian thought, though she was keenly aware that the conversation about Kara and Hughes was being deliberately diverted by Hughes himself.

"I've arranged a meeting for today," he said. Then, looking at his watch, he said, "If we leave now, we should arrive just in time."

"What. *Now* now?" Jillian said.

"I don't think Mr. Laghari is long for this world," Hughes said, adding, "Cancer. The aggressive kind."

Jillian thought about her schedule, already considering what she would have to move to make the trip up to Manchester. She could, of course, ask someone from Greater Manchester Police to make the inquiry, but given the ties Laghari's company had to her investigation, she knew she needed to do this herself.

"One more thing," Hughes said as they moved toward his car. Jillian had decided to leave hers in the parking lot for the time being. "Kara's waiting in my car."

Jillian stopped, looking over at the four-door sedan before her with its darkened windows.

Hughes stopped and turned, then nodding for her to follow, he continued walking. "She's the only one on your team with the background on Laghari. Besides," he added, a smirk crossing his face, "best to get back on the horse as soon as possible, isn't it?"

Jillian took a deep breath and let it out slowly as she began walking toward Hughes's car. This day just kept getting better and better.

CHAPTER 9

What should have been a four-and-a-half-hour car ride would be made just inside four because of the skills of Sebastian Hughes's driver. Despite his colossal frame, he clearly felt at home in the large sedan, which he drove like a race car.

Jillian climbed in through the open door held by Sebastian and looked over at Kara, who nervously said, "Morning, boss."

Jillian just shook her head, saying, "Good morning."

After nearly fifteen minutes of complete silence, Sebastian had turned around from the front passenger seat and said, "So, what brings you two lovely ladies here today?"

Jillian had responded with a knee-jerk, "Oh fuck off," and then suppressed a chuckle, though a thin smile had made it to her lips before she could banish it. She had stolen a quick glance at Kara and seen an expression of complete shock as the young DC looked at her lover's smiling face.

The brazen comment had its desired effect, however, and soon they began discussing what Kara had learned about Raj Laghari and Central UK Imports, with Sebastian filling in his own knowledge and some background from his years in Manchester and as the bodyguard to his former employer.

By the time they arrived at the private hospital where Laghari was admitted, the tenor of the car was, if not exactly congenial, much more relaxed than when they had begun their journey.

The trio walked into the lobby as the driver went to park. Sebastian approached the reception desk and presented himself. After a few minutes, a middle-aged woman in a dark gray suit with pearl earrings and matching choker emerged through one of the frosted glass doors.

Without preamble and with a frown on her face, she said, "Mr. Hughes?"

Sebastian stood and took the offered hand, saying, "Yes. Thank you for agreeing to meet." Turning to Jillian and Kara, he said, "This is Simalla Burman, Raj Laghari's wife."

To say that she was stunning would have been an understatement. Her accent was clearly British, with a touch of New Delhi thrown in. Her slender frame matched her angular jawline, and her dark eyes swiveled toward Jillian and Kara as they too stood up. Still smiling, she said, "And who might you be?"

Jillian took out her warrant card. "I'm Detective Inspector Scotte. This is Detective Constable Devanor."

The smile instantly faded from Simalla's face. She slowly turned her head back to Sebastian and gave him a look of such intensity it should have scared him. Sebastian, however, merely smiled back.

Still looking at Sebastian, Simalla said, "What is this?"

Jillian took a half step forward, forcing the woman to turn her attention back. "We need to speak to your husband regarding the brutal murder of eight women in one of his lorry shipments."

Simalla looked at Jillian impassively for several seconds before she said, "I'm afraid that's not possible. My husband is gravely ill and cannot be disturbed."

"I'm afraid I'll have to insist," Jillian shot back.

A thin trace of a smile crossed Simalla's face before being replaced by a stern and resolute look. Lifting her chin ever so slightly, she dropped her head a bit to make sure her eye contact was perfectly placed with Jillian's. "No," she said with a tone of finality.

Kara, seeing the standoff before her, took a step forward herself. "Mrs. Berman. We can certainly call in for a court order while we wait here in the lobby. Of course," she said, holding the other woman's intense stare, "in such a situation, we can't guarantee that the press won't be monitoring and find out your husband is being treated here."

Everyone standing there knew that what Kara just said was a lie.

The threat, however, was unmistakable. Let us see your husband, or we'll broadcast to the masses that he isn't out of the country but dying of cancer in a very private hospital facility on the outskirts of Manchester.

Kara was banking on the fact that for reasons yet unknown, Mr. Laghari and his wife did not want this information to become public knowledge.

Simalla Berman's face was flushed. She made no attempt to hide her fury at being boxed in this way. After a lengthy pause of consideration, she finally relented. "Fine," she said, then glancing over at Hughes, she said, "but five minutes only, and *just* the women."

This time it was Sebastian, the smile no longer on his face, who said, "No."

It had the same tone Simalla had tried to use with Jillian a moment ago, but there was something in the way it came out, or perhaps it was the shadow behind his eyes. Simalla looked visibly shaken for a brief moment, then sighed audibly and began walking toward the frosted glass door. The trio followed her.

Walking into Raj Laghari's hospital room was like walking into a different building from the hospital-like hallway they had walked down. While there were still machines and tubes and beeping monitors, and even the requisite electronic hospital bed, the rest of the room was appointed like some high-end luxury hotel, or perhaps even a Hyde Park penthouse suite.

Couches, settees, a small table with chairs, a flat-screen television mounted on the wall, and thick carpeting made up most of the room except for a small rectangular space on the floor around the bed that was tiled with the typical bland flooring.

As they entered, an enormous man rose from one of the chairs. As he stood up, he appeared to bristle with physical power. Although heavier and taller than anyone else in the room, he was not unhealthy. He was simply solid.

Simalla made a slight gesture with her right hand, almost as if to say, "It's okay," but the man rose to his full height and glared. He was not looking at Jillian or Kara, but directly at Hughes.

Hughes, having locked eyes with the man, smiled even more broadly than he had been before. Stepping in and closing the door behind him, he now leaned casually against the doorframe, but his eyes never left the towering man, who continued to glare intently back.

Simalla went to the side of her husband's oversized hospital bed and bent to whisper in his ear. The man did not look well. Somewhat emaciated, he lay with multiple tubes connected to various parts of his body and monitors emitting various beeps, waves, and signals.

Raj Laghari looked anything but a powerful mobster. He looked like a man staring death in the face, tired and worn out. His eyes, however, still held something else as he nodded slightly. His wife stepped away, looking at the two detectives standing at the foot of his bed.

His voice, when he spoke, was stronger than his frail frame seemed possible of conjuring. "My wife tells me you want to talk to me."

Jillian was about to say something when the old man continued. "That you had to use a trick from a failed bodyguard of an old friend tells me you, like most of the police in this country, cannot be trusted."

Jillian wasn't about to be told off by this dying thug. "Well, Mr. Laghari, if your office hadn't lied to us about your whereabouts in the first place, we could have called you directly."

Laghari waved a hand dismissively. Coughing a little, he said, "Ask your questions, Detective, then leave me to die in peace."

Jillian looked over at Kara who, after opening her notebook, asked, "Mr. Laghari, what can you tell us about a container shipment that left Liverpool last Monday bound for Calais on one of your lorries with a manifest of paper goods, but which in fact contained the dismembered bodies of eight immigrant women of European descent?"

Laghari looked on in disgust. Turning his head slowly, he ignored her question and stared at Sebastian. "And you," he said, his voice rasping as he labored to breathe. "It's bad enough that you let your old boss, and my good friend, die because you couldn't do your job to protect him. Now you take over his business, and you dare to call on my family on the pretense of needing to speak to me in person, but instead you bring the police to my door. And one of them is a golliwog?"

Sebastian stayed leaning against the door, but his head swiveled ever so slightly so that his eyes could meet Laghari's. Hughes no longer smiled, and as the saying goes, if looks could kill, cancer wouldn't have had anything left to take of Raj Laghari.

Kara, undeterred by the racial slur and determined not to let the two men play their games, said again, "What can you tell us about illegal immigrants found dead in a container being transported by one of your lorries, Mr. Laghari?"

Laghari, clearly unnerved by the look Sebastian Hughes had just given him, snapped, "I've been in this hospital for the last month, you stupid cow. How the hell would I know?" Then he began coughing a deep, guttural cough that made his eyes shut tight. He leaned forward in his bed and his wife gently patted his back. As she did so, she turned to glare at the two women.

Able to catch his breath, Laghari said, "If you want to know about immigrant women in shipping containers, you ought to be looking at Fetushka in effing Liverpool. Now get out of my room." The coughing fit resumed, this time sounding as though he might literally cough up one of his battered lungs.

Kara looked at Jillian, who merely nodded toward the door. As they approached, Simalla Berman stormed up to them. Pointing her finger at Jillian, she said, "You've had your questions, now you leave my husband in peace. Gregorio Fetushka can rot in hell for all I care. You can harass him and his family." Then, with a look of hatred in her eyes, she added, "*Not* mine."

Turning her glare toward Sebastian as the two detectives opened the door to leave, she said, "As for you, you miserable wanker, don't you ever call me or come near my family again."

Sebastian straightened up from leaning against the doorjamb, taking his eyes off the bull-sized bodyguard and fixing them onto Simalla, a grin spreading across his face. "What a disappointment that will be."

With that, they walked out of Laghari's room and out of the hospital to Hughes's waiting car.

CHAPTER 10

Sebastian Hughes held the back door open for Jillian as Kara walked around to the other side. Malcom, Hughes's driver and bodyguard, had gotten out to hold the door for her.

As soon as everyone was settled, Sebastian half turned in his seat. "Where to?"

Jillian said, "What do you know about Gregorio Fetushka?"

"He's been around a long time. Owns one of the largest transport companies in Liverpool," Sebastian said.

"What else?"

Sebastian smiled a knowing smile. "I don't know what he's been up to lately, but he's connected, and not much comes into Liverpool by way of the docks that he doesn't know about."

Jillian looked at her watch and then over at Kara, who glanced away. Turning back to Sebastian, she said, "Do you have time for a detour before we go back to Southampton?"

Sebastian looked over at Malcom and nodded; the big man put the car in gear and pulled away from the curb. Turning back to Jillian, Sebastian said, "At your service, Inspector."

***

EuroXPort was a large building facing a portion of the Port of Liverpool. Massive ships with stacks of shipping containers were in varying states of loading and unloading, similar to ports the world over.

Malcom pulled up by the entrance door and looked over at his boss. "Do you want me to come in?"

Sebastian paused slightly before answering, "No, I don't think so." He bent forward slightly to gaze at the second story of building its bank of tall, floor-to-ceiling windows. "They're not expecting us. I don't think there'll be any trouble. Just stay close."

Malcom nodded and got out to open Kara's door. Sebastian reached for Jillian's door, but she was already halfway out, and the trio walked up the small flight of stairs and into the building.

A few people stood behind a long counter in the lobby, either talking on the phone or to customers. "We'll be with you in a minute," one woman called out.

Jillian was in no mood to wait. She walked up to the woman, flashed her warrant card, and said, "We'd like to speak to Mr. Fetushka."

The woman looked annoyed at having been interrupted while serving a customer. Jillian could see she was contemplating how much to push back when a door to their left opened and a middle-aged gentleman in a black suit, white shirt, and navy-blue tie walked out. He looked distinctly out of place among the dockworkers and casually dressed employees moving around the office behind the counter.

"Thanks, Eileen," he said, nodding to the woman behind the counter as though she had summoned him. He approached Jillian with his hand outstretched. "Hello, how can I help?"

Jillian tilted her head slightly. This man looked and sounded more English than foreign. Taking the offered hand, she said, "Are you Gregorio Fetushka?"

The man chuckled and said, "No, sorry, I'm Monty Unsworth. I work for Mr. Fetushka. And you are?"

Jillian held up her warrant card. "I'm Detective Inspector Scotte, and this is Detective Constable Devanor." She purposefully didn't include Sebastian as she waved her arm back to Kara. "We'd like to speak to Mr. Fetushka about a multiple murder involving a transport that originated from here."

Monty Unsworth frowned. "One of EuroXPort's shipments? When did this happen?"

Kara spoke up. "We're still tracking down where the shipment came from, but we know it originated in Liverpool." She added quickly, "What is it exactly that you do for Mr. Fetushka?"

Unsworth shifted his gaze between Kara and Jillian, and for a brief moment, his eyes flashed over Sebastian before returning to the two detectives. "I manage the finances for him."

Sebastian, who until now had been standing by the wall to the side of the entrance door looking around, said, "So, you're the accountant."

Everyone turned and looked at him, with Jillian giving him her hardest glare. Unsworth opened his mouth to speak, but Jillian turned back around and said, "If you would be so kind as to let Mr. Fetushka know we'd like a word, that would be very helpful."

"I'm afraid he's busy at the moment."

"I'm afraid I'm going to have to insist," Jillian shot back. She was sick and tired of being put off.

The door through which Unsworth had walked opened again, and this time another man dressed in a suit walked out. He was not, however, wearing a tie, and the suit looked like it might rip apart at the seams from the muscles they tried to contain. He looked like a sumo wrestler who was dressed for dinner. The man walked up and stood next to Unsworth.

"Do you have problem, Mr. Monty?" His accent was thick and Eastern European.

The moment he entered, Sebastian had moved off the wall he'd been leaning against and now stood just behind and off to the side of the two detectives. Jillian could feel the tension in the room. The last thing she needed was a testosterone battle. Looking directly at Unsworth, she said, "We simply want to ask Mr. Fetushka a few questions, that's all."

The sumo wrestler spoke before Unsworth could open his mouth. "No one here by dat name. Please leave."

Sebastian now spoke before Jillian could respond. "Or I could just throw you back through that door and we could find Mr. Fetushka ourselves."

The big man locked eyes with Sebastian and squinted slightly. Perhaps he was noticing Hughes for the first time, but whatever it was he saw, he didn't answer immediately. It was Unsworth who spoke. "I'm quite sure that with or without a warrant, any of that sort of behavior by the police will most certainly find you in court."

Kara said, "He's not police," before Jillian could stop her, which caused both the sumo wrestler and Unsworth to look from Kara to Hughes and back.

Jillian had had enough and was about to say something when a voice from behind the counter said loudly, "Monty! Bring them back."

Everyone turned to see an older man in gray slacks, a white shirt, blue tie, and suspenders handing a piece of paper to one of the women working behind the counter. His voice, too, was thickly accented. He was short, overweight, and not particularly handsome, with squinty eyes and a bulbous nose. He turned and walked away before anyone could reply.

Unsworth turned and extended an arm toward the door. "Right this way, Detectives, and uhmmm . . ." He paused, looking over at Sebastian.

Sebastian began walking, his eyes never leaving the larger man, and said, "I'm just here to throw out the rubbish."

Gregorio Fetushka had the stereotypical corner office with an unobstructed view of the Port of Liverpool. It was clean, though his desk held piles of papers and folders that rivaled the disarray of Jillian's own, which was saying something.

Jillian and Kara took the two chairs in front of the massive desk. Fetushka sat behind it, with the hulking sumo wrestler further back against a credenza. Hughes stood behind the detectives, his hands clasped lightly in front of him, but his eyes remained steadily on the bodyguard. Monty Unsworth closed the door behind him as he left.

"What is it you want, Inspector?" Fetushka said, his accent sounding Greek to Jillian.

Jillian explained about the shipping container and that they had been given his name as someone who might know something about it.

Fetushka looked at her as if he'd smelled a rotting piece of fish in a fish market. He looked past her at Hughes and pointed his finger at him. "You," he said. "Do I know you?"

Sebastian remained silent and his stare didn't waver, but he shook his head slowly.

Fetushka pursed his lips. "I know you from somewhere."

"Mr. Fetushka," Kara said, causing the man to turn his scowling face toward her. "What can you tell us about a shipment of eight women of Eastern European descent, which originated from the Port of Liverpool, bound for France last week?"

Ignoring Kara and turning his gaze back to Jillian, Fetushka said, "Are you accusing me of something, Detective Inspector?

"Not at all, Mr. Fetushka," she said. "We were merely hoping you could help us with our inquiries."

Fetushka opened his arms wide, palms facing upward. "I am always happy to help police. However, I know nothing about shipment of illegal women."

"Nobody said they were illegal, Mr. Fetushka," Jillian said.

Fetushka shrugged. "Eastern European women in shipping container bound for France does not take Sherlock Holmes to figure out they are illegal." He laughed out loud, his voice heavy and humorless.

Kara unsmilingly said, "Perhaps if we gave you the shipping container information, it might jog your memory." She held out a sheet of paper for him.

Fetushka looked at her, his dark, small eyes squinting. He did not reach for the papers she held in her hand. "My memory does not need jog. Maybe you speak to harbormaster and jog his memory." He placed his hands on his desk and pushed himself to his feet, indicating that their time was up.

***

"I thought the elephant against the credenza was a nice touch," Sebastian said as they approached the car and Malcom got out to open doors.

"Shut up," Jillian said testily.

"And there's that," Sebastian replied as he climbed into the car.

CHAPTER 11

Jillian woke to the sound of her phone vibrating on the bedside table. Groaning, she reached over and picked it up, noting that it was half-past five in the morning. What got her attention, however, was the caller.

"Boss?" she said, half sitting up in bed but keeping her voice low, trying not to wake Daniella, who was stirring next to her.

"Sorry to call so early," Superintendent Maryanne Sanderson said. "I need to meet with you in person as soon as possible."

That made Jillian's eyes fully open. "Uhm, yes, of course, I can be in London in uhm . . ." she said, trying to do time calculations in her not-quite-awake head.

"Actually, I'm in your neck of the woods. Can you meet me in half an hour?" Sanderson said.

Jillian was now out of bed and already looking for clothes to wear. "Yes, of course. Should I meet you at the Tof?"

"No, can you get down to the Red Funnel Ferries dock?"

"Might be a few minutes late, but I should do, yes," Jillian said.

"Just throw anything on. I'm not bothered with your dress code at the moment," Sanderson said, and something about the way she said "at the moment" gave Jillian pause. Jillian was already on edge; she knew she should probably talk to Sanderson about Kara's "situation," but how and what exactly would she say?

A few minutes past six, Jillian pulled into the parking lot near the popular ferry to the Isle of Wight. At this time of the morning, things were picking up with the business set, who needed to cross to the island. She could see Sanderson standing by the dock, off to the side of where most of the traffic, both on foot and in cars, was heading.

Jillian approached her and watched as she spoke to the man standing next to her, presumably her chauffeur-slash-body-protection officer, who dutifully stepped away as Jillian arrived. She watched as he walked to a nearby black sedan and got in the driver's side.

"Sorry for the early wake-up," Sanderson said, exchanging cheek kisses with Jillian.

Jillian knew Sanderson wouldn't have much time, and she sensed that something was pressing, given that she had driven all the way down from London. So, she simply said, "No problem. What's up?"

Sanderson sighed audibly and looked around a few times, clearly making sure no one was close enough to listen. With all the activity going on with the ferry, the water splashing up against the docks, and the constant din of cars moving this way and that, Jillian was having a hard enough time hearing her boss as it was. The chances of someone overhearing their conversation were zero.

"You went to EuroXPort yesterday," Sanderson said, and it wasn't a question.

"Yes," Jillian began. "How did you . . ." but she never finished.

"Tell me why," Sanderson said bluntly.

Jillian, still on edge, filled her in on their case, the progress that led them to Central UK Imports, and their conversation with Laghari and his wife and then with Gregorio Fetushka.

Sanderson listened attentively, and when Jillian finished, she said, "I need you to leave EuroXPort and Fetushka alone."

Jillian's mouth fell open. "All due respect, mum, they're our biggest lead. Why should we leave . . ." Again, Sanderson didn't let her finish.

"Fetushka has nothing to do with your case," she said flatly.

"I'm sorry?" Jillian said incredulously. She was getting fed up with being told to leave people on her cases alone with no explanation. Sanderson had made a similar request before, though perhaps *request* was too soft a word.

"Walk away from them, Jillian," Sanderson said, her eyes meeting Jillian's directly. "I'm telling you that you are barking up the wrong tree."

"And just how do you know that?" Jillian asked, adding, "mum?"

Again, Sanderson sighed. She tried again, making it clear she was giving Jillian a direct order, but Jillian pushed back, going over the details of the case, the viciousness of the crime, and how there was definitely something wrong about EuroXPort and Fetushka in particular.

"You're not going to let this go, are you?" Sanderson said, adding, "Even if I tell you it could ruin your career?"

Jillian's stomach flipped. She was already worried about her career with the bombshell Kara had dropped on her desk, and now her boss was lobbing another potential explosive. She wasn't sure what she was willing or not willing to do in this case, but if she wasn't allowed to do her job, what was the point of doing it at all? Unsure how to say all that without creating more friction with her boss, however, she kept her mouth shut.

Sanderson looked at her watch and then around her again in all directions.

She was stalling, Jillian thought. That or she really was worried about being overheard. That would explain the face-to-face and the timing and location of the meeting. Or maybe it was everything all together.

Finally, Sanderson turned and looked directly into Jillian's eyes. She stared intently into them for long enough that it became somewhat uncomfortable. Finally, as if making up her mind, she took a deep breath in and said, "I need to tell you something."

Jillian still said nothing, feeling at this point that silence was working far better than anything she could say.

"What I'm about to tell you, less than a dozen people know."

Jillian nodded slightly.

"When I tell you that you cannot, under any circumstances, tell anyone," Sanderson said, "that includes anyone on your team, even Daniella." At this, Sanderson raised her eyebrows, making sure Jillian was paying attention.

She was.

Sanderson continued, "I need to know that I can trust you."

Jillian stood a little straighter and looked right back at her boss. "You have my word," she said.

Sanderson paused again, thinking.

There was nothing Jillian could do or say that would sway her boss one way or the other. Sanderson would have to make up her own mind whether she trusted Jillian. Finally, she turned. "Walk with me."

They began walking alongside the dock, moving further from the ferry crowd.

Sanderson began her tale. "When I was in Norwich, I was just beginning to get noticed. My career was progressing, and I had a good boss who helped me get loads of experience on a variety of cases. He cared for me." Noticing the look on Jillian's face, she added, "Not in that way. More a father-figure, mentor kind of way.

"The more diverse my cases got, however, the more I began to notice things. Things that didn't make sense or didn't add up. Nothing specific, just nagging little things here and there." Sensing a question coming from Jillian, she said, "It doesn't matter what they were. The point was that they wouldn't go away.

"Eventually I went to my boss and confided in him. He let me go through everything and invited me out to his home for dinner with him and his wife to discuss it more. I went, and we spent a few hours after dinner going over everything that was troubling me."

Jillian kept quiet under the adage of "If it isn't broken, don't fix it," and they kept walking.

"In the end," Sanderson continued, "he said that he agreed something wasn't quite right, but said I didn't have nearly enough proof for what I was suggesting. And he was right. I went back to work, but the questions remained.

"I kept looking for more answers, wary now because my boss had warned me that the path I was treading down was a dangerous one. Two months later, he announced he was retiring. I was devastated, not only because he had been such a good boss and mentor to me, but because I feared I might never have someone I could confide in in the future about my concerns. Not anyone I trusted, anyway.

"I told him as much and he gently told me not to worry. He was leaving after a long and distinguished career, and I imagined he just didn't want to take on what I was suggesting at the end, especially as the stakes were very high." Sanderson paused then as they passed a group of people hurrying toward the ferry.

After looking over her shoulder to make sure the group was sufficiently far enough away, she went on. "At his retirement afterparty, back at his home, I was getting ready to leave. I had come to say goodbye, and I was genuinely sorry to see him go. I was also sad that he hadn't taken me seriously and was leaving me when I needed him most. As it turned out, I was doing him a great disservice.

"He grabbed me by the elbow and told me there was someone he wanted me to meet before I left. He then introduced me to someone who would change my life and career forever."

Jillian could do nothing but walk silently beside her boss, hanging on every word.

"I can't go into too much detail, but I spent a considerable amount of time over the next year putting together a team. I call them my Royal Flush."

Jillian looked over at her boss. "What was the team for?"

"We're getting there," Sanderson replied. "The problems I had been noticing pointed to something going on within the police and yet also without."

Jillian's eyebrows knotted together questioningly. Sanderson looked over and smiled. "It's a bit difficult to explain in the abstract and I don't have time to go into specifics, but needless to say, some things were going on that were rotten, and it had to include both people within the police force and some rather big players in organized crime.

"My Royal Flush team was a long-term plan to place some unknown—in some cases, brand-new-out-of-the-academy—undercover operatives in strategic places. We ended up with five people, hence the poker-hand analogy, and over the course of the next year or so, we placed them in various positions with backstories to help them make their marks.

"Four of the five are still in play," Sanderson said. "The Ten had to be pulled back after two years because of health issues. The rest are all still in play. No one in the Met knows about them."

Jillian raised her eyebrows. "No one?"

Sanderson stopped walking and turned to face Jillian, shaking her head. Then she said, "You met a man yesterday who handles Fetushka's finances named Monty?"

"Yes," Jillian replied.

"He is my King." Sanderson said.

"Shit," Jillian said before she realized she'd said it out loud.

"Quite," Sanderson said. "We've spent years getting him into this position. He knows everything and anything there is to know about Fetushka and his business. He's an asset we cannot risk. I spoke to him at length early this morning, and he assures me that Fetushka was not involved in this, and I believe him. He also confirmed for me that when your container arrived in Liverpool, it was inspected and verified prior to being picked up by the transit lorry. There were no body parts inside. Just cleaning supplies."

Sanderson looked at her watch and lifted her arm.

Jillian looked back to where they had started and saw the black sedan turn and head their way.

"Jillian," Sanderson said, "I'm placing a great deal at risk in telling you. Please don't breathe a word of this to anyone. No one on your team must know."

"No," Jillian said, shaking her head, "I won't."

"And you'll leave EuroXPort out of your investigation?"

Jillian nodded. It occurred to her she had completely forgotten the predicament she was in with Kara, but now was not the time to get into it. The two embraced. Sanderson got into her car, and it pulled away heading back to London.

Jillian walked back to her own car, deep in thought. This case, and everyone involved in it, was making her life more complicated by the minute. More than that, though, Jillian had just lost her most promising lead in this case.

"Shit," she said out loud for the second time as she climbed into her car.

CHAPTER 12

Kara Devanor was once again at her desk before anyone else arrived. Aside from a few questions about their meetings, Jillian had said very little on their ride back from Liverpool. The tension, temporarily reduced while they were conducting their interviews of both shipping companies, had returned. The closer they got to Southampton, the more palpable it became.

After another sleepless night, Kara's nerves were stretched thin. Her life was a mess in every respect, no matter how she looked at it. The only thing she could think of doing was to bury herself in work, and so she was going over every aspect of the case, looking for something, anything, that could help the team solve it.

In the back of her mind, she knew it would likely be the last case she worked on with the VCU, and potentially with the Met.

She had been spending most of her time going over reports, logs, all the paperwork that a case like this generated. Now, with her elbows on her desk holding up her head, she was looking at the video of the lorry at the rest stop. As usual, the CCTV was grainy, but it showed the lorry pull into a spot roughly at the time the driver, Ahmal Buggeri, claimed to have stopped, which his driver log corroborated.

The lorry, with its white cab and gray cargo container, parked next to another lorry on the far side from the camera angle. Buggeri got out and entered the rest stop. Video from inside showed him getting food and sitting down to eat it for thirty-five minutes before going to the loo and returning to his lorry. Total time was just under forty-five minutes.

When he went back out, another lorry was parked next to his on the near side, blocking it from the camera view. It had a black cab and a much larger attached container, also black. She watched as Buggeri walked around it and disappear from the CCTV view, but then she saw lights come on from the other side of the black lorry. A minute later, she saw Buggeri's lorry pull out from behind the black one.

Pausing the video, she zoomed in, and although the video was grainy, she could just make out the driver. It was definitely Buggeri.

She watched a little more, checked the registration numbers on both front and back of his lorry, as well as the registration markings on the container it was carrying as it left the rest stop, but everything was as it had been when it pulled in. It just didn't make sense. Someone, at some point, had to switch out the contents of the container, and this was the only place it could have realistically happened.

At that point, Detective Sergeant Listun walked in, saying he saw the boss pulling into the parking lot and that everyone should get ready for the morning brief.

Kara watched as Jillian entered, looking even more perturbed than she had the day before. And when the morning brief started, she found out why.

Jillian wasted no time getting to the point. After arriving back late yesterday, she had told the team to immediately begin digging into EuroXPort and Gregorio Fetushka. Now she needed to walk it back with a good-enough explanation that her sometimes overeager team would believe.

"I'm sorry to do this," she began, "but I've received new information that takes our prime suspect out of the frame."

There was a collective groan around the room. "Apparently, Organized Crime have been looking into Fetushka for some time, which comes as no surprise really, but I've been told that they are absolutely confident that he was not involved in our lorry container or its contents."

"How can they be sure?" DS Listun asked, receiving nods from others in the room.

"That," Jillian said carefully, "they didn't share with me." She held up her hand to silence the quickly vocalized protests from her team. "But . . . *but*," she said louder the second time, "I have been assured that we can cross them off our list."

Kara held up her hand, which was unusual for her. She wasn't quite sure why she did it, but Jillian looked over at her questioningly, so she said, "Guv, when we were there yesterday, there was definitely something off about them."

"I agree," Jillian responded firmly. "I'm not saying they're innocent. There's a reason OC is looking at them, after all. What I'm saying is that in this case, for this crime, they are out of the frame. It's Liverpool's problem to deal with in terms of what they are guilty of. Now, moving on . . ." And with that, she steered the investigation back toward other lines of inquiry.

Kara spent the rest of that day and the next working with the team to chase down numerous dead ends and doing the monotonous and endless paperwork of being a police detective.

Despite her continued unease around her situation with Sebastian Hughes, she rarely had time to speak with her boss because Jillian was on a constant stream of calls and meetings. The few times she saw her were either in a group setting with the rest of the team, or with Listun.

Such was the case two days after they had moved on from EuroXPort when she heard Listun push his rolling chair back from his desk, saying "Shit!" Kara watched as he stood up, motioned for her to join him, and headed over to their boss's office.

Listun knocked on the door and waited for the "come in" from Jillian before opening and preceding Kara inside.

"What's up?" Jillian asked, a stack of folders and papers all over her desk, pen in hand.

Listun sighed loudly. "I just received an email from Manchester CID. They found a body yesterday in what looks like a professional assassination in a car park."

Jillian and Kara both waited for the other shoe to drop.

"It's our lorry driver, Ahmal Buggeri," Listun said.

Jillian dropped her pen on the desk and sighed.

Kara just slumped against the credenza.

"Someone's covering their tracks," Jillian said.

"Looks that way," Listun agreed.

Jillian told Listun to send her the report and then asked where they were on other lines of inquiry, but Kara's mind was already moving. The more people they removed from the equation, the more convinced she became that something had happened at that rest stop.

She returned to her desk and started looking at the rest stop itself. Toward the end of the afternoon, she found something. She looked up at the team. Normally this was the kind of thing she would bounce off Jillian, but that ship had sailed, and although she looked wistfully at her office, she knew she wouldn't go in there.

She thought about DS Listun and his offer to help. She glanced at his desk, where he was busy talking to two other members of the team who were each working on separate cases. His desk, too, was piled high with casework that looked ready to topple onto the floor.

Instead, she called out to Stacey Alston. Stacey was the unit administrator and, as such, held a variety of responsibilities. She had become known for her research prowess, which was what Kara wanted her for.

The two gathered around Kara's computer monitor, and she briefly explained to Stacey what her line of thinking was, showing her the CCTV video. Then she presented the discovery she had just made: A quarter of a mile down the road was an old, abandoned building. It was a concrete structure with a small parking area by the front and a loading dock in the back. The whole thing was enclosed in what looked like chain-link fencing in the satellite photo she had found on the web.

The description of the property was that it was an old meat-processing facility that was up for sale.

"Can you find out as much as possible about this place and how long it's been empty?" Kara asked Stacey.

"Yeah, of course, but it's a bit of a stretch, don't you think?" Stacey asked.

"I know," Kara said, "but there's just something about it."

Stacey looked back at the monitor, clearly not convinced. Kara pressed further. "Look. Look at the entrance of the fence. The grass is all overgrown everywhere, but there are tracks on both sides of the entrance."

"Well, you'd expect that, wouldn't you? It is, after all, the entrance to the place," Stacey replied.

"Yes," Kara said, "but if this place has been empty long enough for all that grass to have grown over, why do those tracks look fresh?"

Stacey pursed her lips thoughtfully. She didn't have an answer.

"Just see what you can find, please," Kara asked, then added, "And see if you can get me in to see it. I'd like to have a look around."

"Will do," Stacey said, and headed back to her desk.

CHAPTER 13

Jillian Scotte was exhausted. The toll of the investigation into the container full of dismembered bodies was infuriating and all-encompassing at the same time. Daniella had an early start, and so it was Jillian who was awoken with a kiss and a coffee but who now lay in bed trying to summon the will to get out of it.

A ring at her front door put paid to that. Checking the video feed from the doorbell did nothing to improve her mood. Throwing on her robe and slippers, she padded to the door and opened it with a sour expression on her face.

Her caller, however, did not mimic her mood. Sebastian Hughes stood with a coffee cup in each hand and his ever-present charming smile. "Good morning. I hope I didn't wake you?"

"I'm running late," Jillian replied, eyeing the coffee. She had let hers go cold by the bedside over the last forty minutes. Looking back up into Hughes's bright eyes, she said simply, "Sebastian, whatever you want, I honestly have neither the time nor the energy for it at the moment."

"Raj Laghari is dead," he said as the smile faded from his face.

Jillian heaved a heavy sigh. She was wondering if she would ever have a day again where someone in this case didn't die. Taking a step back, she opened the door wide and, accepting one coffee from Hughes, invited him in.

As they made their way back to the living room and kitchen area, she said, "When?"

"Actually," Sebastian replied, "he died later that night or early the next morning, depending on your perspective, of the day we saw him."

Jillian looked back over her shoulder. "They kept that pretty quiet if you're just hearing it now."

"Mmm," he said, taking a sip of his coffee. "Not only that, but there hasn't been even the faintest of hiccups in the day-to-day at Central UK Imports. Turns out his wife has been running things there for some time now and no one was the wiser."

"The funeral is next week after the wake," he added.

"I don't think they'll miss us if we don't turn up, do you?" Jillian's sarcastic tone echoed as she walked down the hall toward the bedroom. "Make yourself comfortable while I throw on some clothes."

She got dressed and made a less-than-halfhearted attempt at makeup. She came back into the living room to find Sebastian sitting on the couch, coffee still in hand, scrolling on his phone.

"Was that all you came to say?" Jillian asked.

Putting his phone away, Sebastian said, "No. We need to talk."

"Look," Jillian began, "I'm honestly buried at present, and while I recognize that this mess you and Kara have made needs to get resolved, I really don't have the time . . ."

Sebastian didn't wait for her to finish. "It's tearing her up inside, Jillian." He waited a beat before going on. "She hasn't slept in days. She has trouble focusing. She won't eat."

Jillian opened her mouth to respond, but Sebastian wasn't finished. "I know that she . . . *we* . . . have put you in a difficult situation . . ."

Jillian scoffed.

Hughes continued, "If you're going to fire her, it might be best if you just get on with it. If your friendship with her meant anything to you at all, please think about it from her perspective just for a moment."

Jillian took a deep breath. "I'm not going to fire her."

Hughes's brow furrowed.

Jillian had, in fact, been trying to figure out how she was going to deal with this, and she could only think of one way. "I've decided to take your advice."

Sebastian smiled briefly and pursed his lips, tilting his head slightly.

"I'm going to say that we decided we needed to learn more about you, and we weren't getting anywhere through regular channels like SCD9 and the like, so we decided on a more . . . shall we say . . . face-to-face approach."

"Well," Sebastian said, a huge grin spreading across his face, "not always face-to-face anyway."

Jillian threw her hands up. "Damn it, Sebastian, I'm serious."

The grin faded and Sebastian stood up. "I'm sorry. I couldn't resist."

Jillian grabbed her phone. "Let me call Kara, and perhaps the three of us can meet for coffee and talk this through."

As she dialed the number, Sebastian said, "Actually, I think she's out. When she left this morning, she said she was headed up north to see a building or something."

Jillian frowned as she heard the phone ringing in her ear. "What building?" Sebastian just shrugged.

The phone went to voicemail. Pressing the "end" button, Jillian hit the speed dial for the Tof. When the sergeant on the call desk answered, she asked him if he knew where DC Devanor was. When he said no, she said, "Is there anyone there who does?"

A moment later, Stacey Alston came on the line. Jillian asked if she knew where Kara was and listened for a moment, her eyes intensifying as the conversation went on.

Jillian walked over to the computer she and Daniella shared in the sitting area just off their kitchen. "I'm going to put you on speaker—can you say that again?"

Stacey's voice filled the room. "Yes mum. DC Devanor had an idea while she was watching the CCTV from the rest stop. The one where Ahmal Buggeri pulled in. After he went inside, another lorry pulled up with an LeTransport logo on the side and blocked the CCTV camera view of Buggeri's lorry. DC Devanor's theory was if Buggeri didn't pick up the bodies, then they must have been placed there on his journey, and this was the most likely place."

Jillian was typing away at the keyboard. "Go on," she said.

"Well, we know that neither the container nor Buggeri's vehicle were switched out because all the registrations and markings matched when he entered and left the rest stop. She did, however, find an abandoned building, an old meat-processing plant, a quarter of a mile up the road," Alston said.

Hughes, who was standing in the living room, listened closely and began walking toward where Jillian was typing.

Stacey Alston continued. "Anyway, we looked into it, and we found something interesting. The building used to be owned by an RLET Ltd. corporation which is, or was, the corporation that owned the LeTransport lorries. Anyway, DC Devanor is going there this morning to have a look round at the building. I suppose to see if there's any evidence of it being used to transfer the bodies or what have you."

"You said *or was*—what did you mean?" Jillian said, still looking intently at the monitor in front of her.

"Well, the RLET corporation sold the company some years ago, and it's changed hands a few times again since. We're having a little trouble finding out who actually owns it now."

"Right," Jillian said. "Okay, keep me posted and thanks, Stacey." She hung up.

"Ah hah," Jillian said triumphantly. "I knew I'd heard that name before."

Sebastian just raised his eyebrows as Jillian said, "When she said LeTransport, I knew I'd seen it recently. It was on the report of Buggeri's death in Liverpool yesterday. He was killed in his lorry in a car park and the container he was carrying was from LeTransport."

"That's an awful lot of coincidences around Raj Laghari," Sebastian said.

"Laghari?" Jillian said, looking over at him. "What do you mean?"

"Back when I was in Manchester, he was just building his empire. He started the LeTransport line. Everyone thought it was a French company because of the name, but it really stood for Laghari European Transport," Sebastian said.

"RLET," Jillian chimed in. "Raj Laghari European Transport?"

Hughes nodded. Then he noticed the color drain from Jillian's face. "What is it?"

"Just then, when I was on the phone with Alston," Jillian said. "She said that Kara had wanted to go and see the building and that the letting agent told her the owner would meet her this morning to show her around, given that she was police."

Sebastian's face suddenly became very serious. "If LeTransport owned that building, you can bet it ties back to Laghari, and if Kara's right about it being used to swap out the contents of the lorry . . ."

Jillian jumped in. "And if Simalla Burman has been running the company for some time with Raj Laghari ill, then she would have been the one responsible for it . . ."

Hughes finished her thought. ". . . and there's no way she's going to let Kara look around that building."

Suddenly they were both running out of the house, with Hughes saying that his driver would get them there faster than if she drove herself.

The question was, would they get there in time?

CHAPTER 14

Malcom, Sebastian Hughes's driver, pulled off the motorway and wound the car around the petrol station where the CCTV had shown Ahmal Buggeri taking his break. The tires of Hughes's sedan squealed loudly, as they had for most of the journey, since the over-one-hour trip had taken less than forty minutes. A few moments later, they turned right onto a short entryway in a clearing of the thick trees that lined the road. Before them lay a large building surrounded by a chain-link fence.

An opening in the fence showed Kara's car parked near the entrance, as well as two other vehicles next to it.

"Drop us here, then drive around the back and see what you can find," Sebastian told Malcom, who merely nodded.

Hughes and Jillian got out of the car and began approaching the entrance as the car turned and drove quietly down the side of the building. Jillian was looking up and around the entrance for signs of activity, but there were few windows in what was largely a concrete warehouse that looked like it hadn't been used for some time. The real estate agent's sign hanging on the fence flapped in the breeze behind them.

As they approached the front door, Jillian looked over at Hughes, who now held a gun down by his side in his right hand. Reaching out with his left, he gently pulled on the door and opened it slowly. The entryway had seen better days. As they stepped in, Hughes held the door for Jillian before closing it softly. They could hear faint voices coming from somewhere inside.

Moving across the entryway, they came to a set of interior doors, one of which was slightly open. Hughes moved across it slowly, peering inside. Looking over at Jillian, he shook his head, then opened the door just wide enough to get through.

Jillian, following Hughes, was straining to hear what the voices were saying, but they weren't yet close enough. She stayed behind him as he hugged a wall, moving silently closer and closer to where it opened into a larger room.

The voices were becoming clearer now.

Simalla Burman spoke. "You should have kept your nose out of our affairs, you silly cow."

"Killing a police officer isn't going to keep us out of your affairs, Mrs. Burman," Kara responded, her voice slightly higher than Jillian knew was typical. "I'd venture to say it will have the opposite effect."

Burman's laugh came out as more of a cackle. "No one knows I'm here, and this property isn't listed in my or my late husband's name."

Sebastian had reached the end of the wall, his back now flat against it. Jillian did the same beside him. She watched as he pulled out his cell phone. Opening the camera, he bent down slowly and inched just the edge of the phone around the corner, pressing the capture button silently.

Standing back up, he looked at the photo, angling his phone so Jillian could look as well. The image showed Kara with her back to them. Standing a few feet apart, Simalla Burman and the bull-sized bodyguard they had met in the hospital faced her. The bull had a gun pointed at Kara.

Burman's voice broke the silence. "You'll just be another dead cop found alone in this old warehouse."

Sebastian put the phone back in his jacket pocket, and before Jillian could formulate a thought, he spun around the corner, his gun now raised in front of him. "Or not," he said as he walked over and stood just to the left of Kara. His gun was pointed at the bull.

Jillian walked over and stood on his other side. "We actually were able to trace the old refrigeration company that owned this building back to your fleet of lorries."

Simalla Burman's face flushed with anger. As soon as she saw them, she reached into her purse and pulled out a gun. It was smaller than both her bodyguard's and Hughes's but no less deadly. She was pointing it at Jillian. "I've had about as much of you two meddling in our affairs as I can take."

"As for you," she said, looking over at Hughes, "I don't know what you're playing at with these two slags, but I'm afraid it ends now."

Hughes's eyes never left the bodyguards. "How will that work, exactly?"

There was a pause before Burman spoke. This time, her voice was pitched slightly higher. "I'm well aware of your reputation, Mr. Hughes, but there are two of us and only one of you. I promise you, no matter how quick you think you are, it won't be quick enough. Now, if you would be so kind and put your gun down on the floor in front of you, perhaps we can come to an agreement."

Hughes's mouth twitched with the briefest of smiles. "We both know that's not going to happen."

"Then I'm afraid you leave us no choice," Burman replied.

From somewhere deeper in the building came two rapid gunshots, followed by a third.

Everyone except Sebastian reacted. Burman's head turned in the direction of the sound. Her bodyguard began to turn his head as well. He corrected himself and turned back to face Hughes. But it was too late.

Everything, it seemed to Jillian, happened in slow motion.

Sebastian fired, hitting the bull in the center of his forehead. Then he lunged with his left hand out toward Jillian before pulling the trigger again.

Jillian felt Sebastian shove her shoulder with more force than she would have thought possible, knocking her off balance and to the ground, where she slid away from him.

Burman, hearing the gunshot, had turned back around, firing at the same time Sebastian aimed his gun at her. Because he had been focused on shoving Jillian out of the way, and because Burman had moved slightly as she turned back around, his aim was slightly off. He hit Simalla Burman in the upper chest and knocked her backward.

Burman's aim was also off. Firing where she had expected Jillian to be, her arm pulled slightly and her bullet hit Hughes, who faltered a half step before collapsing onto his back.

Jillian's head was ringing with the echo of the gunshots, that tinny sound that fills the ear and makes all other noise sound as if underwater. She half sat up on the ground, shaking her head gently from side to side to clear it. The first sound she heard was screaming.

Kara, who had been too stunned to move as the firefight ensued rapidly before her eyes, saw Sebastian crumple to the floor. From somewhere deep inside of her, a guttural scream erupted and filled the cavernous empty room. She rushed over and dropped to the floor, hovering over him, seeing a pool of red spreading over his chest.

Her scream turned to a wailing as she reached down and cradled his face in her hands, tears now pouring down her face and falling onto his.

Jillian watched helplessly as she tried to regain her feet, seeing and now hearing Kara's pain clearly as she kneeled over Hughes' unmoving body.

Out of the corner of her eye, Jillian saw movement.

She saw Simalla Burman slowly sitting up, blood spreading across her upper body. She also saw Burman raise her hand and point her gun.

Jillian screamed Kara's name.

She had meant to warn her of the danger. Willing her to somehow lay down flat or move somewhere, anywhere, out of the line of fire.

But her cry, her plea, had the opposite effect. Kara's body straightened, and her tear-streaked face turned toward Jillian.

Burman fired before collapsing lifelessly onto her back. Kara's back arched before she slowly, inevitably, fell forward on top of Hughes, their heads now side by side, one facing up, the other down.

The cries filling the room now were Jillian's. Her own wailing "Noooooooooooo!" stretched out as she scrambled over to the two bodies.

There was a sound behind her as Malcom came running, his gun sweeping the room from side to side and then coming to a stop as he looked down at the bodies.

Jillian was kneeling beside both bodies, red blood now pooling between them. Her hands fumbled as she reached into her pocket for her phone. Dialing, she waited helplessly for what seemed an eternity before it was answered. "This is DI Scotte. Officer needs assistance. One officer down. Need an ambulance *now*!" The last word was both an order and a plea before she gave the address.

Malcom moved methodically over to Burman and her bodyguard, making sure they were dead before standing opposite where Jillian was still kneeling. She looked up and met his eyes. She couldn't read anything on his face, but his expression was hard. Unbelievably, somewhere in the distance, they could already hear sirens.

The sound broke the trance between them. Malcom silently bent down and picked up Hughes's gun where it lay just outside his fallen hand. Then, without a word, he turned and began quickly walking the way he had come, back into the bowels of the building.

Jillian reached out to touch Kara's shoulder. It was still warm, but whether she was breathing, she couldn't tell. She didn't know whether to check for a pulse or move her onto her back and start CPR. The blood leaking out between her and Hughes's bodies as they lay pressed together worried her. Her primary thought was that she could do more harm than good by moving her.

She could hear the sirens loudly now, and a car or cars screeching to a halt outside the entrance. She looked up, expecting a patrol officer, and she had her warrant card opened in one hand, ready to bellow orders to hurry the damn ambulance up.

She didn't expect the armed assault team that barged in rapidly and in force. "Armed police don't move!" they screamed, one after the other. The six men in heavy tactical gear quickly spread out across the room.

Jillian didn't move, save to slowly bring her arm off Kara's shoulder to join the other one holding her warrant card in the air. "I'm DI Scotte."

She waited while the team lead approached her, his assault rifle pointing straight at her. Another officer slightly to his right also had his rifle aimed at her head. She could see their laser lights dancing in the periphery of her vision.

After checking her card and looking at her through his balaclava, the team lead reached up under his throat and keyed his microphone. "I have DI Scotte." Then, looking around quickly, he added, "Count four casualties, status unknown. Room secure." Without waiting for a reply, he glanced at the rest of his team and motioned for three of them to move through the opening at the back where Malcom had gone moments before.

The three men began moving in a line while the other two checked Burman and the bodyguard.

Jillian began to lower her hands and was about to start screaming about the ambulance when a medical team of four came running into the room, each EMT carrying multiple medical packs. One kneeled beside Jillian.

"Are you okay? Is this your blood?" The EMT was a young woman, and her question didn't make sense to Jillian. Looking down as the woman grabbed her wrist, Jillian could see that some of the blood had spilled onto her arm.

Jillian quickly shook her head. "No . . . no, it's not mine . . ."

The woman gently took Jillian's arm and pulled her to the side. Two of the other EMTs took their place on either side of Kara and Sebastian and got to work. The last EMT went to check on Burman and the bodyguard, but came back once he confirmed they were both deceased.

Jillian sat down on the floor helplessly as the medical teams began pulling various items from their bags and doing what they were trained to do.

Suddenly, the lead tactical officer was at her side. "Mum?" he said.

Jillian looked away from the medical technicians and into the face of the man who, moments ago, had his gun pointed at her head. He was holding out a phone. She reached up and took it automatically, holding it to her ear. "Hello?"

"Jillian?" the voice said.

It took a second for Jillian to recognize that the voice was that of Superintendent Maryanne Sanderson.

"Jillian!" Sanderson said again. "Listen to me. Are you listening?"

Jillian nodded silently, then realized she was talking on a phone. "Yes . . . I'm here." She could feel herself going numb.

"We have an emergency helicopter on its way. It will be there in five minutes." When Jillian said nothing, she added, "Jillian, do you understand?"

"Yes." was all Jillian could say.

"The tactical team will take care of everything on scene. Go to the hospital," Sanderson said. "There won't be room for you in the helicopter, but I've got someone coming who will get you to the hospital. His name is Ramston."

"Mmm hmm," Jillian muttered, her eyes inescapably drawn to the EMTs, who had now separated Kara from on top of Hughes. There was blood everywhere, so much blood. She heard Sanderson say, "Let me speak to the officer," and she numbly held the phone out to him.

The tactical officer took the phone and listened. "Yes mum, I'll stay with her until he gets here. Yes mum, understood."

Somewhere in the distance, Jillian could hear the whoosh of the helicopter rotors as it began its approach.

CHAPTER 15
EPILOGUE

Jillian looked down at her bloodstained arm.

She was sitting in a plastic hospital chair somewhere near the surgical theaters. She remembered little about how she got here.

She remembered that DCI Ramston, a tall black man, had come in and whisked her out of the empty building and driven her to the hospital. He had been mercifully quiet on the journey, just asking if she needed anything but otherwise keeping his thoughts to himself.

For her part, Jillian had sat numbly in the passenger seat and stared out the window as the car, with its siren wailing, drove at speed toward the hospital where Kara and Hughes had both been flown.

Once they arrived, however, the quiet DCI had taken charge. His tall, bulky presence and commanding authority quickly put paid to the stalling tactics of the administrative hospital personnel, and before long, Jillian found herself sitting in a corridor with scrubs-clad nurses and doctors moving about. Armed police began setting up a perimeter of access-control points in and out of the area.

A head nurse and one or two surgeons began complaining, and soon a hospital administrator added to the melee, but Ramston was having none of it. He had one ear on his phone and another on the questions of the hospital staff. Suddenly, a more senior administrator appeared and took everyone away, assuring them he would take care of everything.

Ramston hung up his phone, spoke quietly to one of the armed guards, and then approached Jillian where she sat. He kneeled slowly in front of her. "Can I get you anything? Tea, coffee, something to eat?"

For Jillian, everything was hazy, her mind replaying the events of the past hour first at rapid speed, then in slow motion, then in real time all repeatedly. She tried to focus on the kind face of the DCI in front of her.

"No, thank you," she said quietly.

He nodded knowingly. "I'll be just over there if you need me," he said, pointing toward a nursing station where he presently went. He leaned on the counter and began speaking to one of the nurses in front of a computer.

Time passed.

Patients were wheeled in and out of surgery. People in scrubs of various colors walked by. No one said anything to Jillian or the armed police nearby, but they would take a discreet look now and again.

Hours passed. Two, perhaps three—she couldn't really remember when she had arrived. Jillian knew she was in shock, and despite the occasional response to Ramston about food or drink, she didn't move a muscle. Her face was stained with tears she couldn't control. She was, in every conceivable way, exhausted.

Suddenly, she could hear raised voices on the other side of a set of double doors that led into this area of the hospital. The door suddenly swung open, and Superintendent Maryanne Sanderson, in full uniform, came striding through. Alongside her was the senior administrator that had come on the scene earlier.

Ramston approached them both.

"DCI Ramston, Mr. Clark here," Sanderson said, nodding to the administrator, "is going to provide a list of all hospital personnel working both here in the operating theater, as well as the critical recovery section."

Mr. Clark nodded, though not enthusiastically.

Sanderson continued, "I want everyone coming and going checked against that list, and no one"—she raised her voice for emphasis—"and I mean *no one* that isn't on that list gets in. Do I make myself clear?"

Ramston nodded. "Yes mum." He and the administrator returned to the nurses' station together.

Sanderson, holding two cups, walked over to Jillian. She held out one cup. Jillian just looked at it and then up at her boss.

"Take it," Sanderson said, though her voice was much softer now. "It's hot sweet tea. It will help."

Jillian dutifully reached for the cup and held it up to her mouth. Surprisingly, it tasted quite good, and Jillian realized the name on the cup wasn't from the hospital, but likely a shop nearby.

It was Sanderson who now knelt before Jillian. She placed a hand on Jillian's knee, making sure to get her attention. Jillian's eyes met her boss's, but it didn't matter. Her lips were quivering and more tears streamed down her face.

Sanderson squeezed her knee. "They're alive," she said. "I've been told that both Devanor and Hughes will be coming out of surgery soon. They will be moving to a critical care unit just down the hall. Why don't we go there so we can talk and wait for them?"

Jillian's face scrunched up as she did her best to stop crying. They were alive. Kara was alive. No one from the hospital had told her anything other than both wounds were life threatening, and they were in surgery.

Sanderson patted Jillian's knee and stood up. Jillian stood as well, and the two walked down the hallway and around the corner, through a set of doors, and into the critical care recovery unit. They continued down the hallway until they reached a dead end. Two empty rooms were side by side along with a small nurses' station opposite.

It didn't register for Jillian until much later, but the armed police presence had moved with them and set up a new presence at each door to this part of the hospital.

Sanderson indicated two chairs against the wall, and Jillian sat. These chairs were cushioned and more comfortable than the plastic one she had been in.

After taking a sip of her drink, Maryanne said, "Can you walk me through what happened?"

Jillian took a deep breath and began. She explained how they had discovered the building, how Kara had gone ahead to investigate. Sanderson didn't interrupt or ask why she had gone alone. She just let Jillian talk.

Jillian explained how she had been talking to Hughes when she got the call and how they had gone up together. Again, Sanderson didn't interrupt, though Jillian knew at some point she was going to have to explain everything.

Pausing to take a sip of her tea, Jillian explained how they entered the building, how Hughes had stood between her and Kara. The firefight and how he had knocked her to the ground.

At that point, a team of hospital personnel suddenly began moving about, going in and out of the empty recovery rooms. Two gurneys came around the corner. The first had Hughes, with multiple tubes and a breathing apparatus running up and down his body and attached to the side. They moved him carefully into the room on the right.

Sanderson and Jillian stood and watched as Kara came next. Although she didn't have the breathing apparatus on the side of her bed as they wheeled her past, she had far more tubes with machines beeping and whirring.

Dozens of scrubs-clad nurses moved quickly and efficiently into and out of both rooms as they began connecting, transferring, and setting up all the tubes and devices each patient required.

Into this commotion two surgeons appeared, a man and a woman. The male doctor looked at both police officers. "Superintendent?" he asked hesitantly.

"I'm Superintendent Sanderson," Maryanne said, standing up and extending her hand.

"My name is Dr. Keens," the man said, shaking her hand. Then, indicating the other surgeon, he said, "This is Dr. Islemoor."

"This is DI Scotte," Maryanne said, indicating Jillian, and everyone shook hands.

The doctors gestured for Jillian and Maryanne to sit in the chairs, and they stood before them. Dr. Keens turned to his colleague and said, "Why don't you start?"

Dr. Islemoor reached up and removed her surgical cap. "I operated on the female," she said.

Jillian spoke up, "You mean . . ." but Sanderson quickly placed her hand strongly on Jillian's arm, silencing her.

Sanderson said, "Please, go ahead, doctor."

The surgeon, looking a little perplexed, said, "She received a gunshot wound to the back. The bullet penetrated very close to the lumbar area of her spine. Luckily, the bullet didn't get lodged there, but it did some damage further in. I'll get to that in a moment."

Jillian could feel her eyes welling up, and the hand Sanderson had placed on her arm to quiet her a moment earlier reached down and grabbed her hand, holding it tightly.

The doctor continued. "One of our concerns was the nerve damage the bullet did next to the spine. First, however, we had to control the bleeding and survey the damage it did after it moved past the spine. There was severe damage to her uterus. We were ultimately able to stop the bleeding and take a look at the nerve damage."

At this point, the doctor paused. She looked from Maryanne to Jillian and back again. "I think I was able to repair the damage near her spine, but the success, or . . ." Again, she paused. ". . . the success of how well we were able to do it, we won't know until she comes fully out of anesthesia."

Maryanne's voice spoke and there was clearly some strain in it. "You're saying she might be paralyzed?"

The doctor swallowed audibly before replying, "That is one possibility, yes." Not waiting for Jillian and Maryanne to digest the news, she said, "And I'm afraid that's not all."

Both women looked up at the surgeon, afraid to take a breath. "She will very likely need to have a hysterectomy once she heals from this procedure. The damage to her uterus was . . . significant, and I'm afraid, irreparable."

Dr. Islemoor looked back at Dr. Keens.

Clearing his throat, he said, "I operated on the male. He sustained a gunshot wound to the chest, which collapsed one lung."

Jillian felt Maryanne's hand squeeze slightly.

The doctor continued. "There was significant damage from the bullet entry, which caused severe internal bleeding beyond the collapsed lung. We were able to repair the lung and have grafted the opening. The blood loss was more significant than we expected, and the next twenty-four hours will tell us a lot."

The doctors stayed to answer a few more questions, then left. Sanderson stood and moved toward the two recovery rooms, standing between them so she could look into the windows of both simultaneously.

After a while, Jillian spoke up. "Boss," she said with dread in her voice, "there's something I should have told you about both of them that I haven't told you."

Sanderson kept staring into the recovery rooms. Without turning back, she said, "You mean about Devanor and Hughes being a couple? Yes, you bloody well should have." There was a little anger in her tone, but nothing that made her raise her voice.

"I know," Jillian said, standing up and taking a step toward her. "I just couldn't figure out a . . ." Jillian paused then, furrowing her brow. "Wait . . . how . . . how did you know?"

Sanderson stared into Kara's room, then turned her head and stared into Hughes's. After a moment, she half turned, and her eyes met Jillian's. Her voice quivered a bit. "Because Sebastian Hughes is my Ace."

The Story's End

I don't particularly like the term acknowledgement because it's definition is primarily to accept or notice something and what I want to say here is much more important than that.

If you read the first book in this series then you'll know that these stories were born out of the pandemic. At least, most of them. When I stopped answering those writing prompts from the COVID-19 pandemic, I had written one and a half of the stories you find in this volume. The rest, I wrote this past year in 2024.

None of this would have happened without the encouragement, support, and borderline entreaty of many people who enjoyed reading the original stories and the first volume, *Trouble Comes in Threes*. I will forever be indebted to the members of the *Journey Institute Press Writing Prompt Group* who encouraged me to continue with these stories. I am also so very grateful for the many members of my *advanced readers team* who always make these stories much better than I initially tell them. In particular, I am grateful to Claudia and Peggy for always being my biggest champions.

I would be remiss if I didn't mention my incredible editor, Jessica Medberry of InkWhale Editorial. The attention to detail and invaluable work you put into your editing is beyond compare. Any remaining errors are mine and mine alone.

To my wife Dafna for always believing in my and my words. I am nothing without you.

Stories are meant to be told. I hope you enjoy following along with these characters as much as I do, and yes, there will be another book.

MJ

ABOUT THE AUTHOR

Michael Jenet was born in Belgium and moved to the United States when he was seven years old. He is an eight-year veteran of the U.S. Air Force. A self-described "recovering corporate CEO", he now devotes himself full time as the publisher for Journey Institute Press.

An international best-selling and award-winning author, his first two books were in the self-improvement genre. *A Trio of Trouble* is his second work of fiction and the second in the DI Scotte Mystery series.

He lives in Colorado with his wife and family.

Journey Institute Press

Journey Institute Press is a non-profit publishing house created by authors to flip the publishing model for new authors. Created with intention and purpose to provide the highest quality publishing resources available to authors whose stories might otherwise not be told.

JI Press focusses on women, BIPOC, and LGBTQ+ authors without regard to the genre of their work.

As a Publishing House, our goal is to create a supportive, nurturing, and encouraging environment that puts the author above the publisher in the publishing model.

Wordbinders Publishing is an Imprint of Journey Institute Press, a Division of 50 in 52 Journey, Inc.